Holding

The Toymaker

By

Joe Nobody

Edited by:
E. T. Ivester
D. Allen

PrepperPress

Post-apocalyptic Fiction & Survival Nonfiction

Holding Their Own X: The Toymaker

ISBN 978-1-939473-29-5
Printed in the United States of America.
Prepper Press Paperback Edition: May 2015
Prepper Press is a division of Kennebec Publishing, LLC

Other Books by Joe Nobody:

The Archangel Drones

Holding Your Ground: Preparing for Defense if it All Falls Apart

The TEOTWAWKI Tuxedo: Formal Survival Attire

Without Rule of Law: Advanced Skills to Help You Survive

Holding Their Own: A Story of Survival
Holding Their Own II: The Independents
Holding Their Own III: Pedestals of Ash
Holding Their Own IV: The Ascent
Holding Their Own V: The Alpha Chronicles
Holding Their Own VI: Bishop's Song
Holding Their Own VII: Phoenix Star
Holding Their Own IX: The Salt War

The Home Schooled Shootist: Training to Fight with a Carbine

Apocalypse Drift

The Little River Otter

The Olympus Device: Book One
The Olympus Device: Book Two
The Olympus Device: Book Three

Secession: The Storm

The Ebola Wall

Find more titles at

www.JoeNobodyBooks.com

and

www.PrepperPress.com

Foreword by Joe Nobody

For nearly 30 years, I've been exposed to Native American cultures in North America. I've visited countless pueblos, dances, powwows, mesas, and celebrations.

I've dined, prayed, drank, laughed, sheltered, and become friends with dozens of different men and women who have opened their homes and hearts to my family. They come from a number of diverse cultures that many Americans incorrectly lump together into a single category called "American Indians."

Overall, I've found very few differences between the core values of their race and mine. They love their children, want to succeed, relish humor, celebrate art in many forms, and respect honesty. Sound familiar?

To say that Native Americans are this, or that, or the other is doing a disservice to the vast majority of their ranks. That would be like saying all southern men are rednecks and love guns, or that all Texans wear boots with pointed toes. Broad based stereotypes are as inaccurate there as with any diverse culture.

Since I began the Holding Their Own series, I've wanted to explore how various tribes in the Southwest would handle a collapse. Would they do better? Worse? About the same as the rest of America?

From my perspective, of all the social/racial groups in our country, American Indians are the most experienced with apocalyptic events. The last 400 years of their history is ripe with upheaval, betrayal, failed leadership, forced relocation, and bad decision making by all involved.

They have been defeated militarily, abused economically, ravaged by diseases, isolated, and forced off their land numerous times. Certainly sounds like SHTF by any definition I've heard.

And yet they survive, sometimes even thrive.

So how did they do it? What social imprint did those historical events leave in their culture? How much of the Native society of today is influenced by those relatively recent events?

I don't pretend to know the answers to these questions, but I find the subject a fascinating topic for fiction. I hope the reader will as well.

On a final note, the drone technology depicted in this work is real. It exists today, and even the most extreme example can be purchased for about the same price as a top-shelf hunting rifle and optic. So many of my self-reliant friends distrust drone technology, but I am actually embracing it. For preppers, there are several advantages to these gadgets, and I wanted to include a few in this work to seed thought and prime that wonderful pump of self-reliant creativity that I respect so very much.

Enjoy!

Joe

Chapter 1

The underground room was stale and musty, a stagnant space that hadn't experienced sunlight or ventilation for some time.

The specialist rolled back the standard-issue office chair, taking a moment to brush away any dust that might have accumulated. With only the emergency lights illuminating the large chamber, it was difficult to tell if the seat was clean or not. Given the scarcity of water and the fact that all uniforms had to be washed by hand, he wasn't about to take any chances.

"Three minutes!" called out a lieutenant standing by the door. "Three minutes to boot time!" he repeated, using the dim glow of the battery-powered lamps to study his watch.

The specialist glanced over his shoulder, observing a dozen other soldiers waiting for the time to pass. Most were already seated at workstations, the large room filled with several rows of monitors, computer towers, mice, and keyboards. Many of his coworkers were already covered in a glistening coat of perspiration.

"I hope the AC still works," someone commented from two rows back. "All of these computers are going to make this place a roasting oven if it doesn't."

"It's only an hour," replied another soldier. "We can handle it for an hour."

"Two minutes!" called out the LT. "Two minutes until power up!"

Leaning forward, the specialist blew a lungful of air across the keyboard, half expecting a cloud of dust to rise from its surface. None did.

Out of habit, he next rolled around the mouse as if exercising the unpowered device would somehow indicate whether or not it was going to function.

Realizing he was just being silly, the young soldier opened the notebook provided in their briefing a short time ago. Inside was a list of accounts and passwords that he would need once the electricity was restored.

"One minute!" came the shouted countdown. "Let's make every second of this count, people!"

The engineers had predicted that the computers, servers, and network infrastructure would be fine, but the soldiers now seated in the data center had their doubts. The fact that their lieutenant stood brandishing a large fire extinguisher wasn't exactly a confidence builder. The man's refusal to wander far from the door made things all the more tense.

Outside the complex, another team was checking their watches as well. Made up of the few available survivors from the local power company and a small group from the Army Corps of Engineers, all eyes were glued to a large voltage meter connected with Fort Meade's main cluster of transformers.

It was anticlimactic when the meter's needles finally moved, electricity being routed from the WIG – or Washington Interagency Grid. Fort Meade, home to one of the nation's largest collection of computing horsepower, whirred and buzzed with electricity for the first time in nearly two years.

Inside the building, the specialist watched as the fluorescent ceiling lights flickered to life. Expecting explosions, fire, or at least some sizzling smoke, most of the soldiers in the data center eyed the roof above with squinting eyes and deep suspicion.

Immediately following the light came the air. A low hum sounded throughout the complex as HVAC fans began spinning. Evidently, the base's mechanical experts had expertly resurrected the units as cool air began circulating through the room. No one seemed to mind the odor of dust and mold.

"Go, people! Boot 'em up!" barked the LT, fire extinguisher at the ready.

The specialist held his breath and reached for the power button of the server attached to his console and flipped the powerful computer's switch.

There was a drone and whine as the terabytes of disk storage began spinning up, and soon a blinking cursor appeared on the monitor.

Before the specialist could comment, a voice rang out from behind him, "I can't believe it! I'm signing in, sir! It's working."

Soon a chorus of similar reports sounded across the data center as one by one the military computers were started for the first time since the collapse.

After running a quick set of diagnostics to verify his machine was operating within normal parameters, the specialist then flipped the page in his notebook and began typing furiously on the keyboard.

Initially, the engineers had only wanted to power the complex for 15 minutes. Any more than that, they had warned, might lead to fires, blown equipment, or damage to the base's infrastructure. "Charge the lines for 10-15 minutes and let them heat up. Then shut it all down. We'll perform a thorough inspection over the next few weeks, and then you can use up all those computers as long as you want," they had recommended.

But the Pentagon had pushed back, the new president

demanding answers to a host of questions. People were starving, dying of diseases, and killing each other. The recovery had faltered time and again. Scuttlebutt was that the new Commander in Chief was a hard-charging, no bullshit, ex-military officer. According to some, *the man* didn't take no for an answer.

Like Fort Knox held gold, Fort Meade's massive IT capabilities were a vault as well, but of a different sort. Rather than tons of bullion, critical information was stored in the base's massive arrays of electronic storage – knowledge that could help the country recover and ensure her safety.

Each member of the specialist's group had a list of precise tasks to perform in the rationed hour of electricity. Some of them were to run reports, others to check connections with remote facilities. Two of the enlisted personnel were even going to attempt reestablishing satellite communications with allies overseas.

The orchestra of two dozen hands furiously banging on keyboards was soon accompanied by the purr and clack of high-speed laser printers spitting out page after page of reports.

The specialist's job was a bit more complicated. He had been tasked with auditing America's nuclear materials and making sure nothing had slipped through the cracks. While all weapons had been secured during the initial stages of the collapse, it seemed no one had planned for a prolonged outage of communications and electricity. The planners simply had never imagined America would fall so fast, so hard, and for so long. It was frustrating work, his stress amplified by fingers that hadn't manipulated a keyboard in months.

Forty minutes later, he was studying a screen filled with rows and columns of information. One line was blinking red.

Peering up at the now relaxed lieutenant he called, "Sir, we have a problem."

The officer arrived almost immediately, glancing over the operator's shoulder at the monitor's display. "What's that?" he asked, pointing at the red row of numbers.

"Los Alamos National Laboratory, sir. They received a shipment of Cobalt-60 just a month before everything went to hell. According to this record, it was to be used in experiments for the development of a three-stage salted warhead being considered by Congress at the time."

"So?"

"No one's been in contact with Los Alamos since the collapse, sir. Oak Ridge was occupied by the Tennessee National Guard. Savannah River and Livermore had no fission materials on site. The Air Force took over Rocky Flats in Colorado... but Alamos... no one's heard from them for months, sir."

"How much Cobalt-60 is there?"

"A lot, sir. The actual shipment was classified beyond what I can access on this machine, but from the authorizations on this paperwork, you can be assured it was enough that people were worried about it. The Department of Homeland Security even allocated an armed escort."

"Shit."

"Mr. President, we have to send in a team. We've utilized aerial assets, and that analysis has proven inconclusive. While there are some signs of life in and around Los Alamos, our attempts at contacting known individuals from the lab have not produced any results. In addition, sir, the primary research facility appears to have been damaged by fire. If there has been a breach of some sort, we need to know the extent of the damage. If any of the fission materials are missing, we need boots on the ground to ascertain the facts and interview the locals."

The president frowned, "You don't need my permission to send in a team, General. Why are you here?"

The staff officer didn't answer the president's question, at least not directly. Instead, he continued the briefing. "Yes sir, there *is* something else. During one of our flyovers, unusual ground activity was detected. I thought you should be aware of it."

The president accepted a small folder of what appeared to be high-resolution photographs taken from a drone or aircraft. For a few moments, the chief executive studied what looked to be a series of symmetrical grooves cut into the earth, almost as if a giant plow had been dragged across the desert floor.

"What is this?" he asked with a frown, shuffling the images.

"We don't know, sir. Our photo analysis experts can't agree. And the proximity to Los Alamos is troubling. I would like to have our people investigate this area as well."

"Why?"

The general cleared his throat, "Whatever is going on there, sir, it's on a massive scale. Each image in the file covers three square kilometers of ground. We've compared it to older pictures of the same terrain from before the collapse. This is new activity... is apparently well led and organized. The only known entity in that area of the continent that could undertake such an endeavor is the Alliance."

4

The president understood now, fully grasping why one of his senior military officers had driven all the way to Camp David for the briefing. "And this is in New Mexico?"

The general sighed in frustration, "Yes, sir. Not far from the Texas border, but definitely in our... err... territory."

Rising from his perch, the president paced toward the fireplace, seeming to study the flames. He understood the general's pained response; it was a typical reaction in the new Washington.

The Alliance was a large thistle in the crown of thorns he'd inherited after being appointed president. And it was easy to understand why.

After witnessing the entire country nearly tear itself to shreds over the last two years, a backlash had developed amongst the survivors. Now, all across the country, there was a strong prejudice against anyone who held the mantra of "every man for himself." The Alliance was viewed as an entire state populated with such individuals.

While he knew that perception was inaccurate, this wasn't the right place or time to fight that battle. A common foe was what the remaining states of the union needed - at least for the moment. If the people could offload part of their misery onto some distant entity, like the Alliance, then so be it.

The federal government was finally getting its shit in one bag, pulling the people together, inserting itself at local levels, and helping the seemingly lost citizenry find its way. The buzzwords for the new order included, "social inclusion and support." It was a movement that was advancing the recovery from Maine to the Midwest. "We're all in this together," the new leaders of the United States reminded.

It was predictable, the president thought. Two years of famine, disease, and anarchy is enough to make any citizen reevaluate what's truly important in life. An empty stomach and dying family can be quite enlightening.

Organized health care, co-op farming, and military policing were all in the early stages of realization. Most of these seeds were taking root after being planted by a federal presence. Sometimes it had taken extraordinary, draconian measures to pull society out of the apocalyptic mire. Often, the government "farmers" had been forced to resort to heavy-handed techniques and authoritarian practices. Violence was no stranger to the harvest of recovery.

But it was working. The causality rates from starvation, violence, and disease were all beginning to decline. Washington now had electricity for a few hours each day. Nuclear power plants in the Mississippi Delta were coming back online. A few, small sections of the Midwest were even going to have a harvest in the fall. A plant in New Jersey was going to start producing antibiotics next week. Work camps dotted the countryside, thousands of former city dwellers now relocated to tent cities where they planted fields of potatoes and cabbage using hand tools and manual labor.

The president didn't like the socialization of his beloved democracy - not one bit. He cringed every time some report made it clear that individual freedoms were being cast aside "for the greater good of the community." Filling stomachs was now deemed a critical issue even at the expense of liberty. Discipline and rule of law were currently a far higher priority than inalienable rights.

He let it go, always reconciling his passive stance by remembering what he'd encountered before occupying the Oval Office. Back when everyone still called him "The Colonel," he had toured the country multiple times. He'd observed the suffering, smelled the rotting flesh, and stared into the hollow, nearly lifeless eyes of his countrymen. Images of skeleton-like bodies waiting in line for meager rations still occupied his dreams.

He'd witnessed the trenches being excavated outside Chicago, a series of six-foot deep ditches over a mile long and the width of a football field. Graves. Mass graves, stretching to the distant horizon... and being filled by the only available hearses that could handle the tons of dead human flesh – Cook County garbage trucks.

On and on they plodded, rumbling across the frozen cornfield south of Gary, Indiana. A parade of horror that seemed to never end. The Colonel remembered the limbs protruding from the tops and backs of the metal beds. Some had flesh, others mere bone, and with many, it was impossible to tell. The corpses vibrated and jiggled with a sickening limpness as the heavy transports rolled across the plowed rows of unharvested crops.

In a morbid way, The Colonel wished he'd had a camera that day. It was a scene that described the apocalypse far better than any sequence of words his mind could form. The unpicked maize was lifeless and brown, drawn and wrinkled like the face of the old man that was humanity. The light dusting of dirty, gray snow was the dying soul's uncombed beard. The somber, steely sky was a harbinger of the fading winter of life.

The irony of so much food rotting away wasn't lost on anyone who was there. He watched as load after load of cadavers was dumped unceremoniously into the trenches. There hadn't been any fuel for the farmer's tractors and combines. No one had possessed the foresight to realize the diesel hoarded for the sanitation trucks wouldn't be necessary today if someone had simply reallocated it to harvest the crops when they had been fresh in the field.

And that was the crux of the issue. America, the land of plenty, home of immense wealth and natural resources, hadn't fallen from a lack of assets or the ignorance of her people. The greatest society on earth had succumbed to panic, a lack of leadership, and bitter infighting.

The Colonel, now the leader of a not-so-free world, was bound and determined to reverse the suffering and get things back on track. If that meant a temporary suspension of the values he held dear, then so be it. Liberty would be returned once the recovery had achieved momentum. He'd sanction the Constitution he so loved once the people were fed.

On the other hand, the Alliance had been founded on self-reliance. Early on, their leaders had pushed hard for every family to grow gardens, police their own areas, and improve their quality of life without some government entity coming in and taking charge. And that model of recovery was apparently working as well.

The president recalled a conversation with Bishop's wife, Terri, in which they had debated the value of each strategy. Lying in the Texans' rock room with a shank of aircraft frame protruding from his chest, the two of them has passed the time with such philosophical ramblings. He could just hear her words, "But Colonel, wasn't dependency on the government a big part of why the collapse occurred?"

And her point would be difficult to argue.

The president knew the dichotomy between the two approaches wasn't anything new. It was an age-old debate that had divided the American population since the founders had first met to frame the Constitution. Texas, as the Alliance, had manifested itself into the vision of those that supported local governance and a limited federal government.

The United States, on the other hand, was quickly becoming the poster child for those that believed a strong, centralized bureaucracy was the best way to captain the ship.

While the chief executive's brain was in Washington, his heart resided in Texas.

Sighing, the president turned and faced his subordinate. "General, I want to make one thing perfectly clear. While I have personal friends and close ties in the Lone Star State, I will not let those relationships cloud my judgment about what's best for our people and nation. I recited an oath when I took this office, and I fully intend to honor it to the best of my ability."

"I didn't mean to imply anything, sir."

The president waved off the backpedaling with a dismissive

motion of his hand. "Don't worry about it," he muttered, and then redirected the meeting back to its original topic of discussion. "I can't believe Diana and the Alliance leaders would go off the reservation like that, especially without having a single conversation with us. They've never expressed any desire or intent to expand their territory."

"Sir, those people down there in Texas should be united with the rest of the country, joining the fight for recovery. We've always banded together as a nation when faced with a threat. Time and again we've pushed aside our petty, regional differences for a greater good. What would have happened if Texas had decided it didn't want to fight in World War II or Korea?"

"You're jumping to conclusions, General. We don't know that the Alliance has anything to do with Los Alamos or these earthworks. Don't let what you hear around Washington cloud your opinion of those people in Texas. They just have a different way of doing things. So far, they're guilty of nothing more than stepping up to fill a vacuum of leadership," the president advised.

"Yes, sir. Still, their involvement is the only plausible explanation I've heard so far."

"Well, send in a team, and let's get to the bottom of this little mystery. But... and I can't stress this enough, retrieving the weapon-grade nuclear materials is the first priority. Understood?"

"Yes, sir."

The president made for his desk, thinking to continue studying the endless mountains of reports that required his attention. He was surprised to glance up and see the officer still standing in the room. "Is there something else, General?"

"Well... sir.... Yes, there is."

"Go on."

"It's your son, sir. He's a member of the team that is slated to go into New Mexico. I thought you'd want to know."

The president shrugged his shoulders, "My son is a Special Forces operator and a fully coherent adult. He makes his own decisions, and as I stated a dozen times before, he is to receive no special consideration just because I'm presiding over this rambling shit wagon we call a government."

"Yes, sir."

"Dismissed, General."

Chapter 2

"How long has she been missing?"

"About two hours, Grandfather. She, and two other girls were collecting food in the foothills. They heard men approaching and tried to hide. Cover was sparse, and she was separated from the other teens. She has not returned to the village even though she should be able to find her way. My father fears the worse and sent my brother and me to beg your help."

Hack Schneider stroked his bleach-white beard, studying the two teenage Cochiti boys standing in front of his cabin. Flanking the two nervous youth were three Jicarilla Apache warriors, guardians of the old gent. As always, they were on alert, distrustful of anyone approaching his property.

Tall, wiry men, the Apache's faces were painted in streaks of white as if their skeletons were located outside their skin. In addition to the haunting pigment, each bodyguard was adorned with a black leather hood and kilt. The first time Hack had seen them, he'd shuddered at the image. If good, old Mr. Webster had added a picture to his dictionary for the word "fierce," no doubt this is the image he would have chosen. But it was more than that. There was a primordial evil, a particular visual effect that had been intentionally designed hundreds of years ago to incite terror in an enemy's soul. And it worked – even today.

Hack wasn't sure why he warranted 24x7 bodyguards, but someone from their clan was always on duty, rarely spoke, and wouldn't accept any form of payment. There had been more than one occasion that he was glad they had been around.

"What do *you* think?" he inquired of the ferocious-looking gent who was obviously in charge of the security detail today.

The bodyguard shifted his AR15 rifle from one shoulder to the other and replied, "This is up to you, Grandfather. The Cochiti are good neighbors… most of the time."

Nodding his agreement, Hack addressed the two visitors, "Stay here. I'll be back in a moment."

Without another word, he turned and entered the modest cottage, walking straight through to the covered back porch. From there, it was another ten paces to his workshop. While no one had ever seen or heard of the toymaker having family or friends visit his remote, log-sided home, any such guest would have had difficulty identifying the difference between the residence and workshop.

In fact, Hack had designed his "tinkering palace" to be almost twice the square footage of his abode. "I spend far more time there. Why shouldn't it be larger?" he'd informed the perplexed builder.

Unlocking the heavy metal door, Hack flipped on the LED overhead lights and proceeded inside the place where he spent the vast majority of his time. No one was allowed in here. It was strictly off-limits, and even the Apaches respected that rule.

The first notable feature of the sanctum was a montage of pictures and awards practically covering one wall. There were images of a powerful-looking rocket plane, the F-117 Nighthawk Stealth Fighter, a Boeing B-1B bomber, and a host of other exotic aircraft.

Interspaced among the expensively framed photographs was an impressive assortment of certifications, awards, and diplomas. Many of these honors were accompanied by smaller depictions of a younger Hack Schneider, usually perched behind a podium or lectern... or his hand being pumped by a business executive or a Class A uniformed officer.

As he passed, Hack paid no attention to the "wall of fame," his life as an engineer at Lockheed's famous Skunk Works now nothing more than a distant memory.

Everyone estimated Hack to be in his late 60s, but no one knew for sure. With shoulder-length, pure white hair, a tall, wiry build, and upturned eyebrows, the toymaker resembled a storybook wizard. That's where the comparison ended, however, as everyone knew the man possessed far more power than any mythical warlock or fairytale magician.

Mr. Schneider's background was also a mystery. Not a soul knew where he'd worked before retiring to the Caldera. And most were too polite to ask. Northern New Mexico was like much of the southwestern United States in that it was considered rude to question a man about his past unless the information was volunteered. To the best of any survivor's knowledge, the toymaker never broached the subject.

What little was known from before the collapse provided no indication of the man's eventual notoriety in the surrounding settlements. Hack had purchased a small, mountain cabin west of Santa Fe and basically minded his own affairs. A few times a month he'd show up at one of the many craft shows or exhibitions so common in the artsy town, setting up a booth or display to show off his wares.

And what wares they were.

Hack built toys, or more accurately, extremely sophisticated, high technology, well-crafted playthings. His customers knew no age range. Often, his creations were outrageously expensive.

According to local lore and speculation, the toymaker was

most likely an engineer, definitely a craftsman, and obviously an artist. While known for his complex, functional robots, drones, radio controlled vehicles, and other mobile oddities, he also produced works of wooden art, crafted metal conversation pieces, and shaped the occasional item that defied categorization.

His Rube Goldberg machines were considered genius, finely crafted from a mixed bag of lumber leftovers, sculpted from metal remnants, or with repurposed scrap materials.

Once, Hack had pulled into Santa Fe with a scaled diesel-electric locomotive riding in the back of his old, blue Ford pickup. After soliciting a few men to help him unload the behemoth, he'd toured the square, tooting the whistle and offering free rides to the children.

It had been quite the spectacle, Mr. Schneider dressed in overalls, his long white hair flowing from beneath the classic engineer's cap. Straddling the child-sized engine, his spindly knees protruded at an odd angle. He'd gathered onlookers from all over town. He sold the engine that day, pocketing over $3,000 after four train buffs entered into what amounted to a bidding war.

The toymaker's talents were not lost on the local merchants either.

High-end specialty shops began offering his creations, some selling his productions on international auction sites for serious money. Other shopkeepers garnished their storefront displays with his lavish makings, his works drawing attention in the highly competitive tourist ecosystem that was Santa Fe.

But it was his drones that brought Mr. Schneider widespread local fame.

Proceeding into the main room of the extensive facility, he bypassed a hefty lathe and other machine shop-grade equipment, focused on a bench that consumed the entire length of one wall.

Flipping on an even brighter LED light, Hack moved to a small, remote controlled helicopter resting nearby.

Technically, the drone was considered a "quad-copter," its main fuselage in the shape of an "X," with four helicopter-like rotors at the end of each cross member. Built from carbon fiber and sporting a candy apple red paint job, the machine looked like a 2-foot square metallic insect.

Easily picking up the featherweight device, Hack unplugged the solar panels from the drone's battery charger and turned back to his work surface. He began opening cabinets and drawers, using a variety of tools to assemble the desired package of cameras and navigation computer.

11

He returned to the front porch carrying the drone, noting the Natives' reaction of awe when they spotted his toy.

"Gentlemen, I've configured this quad-copter with my best camera for searching at night. I hope it has enough battery life for what we want to accomplish. These things won't fly forever, you know."

"Yes, sir."

Motioning for the still nervous brother to come closer, Hack produced a tablet computer, its brand and logo worn away, its skin marred by frequent use. After a few taps and swipes on the screen, a map of northern New Mexico appeared.

"Point to this map and show me the general area where the girls were foraging," the toymaker directed.

The older brother did as instructed, and then Hack went to work.

It had been a stroke of pure luck that he'd downloaded mapping files before the collapse and the seemingly overnight disappearance of the internet. He often wondered how long the GPS satellites would function without ground control maintenance, but that was a problem for a different day.

Using his finger on the tablet computer's map, the toymaker punched in a series of waypoints, providing a set of directions for his robotic flyer to follow.

"I'll get in my cart, and you can lead the way to the pueblo. We can launch the drone from there. And if we find your sister, you can go and bring her back."

"They are preparing a search party, Grandfather. Several men have volunteered. With your help, we're sure we can find her."

Nodding, Hack went about unplugging the golf cart from its charging station. Soon, the toymaker and one of his Apache shadows were trailing the two Cochiti youth as they rode their horses down the mountain and onto the paved, two-lane New Mexico highway.

Several times, they had to slow and detour around obstacles, the lack of maintenance crews resulting in two rock falls and one section of road that had crumbled after a flash flood. Hack wondered how long it would be before the road was completely impassable.

Glancing over at his passenger, Hack noticed the man's scowl. "You think I'm being a soft hearted old fool going out like this to find the girl, don't you?"

"No, Grandfather, your kindness toward *the people (Native Americans)* is now tribal lore. If you hadn't come to our aid, many of our clan would have starved long ago. More would have died from the Raiders. You're known throughout the nations as our great defender. Why would you ever stop doing such things? It's my job to worry whenever anything unusual occurs."

It was rare for one of the Apache to speak more than a few words. Having little else to occupy his mind, Hack saw an opportunity for an interrogation. "Is that why the Apache send men to protect my home?"

"You don't know?"

"No. Obviously, I do not."

"The great forest fire before the electricity vanished – you saved those men."

Hack remembered back to the time his fellow traveler referenced. Drought had plagued the area for several seasons, numerous forest fires raging across the heavily wooded national forests surrounding Santa Fe. One particularly fast-spreading blaze threatened the toymaker's home and workshop.

It must have been quite the scene that day, the exhausted, dirty team of firefighters approached by the exotic citizen. In his hands was a device that appeared to be some sort of robotic-looking spider with propellers.

According to local legend, Schneider loomed over the area commander and announced, "You're doing this all wrong. Your men are in the wrong place. Now quit fucking around, and get your teams over to Bald Ridge, or you're going to lose control of this fire."

"And just how would you know that, old man?" had come the obvious question.

"Because my little friend here has been flying over the fire with a thermal imaging device, and I've plotted the hotspots from the air. That information, combined with the prevailing wind and undergrowth density, made predicting the fire's advancement child's play. Here, let me show you."

The toymaker had produced a map with numerous notations depicted.

"Fires don't behave rationally or logically," the pessimistic firefighter responded. "I can't go redeploying my men just because some guy walks up and shows me a pretty plaything and a drawing."

Disgusted, Mr. Schneider had given up trying to convince the hardheaded man. The next day proved the toymaker's revelation had indeed been correct, but not one of the fire team remembered or acknowledged his prediction – they were too busy battling an out of control inferno.

It wasn't until two days later that the same desperate chief knocked on the reclusive inventor's door. "I've got a team that's cut off. I've got eight men stranded. The wind changed direction, and now I can't get them out. If I don't do something, they'll all be burned alive. Can your toy help save them?"

He'd been tempted to repeat the man's dismissive words, "Fires don't behave rationally or logically," back to the commander, but thought better of it. Lives were at stake.

Four hours later, guided by the flying robot and the images transferred back to a ground control station, the stranded team reached safety.

"Yes, I remember saving that group of firefighters. What does that have to do with the Apache guarding my cabin?"

"One of those men you rescued was our governor's son. The tribe owed you a debt, not something we take lightly. When the lights dimmed and the whites attacked each other like starving wolves, the council thought you might need protection."

Hack shook his head, the irony of the warrior's words awaking old memories. "I learned some valuable lessons from that day, my friend. 'Always mind your own business.' And 'No good deed goes unpunished.' You see, I thought I was going to be tarred and feathered and then run out of town on a rail for my involvement."

Despite the evident heroic use of his "toy," the local folk's reaction wasn't what Mr. Schneider had expected. Instead of smiling faces and thankful citizens, he'd been shunned at best, nearly assaulted at worst.

The people of Santa Fe were scared of him, or more accurately, his drones. Questions about privacy... the legality and the morality of his winged robots dominated the public discourse. Rumors spread, most greatly exaggerated tales about the capabilities of his tiny flyers. Some people thought the machines could see through walls, others whispering that the mad scientist up on the mountain was listening in on every conversation in the county. Others flagged the old man as a pervert, claiming they'd seen his copters peeking in through the windows of their homes.

Only the Native Americans seemed to smile at him when he made his mandatory visits to town for groceries and supplies. He'd found their reaction odd at the time; now it all made sense.

Hack was more than happy to be out of the limelight, even if the exile was forced. He'd moved to New Mexico for the weather and isolation, not for the area's social life. Still, he could not deny his innate need to make a positive contribution to mankind... somehow, somewhere.

The reaction from the local tribes wasn't lost on the toymaker. When the occasional need to leave his retreat did occur, he found the Native American culture an interesting diversion.

The area was thick with reservations and pueblos, some

dating back to before the time of Christopher Columbus and his famous voyage. In addition to ancient ruins and abandoned cities, there always seemed to be dances, powwows, and mystical ceremonies taking place. The toymaker found a sort of kinship with the Natives' way of interacting with the world.

When society had fallen off a cliff, that bond was made stronger by the dichotomy of reactions Hack watched unfold.

In regular terms, the general population seemed to go crazy. They had been addicted to modern conveniences delivered by electrical power, automobiles that practically drove themselves, and meals they obtained via a drive-thru sack. When all of those "modern conveniences" evaporated, anger and desperation began to surface. Most of Santa Fe was burned to the ground in the riots, neighbor against neighbor violence taking almost as many lives as hunger and diseases.

The reservations and pueblos, on the other hand, didn't seem to be affected at all. The Native Americans had never grown accustomed to the convenience of a local Walmart and so never had to suffer withdrawal from its closing. Additionally, 'the people,' as they called themselves, were accustomed to a life of scarcity, shortage... even poverty. They had never been spoiled by the digital age. When cell phones stopped working, the Natives who had owned them set them aside and shrugged. Mainstream Americans would fight, scream, weep, and yell when they could not command four bars of signal.

Most of the tribes had made considerable efforts to educate their youth in the "old ways." Hunting for survival was still common, as were homesteading skills like making candles, growing maize, and weaving on a loom.

The collapse resulted in shock and trauma for everyone, but it was obvious to Hack that *the people* weathered the storm far better than their white neighbors.

While his cabin was off the grid by geographic necessity, Hack still needed supplies. He was too old to hike the mountains in order to hunt and gather. His solar panels, water well, and in-ground septic covered the basic necessities of shelter, but he still had to eat.

Like everyone else, the speed of the downfall had taken him by surprise. With the cupboard nearly barren, he'd decided to approach one of the friendlier tribes and see if he could strike a barter arrangement. The relationship had prospered from there.

Despite the two Cochiti boys riding their horses at a half gallop, their progress was still painful. A sign of the times, Hack thought. What once took a few minutes now takes so much longer. Time used to be money; now it is life or death.

Turning again to his passenger, Hack asked, "What is your

name? You've been camped out, guarding my place for months, and I still don't know your name."

The Apache smirked, "I don't think you can pronounce my Indian name, but there is an interesting story behind it if you would care to hear?"

"Of course," the inventor replied, always eager to learn new things.

"I asked my mother about my name when I was much younger, and she told me that when my older sister was born, the first thing my father saw when he went outside was the sunrise, so her name is Warming Sky. And then my brother came along, and the first thing my father saw was a soaring hawk, so he was named Wind Rider."

"Okay," Hack replied, "I'm following you so far. What's your name?"

"Two Dogs Fucking."

The inventor's eyes grew wide, his jaw physically dropping. For an uncomfortable moment, Hack didn't know what to do or say, scared any reaction would give insult.

The storyteller bailed him out, breaking into a wide grin, and then letting loose with a belly-deep laugh. Hack knew he'd been had.

"Very funny," the toymaker replied after his passenger's humor had subsided. "You had me there for a minute."

"White people love that joke," the Native American added. "In reality, my name is Jack Smith."

Again, Hack did a double take, not sure if his passenger was pulling his leg once more. "Seriously?"

"Yes, I know it's not all Native-sounding and steeped in tradition, but it *is* the truth."

"And what did you do before the collapse, Mr. Smith?"

"I was a high school PE teacher and baseball coach. I graduated with a degree in education from New Mexico State," the Apache explained.

"Baseball?"

"Love the game for its strategy and pace," Jack responded enthusiastically. "I made it into the Dodgers' minor league system, but just didn't have enough movement on my fastball to make the Bigs. So I went on to teaching and coaching. We went 16 and 5 the last year before it all went to hell."

"That's very interesting, Mr. Smith," Hack noted. "Now that I think about it, I guess a lot of the local folks were into baseball."

The Native waved his hand through the air, "Please, Grandfather, my friends call me Apache Jack, or just Jack, or asshole. I don't like Mr. Smith, it makes me sound like that nerdy guy from that old movie... you know, *Mr. Smith Goes to the*

Senate... or something like that?"

Nodding, Hack did indeed remember the movie. "Okay, Apache Jack it is."

"So now it's my turn. What is your story?"

"I am actually part Native American as well," Hack replied, "Although I didn't even know until my mother was on her deathbed. She was a full-blooded Lakota Sioux who married a shopkeeper from Minnesota. They moved to California shortly after I was born. Until the very end, she never breathed a word about her heritage."

Hack's reminiscing was interrupted by their arrival at the pueblo.

The inventor didn't know the age of this specific village, but he guessed it had been founded hundreds of years prior. Single-story adobe and straw brick structures dominated the landscape, most of the residences quite modest in size.

Only the church's steeple and two large, round-topped kivas protruded from the low-rise skyline dominated by thatched roofs. Even the few trees scattered about seemed to prefer a low profile.

Other than the smattering of pickup trucks and cars parked here and there, it was a timeless community. Many of the homes were equipped with tie-up rails for horses; the streets were narrow, paved only with packed dirt.

Modern-day air conditioners were non-existent, the architecture boasting high ceilings and thick earthen walls that remained cool even in the brutal New Mexico sun. Corner fireplaces and their soot-blackened stacks dotted the landscape, but Hack knew these were mostly for cooking, not environmental control.

The toymaker was led directly to the main square, an expansive, open area used for communal activities and annual ceremonies. The inventor had been here before, one of thousands who attended a lavish dance hosted by the tribe each summer.

This was a different place now. The hundreds of Natives, sporting the full regalia complete with ornamental clothing and painted faces had been replaced by men and women who were clothed in casual blue jeans and western shirts. Instead of smiling faces and welcoming nods, Hack sensed concern and worry in the locals' expressions. The thundering drums of the ceremonial mega-dances had been replaced by the anxious cadence of hushed voices. As soon as Hack exited his cart, everyone fell silent.

"Grandfather, thank you for coming," greeted one elder, approaching with an extended hand.

Another gent came forward, Hack soon learning that the man was the missing girl's uncle, a respected position in the Native American family hierarchy. "Did you bring one of your metal hawks, Grandfather?" the relative asked.

Yes, he'd brought a drone. No, Hack didn't need anything. After a polite exchange, he went straight to work. Removing the flying machine from his cart, he strode briskly to the center of the square. The residents gathered around, struggling to satisfy their curiosity while still trying to maintain a respectable distance.

He didn't need to explain the drone, most of the villagers already having seen his toys in action.

While he ran through a short pre-flight checklist, Hack couldn't help but note the surreal contradiction of the unfolding events.

Here he was, readying to deploy technology that hadn't existed just a few years before. His "metal hawk," as the older members of this tribe described it, was equipped with infrared sensors, proximity detectors, and state-of-the-art battery technology.

Yet, he was surrounded by an ancient society living in what many of his own race would describe as primitive conditions. The new was helping the old tonight.

But it wasn't a one-way relationship.

When his supply of food had been running low, Hack approached a nearby pueblo and offered a trade. He would purpose one of his flying machines to locate game in the surrounding mountains, in exchange for a portion of the hunt.

The tribal leaders had been skeptical at first, but a quick demonstration had quickly brought them to an agreement.

With his flying eyes, Hack could pinpoint herds of elk, sheep, and deer. On a few occasions, he'd even identified roaming groups of cattle that had escaped their home range during the apocalypse. Cows meant milk *and* meat. With his toys scouting overhead, the hunters could save days and days of time wandering the mountains. The supply of meat doubled.

And then there were the Raiders.

New Mexico's remote environment and hostile terrain didn't grant immunity from vagabonds, wandering groups of desperate refugees, and nomadic, criminal gangs.

Some came from Santa Fe and Albuquerque, abandoning the larger cities that had become hellholes of strife and anarchy. Others had only been passing through on the interstate, suddenly finding themselves trapped without fuel or resources.

To the tribes, history was indeed repeating itself, many of the local nations finding their lands, animals, and gardens beset by hostile strangers roaming the countryside. Assault and murder against the Native Americans quickly became everyday events, reminiscent of abuses suffered as much as 400 years before.

It was during one of those early "hunting flights," that the toymaker's screen revealed a group of armed men working their way toward a pueblo, their long guns clear on the computer's display.

Given the early warning, the tribesmen had been waiting in ambush. The resulting gunfight had been brutal, one-sided, and necessary.

A murmur drifted through the crowd when the drone's propellers began spinning, gasps sounding when the small robot shot skyward like a rocket.

The area where the girls had been harvesting was over a mile away from the square, well within the distance Hack's radio could transmit and receive signals. He didn't need the connection to fly the device, its route having been pre-programmed with waypoints and GPS coordinates back at the cabin. What Hack and the gathering elders waited to see was the video link.

With fingers tapping and swiping the tablet, Hack noted the men gathering to peer over his shoulders. He raised the small screen higher to improve their view.

The computer's image changed, a live video feed now streaming from the drone's camera. Again, a buzz of side conversations spread among the gathered men.

Adjusting a control, he ordered the hovering drone to point its gimbal-mounted camera downward, the square and gathered assembly below coming into view.

From 150 feet above their heads, most of the crowd was in focus. "We look like ghosts," noted one of the tribesmen.

"Look at the heat escaping the kiva," noted another. "I told you we needed to fix that roof."

"Hopefully, the missing girl's body heat will stand out against the cooler background of the desert, and we can locate her quickly," Hack explained for the benefit of anyone who hadn't seen his machines function. "Just like when we hunt elk."

Hack tapped the screen, and the drone increased its altitude to 500 feet and then zoomed away, flying rapidly toward its first waypoint. "It will be over the area in a few moments," he informed the gathering. "I ordered the drone to fly a search pattern. All that we can do now is wait and watch."

The pounding of several horses sounded in the square, a party of 15 riders galloping around the corner and pulling up in front of the crowd. They were all men, all brandishing rifles, all wearing paint on their faces and arms.

"I formed a party of our best hunters," the uncle informed the toymaker. "If your metal hawk spots my niece, these men will ride to find her."

All eyes returned to the small screen, several of the men pointing as the drone passed over familiar landmarks. "Look, there's so and so's house," came one comment, another man noting a nearby bridge and a pool of water beneath. "That looks like we might have a beaver damming up the creek," he remarked, impressed with the detail of the video.

"Approaching the search area," Hack announced, hoping to soothe some of the local nerves.

For the first two waypoints, only two rabbits and a groundhog town showed hot on the display. Hack could sense a hopelessness building in the surrounding men.

The flyer was readying to begin its third turn when a group of white spots appeared in the distance. "What the hell?" Hack whispered, his fingers working to change the drone's direction and altitude.

A group of men slowly came into focus, at least three bodies surrounding the pulsating white of a campfire.

Ordering the drone to approach slowly, the image began to show more and more detail as the camera moved closer.

The strangers were armed... heavily armed. Hack could make out load vests, military grade weapons, helmets and other equipment that identified the trespassers as military or law enforcement. "I don't know who these interlopers are, but they have come prepared for a war," the toymaker mused.

And then a fourth hotspot showed on the screen, this one smaller, just outside the camp.

"There she is," Hack declared, pointing at the clear outline of a small female in a crouched position. "She's right next to their camp.... What is she doing?"

One of the men examining the screen from the edge of the crowd shouted, "They've taken her prisoner!"

Another spectator had a different point of view, countering with, "No, it looks like she hid from them and has gotten trapped. They're too close for her to escape!"

A din arose from the gathered throng, all of the combatants competing to voice their opinions at once. It was the uncle's words that rose above the clamor and then silenced the crowd. "None of this matters!" he shouted. "They are trespassers on our land and armed for battle. For many years, white men have used their weapons to snatch food from the very mouths of our children. How can we trust them now? Did these travelers come to the pueblo and announce their arrival? No, they hide in the mountains and wait for their opportunity to pillage our settlements and make slaves of our people," the uncle paused to make sure his audience was considering his words before continuing his soliloquy. "And already they have taken their first captive."

Hack scanned the mass, seeing several heads nodding in agreement. Before he could make an observation, the uncle turned to the gathered hunting party and implored, "You have the information you need. Will you not go now and rescue my niece?"

"Hold on," Hack barked, "Wait just a minute. Before you go rushing off, you need to understand those three men aren't the typical Raiders. They look like U.S. military to me... maybe cops or deputies. Whoever they are, you need to be extra careful. They're armed to the teeth, and the girl is very close to their camp."

"Show us where they are, Grandfather, and we'll bring her back... along with their heads," spouted the lead hunter.

Hack didn't like it but could sense the determination of the men surrounding him. Nodding, his eyes returned to the tablet where he began to manipulate the software.

A frown formed on the toymaker's face when he realized the girl's location. Looking up with concern, he announced, "They're right on the southern edge of the project. Directly above where the men have been digging for the last few days."

Before he could form any other words, a chorus of hoots, whoops, and blood-curdling screams rose up from the riders. With a wave of his arm signaling for the others to follow, the leader spurred his mount, and the hunting party was storming out of the square accompanied by the rolling thunder of hooves.

Chapter 3

The wind had been kicking up dust devils all afternoon. By the time Bishop was ready to turn in, he knew a storm was on the way. He could smell the moisture in the air, a rarity for the arid environment.

"Good... we need rain," the Texan observed.

Scanning his small patch of West Texas dirt one last time before entering the RV, he noticed flashes of lightning to the west, their strobes illuminating the majestic outline of the Chisos Mountains in the distance. "A storm at that. I wonder if the thunder will frighten Hunter?" he worried.

Terri was in Alpha with their son, visiting Diana and finalizing wedding plans. No doubt there was a hefty dose of girl stuff involved as well. She'd begged him to come along and be around people for a change, but there were too many chores on his list. Always too many. Besides, Terri was more akin to the city life, and he'd just dampen the mood worrying about this, that, or the other back at the ranch.

The harsh Chihuahuan Desert had been contrary as of late, the land making it difficult to feed his family and make an honest living. That, and a streak of bad luck weighed on Bishop's mind every night and day.

Mr. Beltran had advanced him six head of seed stock, the small herd of cattle comprised of an aging bull and five serviceable cows. One had fallen to her death, the victim of a rockslide and grazing too close to the steep ridge. Another had contracted disease and expired. Veterinarians were a luxury since the collapse. Even when an animal doc could be contacted in time, medications to treat sick stock were seldom available.

One calf was on the way, but even if she delivered without incident, the headcount was in decline. At this rate, it would be years before he could butcher for table beef. Initially disappointed in just the one pregnancy, an old-time rancher at the Meraton market had set Bishop straight. "Bovine are skittish creatures. You've introduced them to a new environment. You're lucky to have one seed take root. Patience, my friend, patience."

And then there was hunting, or more appropriately, the lack thereof.

The Texan had grown up in the area, scouted the surrounding mountains and valleys throughout his youth. Even after moving to Houston as a younger man, he'd returned to the ranch periodically, spending a week roaming the hills and harvesting the occasional deer. In all those years, he'd never seen such a lack of game.

He supposed it was due to people having to hunt for food. He'd read somewhere that during the Great Depression, a few species of White-tail deer had been hunted to extinction. Folks had to eat.

Then there was the competition introduced by his herd. He'd observed both species grazing on the same plants. Even the local jackrabbits dined at the same green-counter. Perhaps his cattle were driving the other animals away to lusher pasture.

Bishop entered the RV, opening the fridge and pouring a cup of cold water. The drink reminded him of the need to repair the shaft on the windmill pump in the south canyon. He'd get on that in the morning.

A quick shower and scrub with homemade soap left him feeling a little better. He did have air conditioning. He didn't have to carry a rifle with him every moment of the day. He wasn't worried about Terri and Hunter's safety. Things could be worse... things had been worse.

"After I fix the well pump, I'll go higher into the mountains tomorrow afternoon. I bet the rain will bring the deer down, and maybe I'll have some venison when Terri gets back," he whispered to the empty camper.

He stretched out on the bed, forcing the worries of the day from his mind. Terri would be back in two days, and he'd welcome her home with fresh meat and a garden that was beginning to produce. It would all be okay.

Before sleep came, his mind drifted back to his childhood on the ranch. At the time, he'd thought his father had been a gruff, old worrier, never able to relax or enjoy life. The man had possessed little sense of humor, and even less tolerance for the "wasteful activities," of recreation or fun. Bishop couldn't remember his dad ever reading a book or going to see a movie at the Alpha Bijou. The demands of ranch life did not allow for vacations or frivolous trips out of town.

For years, Bishop had written off his father's outlook as a product of scars from the Vietnam War, but now, older and wiser, the Texan had his doubts about that conclusion.

It seemed like every day his thoughts would drift back to old memories of the lessons that the father had tried to instill in the son. Work ethic, honesty, ability to get along with other men, how to fight, and knowing when it was better to run.

It seemed like there was always a conflict between the two of them. Bishop was adventurous, curious, and easily distracted. His father made every attempt to hammer home the skills and knowledge that could be used in the real world, often frustrated by his son's interest in places and people far away from the desolate, West Texas ranch.

"You need to learn about livestock, the economics of ranching, and how the cost of feed makes the difference between beans for supper or steak," his dad would preach. "You can't call a vet for every sick animal – the bills would eat up a year's profit in a month. Knowing how to run a fence can save a man hundreds in the cost of wire and posts. Learning when to sell and when to hold your stock means money in your pocket and food on the table. Get your head out of the clouds, boy. The only thing we know will be here tomorrow is the land. Learn to live off of it, and you'll be a better man for the effort."

It had all seemed so harsh to young Bishop. He saw magazines and pictures at school, images of cities and landscapes that seemed so different than his native Texas. Didn't his father know there were other ways to make a living? Didn't the old man realize there was another world out there?

Now, older and with experience under his belt, Bishop understood his father's perspective. Given the responsibilities of trying to feed his own family, his father's approach didn't seem so harsh or outdated.

"I'd give my best rifle to spend a day with my dad," Bishop whispered. "I wish I'd paid more attention. Those lessons would help me now. I could pass them onto Hunter. He might need them later."

Despite the soft pillow and clean sheets, sleep proved difficult. Bishop's mind eventually slowed, it's whirling cycle surrendering to a body feeling the effects of a hard day's toil.

"I'll take the first watch," Chief Master Sergeant Grissom announced, throwing the remainder of his coffee into the fire and watching the sparks and steam sizzle into the night. "I'll wake you in three hours."

"Be careful," teased Sergeant Jones. "We're in Indian country."

"I like my scalp just the way it is," added the lieutenant, unrolling his sleeping bag. "The women back at Fort Bragg would never forgive you if a savage's tomahawk fucks up my rugged, but handsome profile. Now, Jones over there," he continued, nodding toward the third man, "he could use a little cosmetic surgery. Boyish good looks have gone out of style."

"Whatever," Grissom grunted. "I guess I should consider it a privilege to stand guard over your beauty sleep, eh LT?"

"All of you '*Chair Force*' studs should be proud to serve with us Army men," Jones countered. "It'll enlarge your nut sack and grow chest hair. Make a man out of you."

Rolling his eyes, Sergeant Grissom ignored the twin insults to his service and manhood. He'd long ago grown used to the bravado of the U.S. Army's Special Forces operators. The banter was predictable.

Grissom grunted, still shaking his head over the exchange. Bending to heft his rifle and night vision, he moved away from the fire and began thinking about the pattern he would follow during his stint on watch.

Being in the U.S. Air Force had been a deliberate choice. Signing up to be a Pararescue Specialist or PJ (abbreviated from the original Para Jumper) had been his ultimate goal. After almost two years of the most arduous training in the military, Grissom had graduated and joined the teams.

For those in the know, PJs commanded the same respect as Navy SEALS, Green Berets, and the CAG. In fact, most of Grissom's deployments had been with integrated teams from those same units.

Grissom had wanted to serve with the PJs because their core objective was to save lives. Their primary mission was to rescue downed pilots from the most hostile territories and fight their way back to friendly lines if necessary.

He'd attended all of the elite schools, from Army Airborne training at Fort Benning to the combat diver course in Panama City, Florida.

After receiving the same level of combat instruction as any Special Forces operator, the PJs were only halfway through their curriculum. Next came nearly a year of specialized medical training, multiple survival courses, and a constant diet of refresher exercises. To be a PJ required heart *and* brains.

The sergeant meandered his way up the ridge from the bivouac, wanting to access the higher ground so he could gain a better perspective of their surroundings. In reality, he was still curious about their secondary objective, motivated to study the earth-moving activities in detail.

Despite the good-natured banter from the soldiers below, Grissom wasn't really worried about being discovered. They were only going to be in the area for a short period of time – a quick insertion, reconnaissance, and then orderly egress.

Their primary objective, Los Alamos, had been a mixed bag. They had found the massive, steel vaults at the labs still intact, their Geiger counter detecting no evidence of any radiation leaks. Grissom had radioed in the report, including video images via the satellite phone's datalink. The brass back at the base seemed pleased with the results. They could now safely send in another team of specialists for the preparation and transport of the nuclear materials.

But there was bad news as well. Large sections of the laboratory and its sophisticated array of equipment had been destroyed by fire. The undamaged parts had been thoroughly looted. Another national asset lost to the apocalypse.

The town surrounding the massive research facility was entirely abandoned, the team discovering only a few clean-picked skeletons and random piles of sun-bleached bones to account for the thousands of engineers and scientists that had once occupied the area. They had found most of the garages void of automobiles, a sure sign that the brain trust had bugged out when things had started getting bad.

Grissom hoped most of them had made it.

It was the secondary objective that now troubled the sergeant. He'd never seen anything like the activity they'd found in the valley below.

Vast sections of earth had been disturbed, evidence of excavation, movement, and grading throughout the valley. Massive berms had been raised, accompanying a complex system of what appeared to be locks and canals. It had all puzzled the analysts studying the aerial photographs, and now, despite his team's close-up inspection, he still didn't have a clue.

Grissom was nothing if not curious. This was normally a positive attribute, but occasionally could get him into hot water. He loved to solve mysteries, and that sometimes led to quandaries.

He reached the pinnacle of the rise, staying low for a moment as he scanned the horizon with his night vision. As expected, there wasn't any movement or unusual shapes displayed in the green and black world created by the device's light amplification tube.

Satisfied that his team was still undetected, Grissom stepped higher and began studying the valley below. He had to admit, it was all just plain weird.

In a way, the scene reminded the sergeant of old pictures he'd once seen, a series of photographs taken during the construction of the Panama Canal.

While the activity below was on a smaller scale, it was still a substantial undertaking, collapse of society or not. And it didn't make one bit of sense. The nearest city was Santa Fe, but everyone knew that town had been mostly destroyed by fire and looting. Albuquerque was almost as bad, both metropolitan areas practically void of inhabitants.

The surrounding territory was desolate, sparsely populated,

and mostly comprised of Native American reservations, tribal lands, and National Forests. Who was moving all that dirt down there... and why?

The project below would have represented a massive undertaking even before the loss of fuel, heavy equipment, and computer aided drafting. Now, without those capabilities, the scale and complexity of the operation just didn't make any sense.

One of the analysts back at the Pentagon had even gone so far as to speculate that the scientists and engineers at Los Alamos were responsible. One theory had it that someone was digging a massive burial ground for the nuclear materials known to be at the lab.

But that concept had quickly been shot down. There were less than 100 pounds of fissionable material in all of the laboratory's sprawling infrastructure, and that wouldn't require such a big hole.

Grissom didn't know who was running the show down in the valley, but he was reasonably sure it had nothing to do with nukes. The involvement of Los Alamos scientists was still a possibility, but the PJ had his doubts.

Forcing his mind to refocus on the job at hand, the operator began quietly circling the camp, eyes and ears prying the darkness, searching for any sign of trouble. "Don't let curiosity kill the PJ-cat," he whispered.

Hack wanted to keep the drone above the intruders and observe the encounter in real time, but that was impossible. The terrain between the pueblo and the valley was too difficult for the hunting party to make good time, especially in low light conditions, and his batteries were limited.

Sighing at the flying machine's power indicator, he punched a series of buttons and ordered the drone home.

"I know you all want to watch, but my machine is out of juice," he explained to the gathered onlookers. "The hunting party will bring the girl back, I'm sure."

"You've helped beyond measure," replied the uncle, placing a reassuring hand on the inventor's shoulder. "Would you like any food or drink while we wait?"

"No thank you, I'm fine."

The crowd milled around for several minutes, Hack catching bits and pieces of the low conversations while he waited. Everyone was clearly keyed up, the family members of the hunting party both proud of their kin's participation in the rescue, and worried at the same time about their wellbeing.

At no time did the toymaker detect any hesitation or second-guessing of the project. Hack was unsure if the locals just hadn't put two and two together... or if he was just paranoid.

This is all related, he thought. There's no other reason for military men to be in that area. Somehow, they're on to us.

Someone pointed skyward, and then the drone was hovering overhead. Without Hack touching the tablet, the flying robot began its descent into the middle of the square.

After his toy had landed, Hack performed a quick check-over of his device and then returned it to his car. All along, his Apache shadow loomed close by.

"There's nothing more for us to do now but wait," he informed his bodyguard. "I want to stay here and talk to the hunting party when they return. If they capture any of the strangers alive, I want to speak with them as well."

Apache Jack grunted, "They won't take anyone alive, Grandfather. You know that. Still, it will be good to see the girl reunited with her family."

Hack nodded, knowing his companion's words were accurate. The local tribes had stopped taking any prisoners long ago. They would, however, bring back the equipment and personal effects from the bodies, and that might help explain the purpose of the strangers' trip. The guard sensed his apprehension. "You are troubled, Grandfather. Is there something else?"

"I don't like military men spying on the project," Hack replied. "If there is any government presence remaining in Washington, they're not going to like what we're doing. I've long hoped our joint venture would be completed before anyone discovered our handiwork."

"More than any white man since your kind came to our lands, you have helped the people, Grandfather. From my brothers the Mescalero in the south to the Navajo in the west, the nations are uniting behind the project. Our time has come. It's our turn, and nothing is going to stop us."

Hack didn't respond at first, moving to lean against the hood of his cart. He'd heard similar words from several of the local leaders, and in a way, they were right.

It had all started innocently enough.

Given the success of his drones assisting with security and the hunts, he'd been experimenting with equipping the metal hawks with ground-contouring radar.

He'd earned the handle "Hack" back in the early days at the Skunk Works, quickly developing a reputation for "hacking" together solutions using existing hardware and software. The name had stuck, and besides, he thought it sounded far better than "Ruben," the name given by his mother.

Using scavenged components from a police radar gun and old cell phones, he'd been "hacking" together a device that would provide detailed mapping of the surrounding territory. If they were to survive long term, the tribes were going to be forced into large-scale farming.

That plan required tillable land, water for irrigation, and manageable overland routes to plant and distribute the harvest.

His hack had worked, downloading detailed terrain and elevation data into one of the inventor's more powerful computers.

Hack could still remember the day it had dawned on him that the valley was ripe for irrigation. He'd been studying the high output, agricultural regions, such as those in California and Texas, and discovered the surrounding desert was geographically predisposed for just such a project. But where to find that much water?

The answer was obvious – the Rio Grande River.

Flowing from north of them in Colorado, the Rio Grande wasn't much more than a broad stream as it passed through Santa Fe and flowed south where it eventually formed the border between Texas and Mexico.

Hack quickly discovered that the limited water supply was partly due to the waterway's split just north of the valley. There, the Pecos River branched off, taking a separate route toward central Texas. The two rivers eventually met again along the Mexican border before flowing into the Gulf of Mexico at Brownsville, Texas.

But what if the Pecos was damned and its flow diverted into the Rio Grande's channel? There would be plenty of water to turn the entire valley green with crops. There would be more than enough food to feed the tribes.

He'd presented his idea gradually, talking with a governor here, an elder there. Would the Nations buy into such a project?

"We can establish one of the most productive, fertile regions in the world," he explained at one council meeting. "We've all been living for years off the corn and wheat production from the Midwest. Since the collapse, that source is no longer available. Those fields may never be planted again."

At one of the powwows, a group of dignitaries from the Hopi tribe was visiting. After the presentation, one of the foreign chiefs approached Hack and asked, "Do you have the tablet?"

"Sir? Do you mean a tablet computer?"

"No, I'm speaking of the tablet of prophecy. Are you the

elder brother?"

Hack was puzzled, his bewildered expression answering the chief's question. The old man was polite enough to explain, "My people were led into this world by two brothers. The younger, and his followers, stayed here in what is now called the Southwest. The older brother traveled east, into the morning sun. We believe that when it looks like our world is about to end, the older brother will return and save our people."

Hack shook his head, "I'm just a man, sir. I may have a bit more knowledge than some other men, but I am flesh and blood, just like you."

The chief was skeptical, giving Hack a slow look-over from head to toe, his eyes seemingly drawn to the inventor's long white hair. Finally, in a low voice, he expanded, "Our prophecy calls the elder brother the 'True White Brother.' And you are very white."

The old man then turned and pointed to the bright red drone Hack had brought along for a demonstration. "Our legend also states that the True White Brother's followers will be red."

"That's just a coincidence," Hack said, waving off the observation with a friendly gesture. "Red is my favorite color, so I paint many of my toys with the same pigment."

"I see," nodded the chief. "Thank you for your honesty, and thank you for helping the people. The lands of the Hopi are some distance away, but I will pledge our resources to this project if the local leadership decides to pursue your ideas."

The chief started to turn away but then paused. Turning back he said, "Would several, hefty bulldozers and other earthmoving machines help?"

Hack's eyes grew wide. "Yes, yes, they would help immensely."

"Before the lights flickered out for the last time, our tribe was clearing land for a new construction project. The workers never returned for their machines, and they've been sitting still ever since. Some of our men wanted to take the fuel truck that sits at the location, but the council wouldn't let them. I suppose, after all this time, we could make a claim and use it for such a grand purpose."

The toymaker's mind immediately began racing with options. Would the engines start? Would the diesel fuel be usable after sitting for months and months? Did he know enough to make them function?

A month later, work crews started showing up, surveying, placing stakes in the ground, and assigning local volunteers to various tasks.

As it turned out, the Hopi's diesel fuel was worthless,

nothing more than a tank full of lime green algae.

But Hack had another solution – wood gas.

The surrounding mountains were thick with forests. Wood was in plentiful supply. In less than a week, he had the first refinery producing fuel. A month later, using his model and scavenged parts, the methane-based gas was being produced in nearly every pueblo.

Soon there were giant bulldozers working alongside the legions of laborers. Shovels were in short supply, the demand forcing two raiding parties to enter the ashes of Santa Fe and Albuquerque to pillage hardware stores and warehouses for anything that would move dirt.

Hack was using every ancient engineering trick in the book to help move earth and build the infrastructure required to irrigate the valley. Water wheels, rail cars similar to those used in the early days of underground mines, and even homemade explosives were now common sights in the desert.

Everyone began calling the project "Valley Green," and the name was apt. They truly were going to turn the basin the color of emeralds.

Only once did Hack think about the impact on those downstream. If his scheme worked, both the Rio Grande and the Pecos rivers would cease to exist outside of New Mexico. One of the elders had family in Texas and voiced concern over their wellbeing if the river dried up completely.

"They can move here and enjoy a full stomach every day," one of the governors responded. "They can come home."

Bishop's hand was reaching for the bedside rifle before his mind could climb from the depths of REM-sleep. With a racing heart and unsure legs, Bishop swung his feet over the edge of the mattress, eyes probing the darkness, scanning for the threat.

"The camper is under attack!" his foggy mind was screaming.

But it didn't make any sense. What kind of attack made such a roar? What kind of weapon sounded like a jet engine on the roof?

With rifle high and sweeping, he negotiated the narrow passage to the main salon. He was alone. There weren't any bullets tearing through the trailer's thin, aluminized skin. No explosions rocked his world.

"Is some piss midget landing an airliner on my RV?" was his

next thought.

Padding to the door, Bishop cracked it open and had his answer. Hail.

Gusting wind was driving the marble-sized chunks of ice nearly horizontal, pelting both the RV's top and sides. Relieved that he wasn't facing armed vagabonds with some sort of heavy weapon, Bishop exhaled and studied the storm through the door's narrow opening. So rare was the weather phenomena, he stuck a bare arm out the narrow opening without thinking.

Pulling back the stinging limb, Bishop set the rifle down and rubbed his skin. His first thought was of the cattle, but he quickly dismissed any worry there. Their thick hide would withstand the assaulting ice.

The camper would be okay as long as the hail didn't break a window. His beloved pickup was with Terri in Alpha. The bat cave was a fortress.

The garden!

"Shit!" he snapped, rushing back to the bedroom for his boots. He emerged a few moments later, leather slicker pulled over his head, flashlight in hand.

The ground was already covered with an inch of white, the Texan's boots making crunching noises as he rushed toward the garden. The canyon looked surreal, the snow-like layer reflecting the beam of his torch as he fought to protect his face from the biting balls of pain.

Before the garden plot came into view, he had suspected what he would find. For a moment, he considered turning back for shelter. "There's nothing you can do about it anyway," he chided himself. But he had to know... had to see.

Bare stalks appeared in the flashlight's pool of illumination, soon followed by stripped vines, shredded leaves, and green debris scattered on the ground.

"No," Bishop whispered, his agony bleeding through in that one word. His chin dropped low to his chest, the raging storm distant and forgotten. He had to take his eyes away from the disaster. "I worked so hard... all that time... babied every single seed, celebrated every sprout," he mumbled.

Dejected, the Texan merely turned and headed back for the camper. There wasn't anything he could do.

Sergeant Grissom's face brightened as he scanned the valley with his night vision. The dark world of greens and blacks displayed through the device were showing him a different pattern of shape and contour. It came to him in a rush - he knew the purpose of the activities in the valley.

Someone was building irrigation channels... and a bunch of them at that.

It was so obvious through the NVD. He was sure that's what all the fuss had been about.

Pulling a map from his chest rig, he ducked low behind an outcropping in order to shine his flashlight on the chart. Yes, there it was; the Rio Grande River was less than a kilometer away. Now, the development all made sense.

But who could have possibly organized such a massive project? That mystery wouldn't be solved until they could see the workers and equipment, hopefully in the morning.

Grissom was so excited by his discovery, he thought to wake the other team members and announce his sleuthy prowess. "I'll be rousting them soon enough," he whispered. "Let 'em sleep. They're Army after all and need all the rest they can muster."

Re-folding his map, the PJ decided he couldn't wait to share his discovery. As he climbed back to the overlook, the sergeant connected his night vision to the Panther Sat-Phone using a cord from his load vest. After double-checking the connection, he punched a sequence of numbers into the small com-unit's keypad.

Just like placing a cell call before the collapse, Grissom heard a ringing on the other end. A voice answered, "CONUS CIC (continental US combat information center), state your business."

"This is Rat-pack 3. Repeat, this is Rat-pack 3. SITREP (situation report) and upload to follow."

"Wait one," replied the voice.

Another voice came on the line a few seconds later, "Go, Rat-pack 3."

"This is Grissom. We've obtained eyes on the earthworks, and I believe I know what they are. Someone is preparing to dam the Rio Grande River and channel the flow through a series of irrigation channels. Video to follow."

Turning on his night vision device, Grissom acted like he was any old vacationer filming a tourist attraction. He scanned the valley below with his NVD, all the while whispering a commentary through the Satphone. "These are the entry channels here at the north end of the valley. They branch out approximately every point-five click into the retaining pools over there. If you check the topography of my AO (area of operations), you'll see this all fits."

He continued his report for almost two minutes.

"Wait one while I verify the video was received," the hollow voice from space responded.

Grissom unplugged his NVD and was returning it to his weapon when the sound of a human whimper made him freeze. It was close... damn close.

Whispering and going to an alert crouch at the same time, he said, "Contact. Wait one," into the Satphone. He tucked the still connected device into his vest in order to have both hands free for his weapon.

Some intuition told Grissom that the source of the noise was not a threat, but his grip never relaxed on the carbine on his shoulder. He progressed slowly, without a sound, his eyes desperately scanning the rocky surroundings for the source.

The night vision found her, balled up in an indentation of rock and covered with dead scrub. "What are you doing here?" were Grissom's first words, quickly followed by, "I won't hurt you. Come on out."

But she didn't move.

Chancing his flashlight again, the PJ's beam illuminated a young girl, eyes wide with terror, face covered with tears, dirt, and mucus. "Come on out," he coaxed softly. "You're okay. I won't hurt you."

Shivering with fear and squinting from his light, she refused to move.

Grissom took a step toward her, thinking to offer the girl a drink and tempt her out of the narrow nook.

Taking a deep breath, she screamed with lungs full of horror.

At that moment, all hell broke loose on the ridge.

The hunting party hadn't been in position just yet, dividing their number and moving slowly to encircle the camp. Prompted by the girl's cry of terror, they had been forced to launch the attack early.

Grissom heard a shot from below at the same moment a shadow came flying over the rock formation, the leaping attacker catching him full on. The two combatants hit the ground hard, rolling into a desperate struggle.

Surprise was with the hunters. Weapons, skills, and conditioning with the soldiers. Around the dying fire, Jones was out of his sleeping bag first, managing to kill a charging man with a shot from his sidearm. The LT soon joined the fray, bringing his M4 to bear and spraying at the shadows.

No soldier likes to fight at night, the lack of perception afforded by the human eye serving to handicap the brain's ability in executing the skills necessary for battle. Close quarters, hand-

34

to-hand fighting without light was a nightmare.

In they came, shooting, screaming war cries, and wielding edged weapons. The Green Berets were savvy, hardened men, and gave back all they could.

Shots, rifle butt-strokes, and finally landing fists sounded from the camp. The grunts of straining men pushing their adrenaline-charged bodies to the limit of physical strength and mental endurance.

Grissom had his own struggle, three of the hunters determined to kill the PJ by any means. Just as he managed to dispose of the flying attacker with a series of blows to the head, two others were there, one wielding a tomahawk, the second bringing his rifle to bear.

The first shot hit the PJ in the shoulder, his body armor stopping the round from penetrating, but doing little to thwart the numbing impact of the bullet's energy.

Sidestepping the downward arch of the hatchet, Grissom shot the wielder in the chest with a short burst as the man with the rifle worked the bolt for a second attempt.

The sergeant was bringing his weapon around to address the remaining assaulter when the Cochiti warrior made the decision he wasn't going to be able to cycle his weapon in time. With a battle cry brimming with bloodlust, he threw his rifle at Grissom and charged low, the shining steel of a long knife appearing in his hand.

The 30-06 deer rifle impacted on the sergeant's forearm with enough force to foul his aim, throwing his burst wide. There wasn't time to correct, the howling attacker bowling into Grissom's chest before he could adjust.

Slashing, sharp steel flashed brightly in the quarter moon, the screaming warrior's arm a streaking mirage of death. Again, the PJ's equipment saved his life, the knife's blow bouncing harmlessly off his Kevlar helmet. He managed to grasp the foe's wrist with both hands, twisting with every ounce of force his muscular arms could leverage.

Something on the warrior's arm gave way, unable to withstand the torque Grissom was applying. With his throat growling a howl of pain, he rolled off of the PJ and scrambled to regain his feet.

Grissom did the same, struggling to stand while his numb hand tried to grip the carbine still strapped to his chest.

Again came a charge and flashing blade, this time in the opposite hand. The sergeant easily blocked the knife with his rifle and then shoved his attacker back in order to gain the space for a shot.

A lightning bolt of pain roared through Grissom's shoulder

before he could dispose of the man with the knife. With a look of shock and surprise, he half turned to see the young girl behind him, raising her own blade, readying to stab him again.

In a flash of desperation, the PJ grabbed her descending wrist and spun her lightweight body around, using her as a shield to stop the larger male's charge. It was a momentary standoff.

Grissom was having trouble thinking clearly, unable to lift his weapon while holding onto the squirming girl. Both his enemy and he slowly circled each other low, in combat crouches, waiting for any opening.

Below, Jones went down with a well-thrown tomahawk buried in his throat. He fell on the dead bodies of three foe littering the forest floor at his feet.

The LT had managed to maneuver to a position where his back was against the trunk of a large pine, but the officer didn't last long. He'd been sleeping without his armor and finally slumped to the ground after taking a third bullet to the chest.

As suddenly as it had started, the fight was over, only the moans of the wounded filling the New Mexico night.

Grissom sensed his comrades below had fallen. Using words the PJ didn't understand, his antagonist yelled to his mates. The sound of numerous footfalls climbing up the ridge made the meaning all too clear – help was on the way, and they weren't coming to rescue the sergeant.

The PJ shoved the girl toward his attacker, following her flying body to get in close. A brutal thrust of his rifle butt sent the knife wielder to his knees.

Grissom turned to run, the sound of a snapping branch telling him the reinforcements had arrived.

He pivoted to spray where he sensed they were. A brilliant white light blinded the sergeant as a bolt of pain shot through his skull.

He saw the ground rising toward his face. With the earth spinning out of control, his life force was being pulled away. A glow of twin orbs appeared, two faces showing in the distorted light. One was David, his son, the other Samantha, his beloved daughter. "I love you," his heart proclaimed. "I'll miss you."

And then the world went black.

Chapter 4

It was much later than he'd anticipated before the hunting party returned. Hack knew instantly that things had not gone according to plan.

Rather than entering the pueblo with thundering hooves and shouts of victory, the caravan of horseflesh plodded in at a snail's pace. Even in the dim light, it was clear that several of the riders were returning draped over their saddles.

Mothers and fathers streamed in from nowhere, most of them scooting close to see if their sons were among the dead. Out of the 20 men who'd left on a mission of rescue and vengeance, only 11 returned upright in the saddle.

It was with some relief that the girl, the catalyst of the entire affair, was unharmed. Riding in front of one of the men, her uncle helped the young lady down.

And then the wailing started.

Hack stayed back, letting the village deal with its reaction of remorse and disgust. He'd tried to warn the rescuers before they had ridden out.

Mothers screamed their sons' names, fathers and uncles trying to comfort the hysterical, grieving women.

Hack watched as three bodies were unceremoniously pushed from one saddle, their limp forms slamming to the ground in a heap.

He approached the corpses, compelled by the need for answers to the hundred questions that were surging through his mind.

As he strolled across the square, the entire mood of the throng changed. Like someone had flipped a switch, one of the grieving mothers wiggled away from her husband, bent and hoisted a rock and then rushed at the dead interlopers. With an ear-splitting scream, she pummeled a soldier's remains with her stone. A moment later, there were dozens of women following her example.

Hack was taken aback by the viciousness of the display, the women cursing and throwing as fast as their arms could move. Apache Jack appeared at his side. "They would administer the same punishment to a prisoner," he noted. "Sometimes it is best not to be taken alive."

And that's when one of the bodies moaned.

"One of them *is* still alive," Hack turned and shouted to the uncle. "I want to talk to him... get answers to my questions. Please stop them."

But no one seemed to heed Hack's request, the assault continuing without interference. Hack quickly directed his entreaty to the girl's uncle, "Please, sir, please stop them! I think these men were spying on our project, and the only way I can be sure is to interrogate the survivor."

Several of the older men huddled, a few throwing glances at the toymaker during the brief discussion. Finally, one of them separated from the others and said, "Only for you, Grandfather. And when you're through, we want him back."

Stepping forward toward the women, the uncle shouted and barked a series of words. It took three more attempts before the assault was halted.

Hack rushed forward, bending over the man he hoped was still breathing. The pulse was weak, but there. He turned to the Apache and instructed, "Load this man onto my cart. We need to keep him alive long enough for me to ask a few questions."

As soon as he was sure the victim was being loaded, Hack spotted a young warrior briefing the tribal elders, presenting them with everything the warriors had discovered at the camp and removed from the dead.

Hack shouldered his way through the crowd, taking a knee to examine the loot.

There were three M4 carbine rifles, the short-barreled variety, all equipped with cancelation devices. "Not regular infantry," he noted. "Probably Special Forces."

Picking up one of the captured night vision goggles, he half turned to the Apache and exchanged a knowing nod. "Definitely Special Forces."

The dead soldiers' dog tags had been removed, along with their boots, wallets, and all of the contents of the packs. No one protested as Hack sorted through it all.

"These men were carrying 3-day assault packs and minimal ammunition. They were here to gather intelligence. I fear that they were intentionally positioned here to spy on the project."

The missing girl's uncle appeared in the circle of men, his face neutral. "They didn't kidnap my niece," he admitted with a sad voice. "She was hiding from them. Until the last moments, they didn't know she was there."

"How many got away?" Hack asked, ignoring the uncle's admission.

"No one escaped us," came the report. "They moved like ghosts and fought like demons, but there were only three."

Hack turned to the local chief, "I have no use for the weapons, but I would like to examine the rest of their equipment and belongings. Is that acceptable?"

"Yes. But when you are finished, all of the captured

equipment should be distributed to the families of the dead men. It is tradition," replied the headman.

"Will do," Hack replied, knowing that some of the hardware carried by the trespassers would feed the widows and orphans for a year.

Without another word, the toymaker pivoted and began walking with purpose back to his car. "This is very troubling," he confided in the Apache. "Very troubling indeed."

The president was completing his nightly routine, preparing to turn in after another day of frustration.

Enjoying his evening vice of a cigar and two fingers of brandy, the chief executive reflected on the events of the day. Like any commander, he tallied the small wins and losses, his mental scorecard used to judge the effectiveness of the campaign overall. Did he win today? How badly did he lose? It was a long-time habit, common in such competitive men.

"If I were a baseball coach, I wouldn't be expecting to have my contract renewed," he whispered to the empty room. "If I were commanding an infantry platoon, I'd anticipate being relieved."

But what really was bothering him the most was missing the time he'd set aside to be with his grandchildren.

Sure, they were safe and sound at Camp David, far better off than the vast majority of their generation. David and Samantha lived inside the iron ring of security provided by the Secret Service, were well fed, received private tutoring, and slept in a warm, dry place.

But the grandfather knew they needed more than just three squares to mature into rounded, adaptable adults. They needed family and love.

A polite knock on the door interrupted the president's bout of introspection, the Commander in Chief surprised by the appearance of an Army chaplain and one of the generals.

Before he even greeted the two arrivals, he realized the purpose of their visit. His son.

The chaplain began, "Sir, my apologies for interrupting you so late, but we thought...."

The president didn't let the man finish, "Dead? Confirmed? Missing? Where?"

The general stepped forward and cleared his throat. "Missing, presumed dead, sir. New Mexico."

"And how do we know that, General? I thought he deployed

on that mission only a short time ago?"

"He was in the middle of uploading a situation report when his team was attacked, sir. The satellite phone he was using remained connected for some time."

"I want to hear it," the president barked, his tone harsher than intended. Softer, he added, "Please."

"Sir, I'm not sure that is a good idea at this time," the chaplain interjected. "If you would care to sit and discuss the situation, I'd be happy to...."

Again the president interrupted. "While I appreciate your position and concern, Chaplain, I'm in no need of such unearthly support at the moment. I would like to hear the tape, General."

"Yes, sir," replied the senior officer, moving to pick up a nearby phone. After a series of inaudible orders, he returned the receiver to the cradle and reported, "It will be here in a few minutes, sir."

The president fought hard to keep his emotion in check. While any normal father would be free to express whatever anger, remorse, or grieving he experienced, the chief executive was not a normal parent.

As the time passed slowly by, the president tried everything he could think of to keep himself calm. Internally, he argued that millions of parents had received similar visits. He tried to find solace in the fact he hadn't physically seen his son's body, and until that moment arrived, there was always hope.

His troubled mind then journeyed to the core of support that had carried him through so many similar difficult times. Fundamentally, the president's mind functioned with a profound military influence. He tried to justify his son's death with all of the tired excuses. He was serving his country. He was doing what he wanted to do. He died for a purpose and with honor.

None of it worked.

And then thoughts of Samantha and David came rushing to the forefront of his thinking, a tidal wave of guilt crashing against his soul. Missing his scheduled time with them took on a new, immensely painful meaning.

Staggered by it all, the president lost his grip on his brandy glass, the heavy crystal impacting the floor with a loud thud and shattering rattle.

The Secret Service instantly appeared, drawn by the sound of the broken tumbler. They helped the dazed father to a nearby chair, one of the agents on his radio calling for a surgeon.

A hundred questions came at the president, seemingly all at once. Are you okay, sir? Are you experiencing any shortness of breath, sir? Are you feeling any pain, sir?

In a way, the barrage of inquiries was helpful, angering the president so much that his thoughts were temporarily distracted from his son.

"Would all of you fucking mother hens get the hell out of my face?" he growled. "I'm just fine, thank you. I dropped a glass for Christ's sake. Can't a man be clumsy every now and then without it being a national emergency?"

The triad was interrupted by the arrival of a junior officer caring a laptop computer.

"I don't think it's a good time to listen to this transmission," someone said, but the president would have none of it.

The chief executive, surrounded by staff, huddled over the computer's small speakers, his experienced ear dissecting every word and sound. Three times he asked that the recording be paused and rewound.

When it was over, he stared up at the general and said, "I admit that it sounds like my son was badly wounded or killed, but there's no proof. I assume he will be listed as missing in action?"

"Yes, Mr. President, that is standard procedure."

The POTUS rose from his perch, ambling to the fireplace with a blank expression. After a bit, he spoke, his voice filled with the ice of revenge, "If the Alliance is to blame for this tragedy, I will personally lead the 4th Infantry Division right into Alpha and kick their sorry asses."

Not a single person in the room doubted his words.

Realizing he was on the edge of appearing vengeful and out of control, the president forced down the rage that threatened to boil over. "And, we need to get a team into Los Alamos pronto. Right now. If someone is playing empire-builder in that part of the nation, I want that nuclear material out of their reach."

"Yes, Mr. President," acknowledged the general.

"One last thing, gentlemen, I will inform my grandchildren about their father as soon as more facts are known. I want to do this personally. No one is to breathe a word of this to them. Is that understood?"

After the chorus of "Yes, sir," and "Of course, Mr. President," died down, all of the visitors quickly filed out of the room, leaving a man who suddenly found himself feeling more like a helpless father than a powerful leader.

Grissom was sure he'd died in battle and been cast into hell.

Overcoming the throbbing behind his temples, the sergeant

struggled to open his eyes. There, lurking a short distance away, was surely a demon.

The evil being possessed the shape of a man, but that's where the resemblance ended. White streaks of ash crisscrossed its face; bones were braided in the beast's dark mane.

Unable to look away, Grissom squinted to clear his vision. *Since when do the devil's troopers carry AR15s?* his aching, confused brain managed to wonder. *And wear wristwatches?*

The Apache standing guard over the prisoner sensed his charge was awake. Stepping closer to examine the bound captive, the tall warrior strode to the door and barked a few words to his superior.

Grissom was again confused when another mythical figure appeared. This time the apparition seemed more like an angel than a fiend, its flowing white hair and kind eyes in stark contrast to the other creature in the room.

"Sergeant Grissom, I presume?" Hack asked.

"Yes," the PJ croaked. "Am I dead?"

"No, not yet," came the honest response. "Are you in much pain?"

"Yes," the soldier replied as he began gingerly testing his limbs.

"You have a stab wound just below your left shoulder blade, but it has stopped bleeding. I did my best to bandage it. I hope you'll pardon my sloppy work. Your right shoulder is severely bruised. But the worst of it is the blow you suffered to the back of your head. That had me concerned."

Grissom's medical training took over, "Do you have any aspirin? There's some in my med-kit if you don't. It would help to thin the blood."

Hack produced a bottle of water and two tablets from his jacket pocket, and proceeded to help the bound man swallow and drink. "So you're a Para rescuer. I've read about your training. Impressive."

"And you would be?"

"You can call me Hack," the toymaker responded. "Most of the locals call me Grandfather. My real name is Schneider."

Hack watched as Grissom slowly recovered, eventually helping the man to sit upright on the cot. "I have some questions for you, Sergeant. Now I know enough about Special Forces operators to know you're pretty tough men. My Native American friends think you'll require certain painful inducements to answer my inquiries, but I disagree. We're not at war. I'm not your enemy."

Wincing from the pain, the prisoner responded with a smirk. "Given how my head and body feel, you could have fooled me. If

I'm not your enemy, I'd sure hate to see how these people greet one."

Hack chuckled, "They thought you were some vagabond that had kidnapped a village girl."

The statement helped clear Grissom's thoughts, opening a door for his memory to refresh. "Yes, I remember the girl. We had no idea she was there. So now that we have that all cleared up, why are my hands and feet still bound? Why is there an armed guard... or whatever you call that thing... leering over me?"

"Because we're still not sure exactly why you were trespassing on reservation land. Hell, for all we know, you and your friends were some rogue deserters come to loot and pillage the neighborhood."

The sergeant shook his head, the painful movement producing another grimace. "No, we aren't deserters. But just in case I'm lying, why don't you haul me back to the nearest U.S. military base and let me prove it?"

Hack ignored the request, producing Grissom's Geiger counter from his jacket. "And why would a team of Special Forces men be carrying a radiation detector around with them?"

"That's classified."

Hack leaned back, his cold eyes studying the captive with an intensity that made Grissom want to squirm. "I think that's a very legitimate question, young man. For all I know, some crazy person has detonated a nuke or made off with a bomb and you're chasing him. My neighbors and I might be in danger, and there you sit, withholding information that could save lives."

"You and the people in this area are in no danger from radiation or any nuclear weapon. That much I can divulge."

"So why are you here?"

The sergeant hesitated, trying to decide just exactly how much he should say to the exotic weirdo that was holding him prisoner. Technically, he could find no reason to withhold information, but some inner voice was telling him that Hack was dangerous... or at least not a friend.

Seeing his captive pause, Hack decided to up the ante. "Look, Sergeant, I'm not the head honcho around here. That role is shared among the governors and chiefs of the surrounding pueblos. Right now, down in the valley, there are a bunch of grieving widows and mothers who are planning a rather unpleasant demise for a man who butchered their family members. They're quite creative, I might add. They've had thousands of years to refine their tortures," he paused to allow the captive's imagination a moment to register before continuing. "Now, I'm not without influence. If you cooperate, I might be able to convince them to spare your life. On the other hand, I've seen

43

what these people do to prisoners, and it is most unpleasant."

Hack shuddered as he recalled the images and then continued. "They will shove a small knife up your anus a few times, and then stake you down naked on an ant hill. Have you ever seen our desert army ants? They're the size of my thumb and have incisors that can cut through moose hide. The last trespasser my friends caught... well... I could hear his screams all the way up here. He lasted almost 20 hours, God rest his soul."

Grissom, with significant effort, ignored the threat.

Shrugging, Hack rose from his perch. "Up to you, Sergeant. If you don't help me, there's very little I can do to help you."

"Those men attacked us!" the PJ protested. "We were only defending ourselves, and you fucking know it. I'm a representative of the U.S. military. Why would you let them torture and murder a man who was doing nothing more than serving his country?"

Hack shook his head, obviously frustrated that the young soldier didn't get it. "If you hadn't been trespassing on reservation land, none of this would have happened. No one would have died. Yet, my neighbors can be mellow, benevolent souls. They might understand that accidents do happen, especially in these troubled times. But you're giving me nothing here, Sergeant. Nada. Zip. So the only conclusion I can make is that your intentions were nefarious." The older man shifted his position in order to stare at the prisoner straight in the eye. "As far as the U.S. military receiving any brownie points? We're talking about American Indians here. Did you ever study history regarding the treatment of America's native peoples? Do you really expect them to give invading soldiers a break?"

Grissom's mind was racing a thousand miles per hour. Cursing the pain that was adding to his confusion, he struggled to come up with a response. When Hack turned and motioned to the guard with a finger going across his throat, the sergeant wanted to puke.

Hack decided to give it one last try. "Sergeant, please be reasonable. You're going to tell us what we want to know eventually. Why not speak up now rather than when you're begging my friends to kill you quickly as you suffer those ferocious insects eating your bowels from the inside out?"

Grissom knew the man had a point. Everybody talked eventually. There was no military reason to delay the inevitable. Rescue, at least in the short term, was unlikely. He decided to buy time with partial information. "The irrigation system you're building down in the valley was spotted via aerial reconnaissance. My superiors sent in my team to check it out."

44

Hack scratched his chin while staring hard at the captive. Exhaling with disappointment, he said, "Oh, come on, Sergeant. Do you really think I'm that stupid? That little tidbit of a story is just plain insulting."

"It's the truth," Grissom pleaded.

"Bullshit!" the toymaker snapped. "Why would anybody need a Geiger counter to check on an irrigation project? Why were you on the wrong side of the valley? Why not just drive up to the reservation's border and ask rather than sneak around in the woods?"

Again, the PJ cursed his throbbing head. Apparently, he wasn't thinking clearly, and it was getting him in trouble. The man interrogating him was no fool. He needed to be careful, yet silence wasn't an option. "What do you mean the wrong side of the valley? I have no idea what you're talking about."

"You were on the western rim of the valley. On the Los Alamos..." Hack stopped mid-sentence, his eyes growing wide. "You were in Los Alamos with a Geiger counter. There are nuclear materials at the lab... and when the military used a drone to scout the area, they spotted our project. Now this all makes sense."

Grissom was amazed at how quickly his captor had put two and two together. But Hack wasn't done.

Pacing now, the toymaker continued to mumble his rambling logic as he talked aloud, sorting out the explanation to the puzzle. "There must be a problem with the nuclear materials at the lab. The Pentagon is worried about it, or at least concerned enough to dedicate vital resources like a Special Forces team. A radiation leak? No, you didn't have any protective suits or breathers. There must be something valuable there...."

Hack abruptly stopped, turning to Apache Jack. "We are going to Los Alamos. We will need some additional men."

"Yes, Grandfather," came the reply. "I'll see to it."

Turning back to face his prisoner, Hack's smirk was brimming with confidence. "Thank you, Sergeant. I think you've just provided me with a solution that will protect our little irrigation project. Now if you'll excuse me, I've got to go and research the hazardous materials storage units at Los Alamos."

Grissom knew immediately where Hack's mind was going, and it made him ill.

They looked like a wagon train from a B-grade Western,

straining teams of horses pulling dilapidated, weathered wagons through the scenic valley.

Surrounding the rusty wheels and horseflesh were the mounted scouts and warriors. With rifles pointed skyward and resting on saddle leather, some were Santa Domingo, others Cochiti. The toymaker's Apache escorts made up the rest.

Hack had instructed the elders to prepare enough food and supplies for a three-day excursion. Not knowing what to expect, he'd also suggested a significant amount of ammunition be added to the manifest. That had taken the entire cargo area of one of the wagons.

And then there was the anticipated looting.

Everyone around the Caldera knew Los Alamos had been abandoned less than a year after the electricity had vanished. The mountain town's unmaintained sewers had bled into the water supply after a heavy spring rain. Disease had racked the population in a matter of days. The survivors had fled in droves.

Since then, the larger and closer cities of Santa Fe and Albuquerque had been more accessible targets for the tribe's scavenging parties to plunder. Los Alamos, at its peak, had attracted only about 12,000 residents, and many had survived and consumed supplies for months after the collapse. Early scouting expeditions had found the town nearly void of items high on the looters' priority lists.

But that didn't mean that the entire area was void of valuable assets. Since Hack and his party were going to be making the difficult trip anyway, why not bring along an extra wagon or two to fill with anything useful?

The highest priority, however, wasn't batteries, medical supplies, foodstuffs, or weapons. Hack wanted to harvest the nuclear materials from the lab. With those in his possession, he could protect the tribes and the Valley Green project. Thus, the extra wagons.

The ex-engineer had no illusions of converting his small patch of New Mexico into a global nuclear power. He knew enough to realize that building a fission bomb required extensive capabilities and knowledge that were beyond his grasp.

But radioactive materials had more than one use.

For years at the Skunk Works, the threat of a terrorist's dirty bomb had been a perplexing problem for those who earned their living protecting the USA. Hack had worked on aircraft-mounted sensors and early detection devices more than once in his career.

There had also been a project that revolved around performing damage assessment if a U.S. city ever experienced the horror of a dirty bomb detonation.

The toymaker knew that the concept struck fear into the hearts of the bravest of men. He fully understood how political leaders reacted to the ramifications of the threat.

If he could safely capture whatever the Los Alamos labs held in their vaults, it would be a potent deterrent for anyone trying to interfere with their project... or the tribes in general.

The chiefs and governors had grasped this immediately. "If we had commanded this capability three hundred years ago," remarked one of the council elders, "the whites would be the ones relegated to life on reservations."

The constant plodding of hooves on pavement was causing Hack to grow drowsy. He was fighting a nearly constant stream of yawning when the outline of Los Alamos appeared over the crest of a rise.

From a distance, the mountain city looked like any other town bathed in the afternoon sun. With beautiful vistas and diverse surroundings, Hack had to admit that the government had made a wise decision back in the 40s when they had established the Manhattan Project at the remote locale.

An hour later, the entourage was entering the outskirts, bumping along at the horse's uphill pace.

Up close, the appearance of the berg was completely different.

Weeds and vines had taken root in practically every crack and crevice. In some areas, piles of windblown debris had accumulated as high as a man's waist.

Dust covered surfaces that the human mind was accustomed to seeing clean. What windows were still intact were darkened by a disturbingly thick layer of grime. The few automobiles they passed were coated in the same filth. Many of the tires were flat, some displaying unmistakable signs of dry rot.

The lead rider reigned his horse to stop at the intersection of two main streets. All eyes turned back to Hack's wagon, eager for his instructions.

The toymaker had memorized the town's street grid and layout. Motioning for a few of the leaders to gather around, he began issuing instructions.

The Natives had taken to calling them Locusts, and Hack thought the description was apt.

According to the tribe's recently minted lore, the first few attempts at scavenging had failed miserably. It had taken some time and experience to refine the art of looting.

The first issue had been security. In the early days of the apocalypse, it was often difficult to tell when a town or city was unoccupied. Regardless of the current census, electric lights didn't shine at night. Lawn mowers didn't hum as they trimmed yards. Children didn't run laughing and shouting in the yard.

The Locusts, after being ambushed and shot up on more than one occasion, had learned to apply the same skills used in tracking wild game. Their first sign always involved water.

Humans had taken to mimicking deer and elk, requiring a visit to the local watering hole one or more times per day. A home or building with buckets outside was a sure sign of a resident. A worn path to the nearest creek or lake was another telling indication of human habitation.

Scat was an obvious clue. Like all members of the animal kingdom, people produced waste and often weren't very clever about hiding the evidence of their deeds. And it was more than just the presence of bodily byproducts that gave them away.

People, even after the collapse, produced garbage. Hack had heard of the Locusts avoiding potential trouble spots after finding skinned animal hides, piles of rotting intestines, and other signs of hunter/gathers.

Clothing wore out and was discarded. Stashes of food were still being discovered, producing wrappers and packaging. One popular campfire story related the tale of a Locust discovering a can of soda outside of a warehouse in Santa Fe. Common houseflies were swarming the empty container, a sure sign that it still held the residue of sugar. Three heavily armed rogues were seen leaving the building just a few minutes later. A firefight had been avoided.

Eventually, Hack and his flying cameras were employed in the effort to avoid confrontation. The drones could more easily identify occupying humans and surveil their activity, but even that method wasn't foolproof.

Over time, the Natives began to map out the pockets of surviving humanity that still existed throughout the area. The elders decreed it law that the Locusts were not to take from others. If valuables were found abandoned, then they were fair game. Stealing was forbidden.

While the intent of such a rule was noble, the practical application was not. What if two independent parties happened upon a cache at the same time? After numerous such violent encounters, it soon became clear that combat skills were a high priority for any person wanting to be a Locust.

Protocols had developed. Scouting, stalking, and other tactical methods became common practice. Like any other occupation in the post-apocalyptic world, there were masters and apprentices, managers and worker bees.

And what to scavenge? Often, when a new, untouched location was found, there were more goods than could be carried off by a small team of individuals. Which items were the most valuable? Just like every other aspect of an economy, supply was soon driven by demand.

Brokerages quickly appeared, each pueblo supporting its own branch office. Residents would visit the local broker and place an order for needed supplies. Haggling would ensue. Eventually a "procurement ticket" would be generated and a wish list formed from the collective supply needs of the community. When the Locusts went hunting, they carried a list of priorities.

Over time, the scavengers refined their production capabilities to include what everyone called "mining." If a team of Locusts uncovered a particularly large trove of treasures, they would stake a claim and then spread the word. Like ants ravaging a picnic pie, the gatherers would travel from far and wide, carrying off the goods until nothing was left, paying a percentage to the original prospectors.

It was a team of Locusts that Hack addressed first.

"The primary business district is located in that direction," he indicated, pointing down the street. "Less than a mile further is where the neighborhoods of upscale homes begin. Take two wagons and your shopping list. We'll meet you back at this intersection in four hours."

Without any comment, the Locusts separated and began moving toward the primary scavenging area.

As Hack watched them go, the remaining members of the expedition drew closer, waiting for his guidance.

This group was comprised mostly of armed males. Hack hoped their firepower wouldn't be necessary, but in the days of anarchy, one never knew.

"We will travel to the laboratory's main complex," he began. "We're looking for a building that will most likely have radiation warning signs that look like this," he said, holding up a tablet computer with an image on the screen.

"Inside one of these structures is a vault, not unlike what we've all seen inside of a bank. That's where our prize will be located."

The onlookers all acknowledged their understanding, many heads nodding up and down.

"Once we locate the vault, I'll take over from there. I'm probably going to have to use explosives to breach the door. And there's a risk in that. If I compromise the nuclear material's storage containers, then anyone close by will get sick... probably die. So I need everyone to stay back until I signal the 'all clear.' Is that understood?"

Again, the throng expressed comprehension.

Hack was about to continue when a distant thumping noise sounded over the mountain. Pausing to listen, the toymaker realized instantly what it was.

With wide, excited eyes, he turned back to his followers and said, "There's a helicopter coming in. It's probably the U.S. Army searching for the same prize we're after. Everyone get out of sight! Quickly!"

The horses sensed the sudden surge of stress that shot through their human masters. That, and the abrupt, harsh commands made the animals jumpy and difficult to control. But the Natives were excellent riders, and soon the caravan was moving away from the open pavement and seeking shelter wherever it could be found.

"Shit," Hack confided to his Apache friend and caretaker, "The soldiers on our ridge must have gotten a message out before they were killed."

"Should we leave, Grandfather?"

Stroking his beard, Hack thought about their options. Finally brightening, he answered, "No. This might actually be a positive development. Gather all of the men who can fight. Tell them to pack all of the ammunition they can carry. We can make this work to our advantage."

While the warrior scurried off to do as the toymaker commanded, Hack ventured to the back of his wagon and uncovered one of his drones. The sound of the approaching machines now made it clear that more than one bird was inbound, and the whirlybirds were getting close.

With his fingers flying over the tablet's controls, Hack quickly programmed instructions for his flying robot. The first helicopter zoomed over the town just as he'd finished.

All in all, four helicopters passed overhead, their destination being the laboratory's massive complex of structures. "You're going to lead me right to the goodies," Hack whispered, making the final preparations to launch his machine.

With a smile, he hit the command on his computer and then stood back as the small flyer shot skyward. A few moments later, with several of the Apache watching the computer's display over his shoulder, Hack began to receive images from the aerial camera.

The helicopters were easy enough to spot, having landed in the lab's main parking lot. Evidently, the visitors didn't expect to stay long, the main rotors still spinning at an idle speed.

Hack could see three or four men exiting each bird. Some

were armed with battle rifles, others carrying suitcase-like packs and boxes.

The toymaker guided his drone higher, wanting to make sure he didn't lose sight of the location where the government's men were going. It then occurred to him that their destination didn't matter. They would open the vault. They would prepare the nuclear materials for safe transport and then return to the copters.

Motioning for his bodyguard to come closer, Hack explained his reasoning in a few sentences. With a nod and a smile, the Apache said, "We can make sure those whirlybirds don't leave."

"Do you see how their security men have fanned out?"

"Yes. I would do the same. This won't be difficult, Grandfather. We are many. They are few, and we have surprise on our side."

"Okay, but don't attack until you see the others returning with the goods. And exercise great caution. We must not shoot up whatever cases they are carrying."

"And what about the aircraft? Do you want them destroyed?"

Again, Hack had to think it through. "No," he responded. "Try to leave them airworthy, and don't kill more than is necessary. The men who entered the buildings are probably scientists, not military. We want our friends in Washington to know we have their property. This will send an unmistakable message."

Nodding, the Apache turned to his men and began barking orders. A few moments later, the war party was stalking through the streets, moving swiftly toward the lab's parking lot.

Hack lingered back for a bit, observing the proceedings from his airborne toy. *Better an old man like me lend moral support than get in the way,* he mused.

Twenty minutes passed quickly, the drone's battery level falling to a critical level. Shaking his head in disgust, he ordered the flyer home.

Despite his age and lack of fighting skills, Hack still wanted to see what was happening. After his pet had landed securely by the wagons, he began making his way toward the labs and the waiting Apache.

He was trying to stay low and quiet, slithering slowly from building to tree in order to remain unobserved. Out of nowhere a young warrior appeared at his side, scaring the hell out of Hack.

Without a word, the younger man began hustling Hack through a series of side streets and ravines. Three minutes later, the toymaker found himself beside a rather annoyed looking Apache Jack. "What are you doing, Grandfather? Do you want to get yourself killed?"

"I wanted to see. I need to see."

Shaking his head in disgust, the Native returned to his primary objective, watching the armed men surrounding the still-running helicopters.

Hack was not sure how much time passed before the retrieval teams reappeared from the lab's complex of structures. The first hint of the pending arrival had been one of the perimeter defenders holding his hand up to an earpiece and listening. The guards became very alert after that.

Movement appeared between the buildings, a short procession of men parading back toward the lot, several carrying what appeared to be a set of common beer coolers. They strolled out of the lab's main gate like they were on the way to a football tailgating party with an ice chest full of brewskis.

Hack exchanged looks with the Apache and nodded. "That's what we're after. That's the prize in those chests."

The Indians waited until the goods were halfway back to the helicopters. Hack heard the man next to him unsafe his weapon, and then all hell erupted in Los Alamos.

The Natives sprang their trap with deft skill and unquestionable bravery. Gunshots rang out all around the perimeter, most of the security force falling in the first few seconds.

Hack saw another group of his friends rise from a row of overgrown shrubbery not far from the men carrying the nuclear containers. Anyone who didn't hit the ground immediately was shot.

One of the helicopter pilots must have decided on an escape, the sound of his engine making it clear he intended to take off. In seconds, he was looking at three rifles pointed at his bubble canopy. Wisely, he changed his mind.

And then it was over, the victorious Natives yelling and whooping in celebration.

"Stay here, Grandfather," ordered the Apache. "I will send a man back as soon as I am sure it is safe."

Hack did as he was told, watching as the bushwhackers disarmed and searched both the survivors and the dead.

It was only a few minutes before Hack's escort arrived to retrieve him. Three of the senior Apache surrounding the toymaker as he approached the captives.

Hack didn't care about the men from the helicopters. He made for the coolers.

What he found were four heavy, thick stainless steel and lead boxes, each equipped with stout-looking seals and numerous warning stickers plastered all over the exterior.

Pulling the PJ's Geiger counter from his pocket, Hack scanned the exterior of containers. With relief, he found they hadn't suffered any damage during the battle.

"Who *are* you people?" one of the captives shouted indignantly. "Stay away from those containers. You don't know what's inside of those! You'll kill us all if you open those boxes!"

Hack walked over to the protesting man and took a knee beside the prone fellow. "And you might be?"

"I'm Dr. Roland S. Pataki, head of research at Oak Ridge National Laboratories," announced the prisoner. "Who are you people, and why are you doing this? We are here on the authority of the...."

Hack put a finger to his lip, ordering the man to be silent. "Welcome to New Mexico, Doctor. I regret to inform you that you no longer will be burdened with that cargo. Furthermore, I would suggest you shut up and do what these young men command. They aren't the most patient gentlemen on the planet."

Then, without waiting for a response, Hack strolled over to a younger captive. "I have a message for you to deliver. Tell your superiors that the joint Native American Nations of New Mexico have taken possession of these nuclear materials. Tell them that we only want to be left alone. If they try anything... anything at all to interfere with us, I will scatter a radioactive cloud from here to the Mississippi River and make the land uninhabitable for the next 1,000 years. Do you understand?"

The man nodded nervously.

"Repeat it back to me," Hack ordered.

Finally satisfied that his message would be properly relayed, Hack turned to the Apache leader and said, "Let them go. Take the boxes and all of their weapons and disable their radios. Then let them fly back to wherever. We need to get those containers back to my cabin ASAP."

"Yes, Grandfather."

Chapter 5

"Okay, next on the list is the floral arrangements," Terri announced, moving her pencil one line down on the pad in front of her.

"Really?" Nick hesitated, throwing a frustrated glance at Diana. "We're living in a post-apocalyptic world where half of the people aren't eating enough, and we're going to have flowers at the wedding? Are you gals going to get on the shortwave and dial up 1-800 BOUQUETS?"

Terri tossed a wadded up sheet of paper at the less than enthusiastic, testosterone-charged half of the wedding party. "They don't have to be fancy flowers," Terri countered, "but at least the reception should have some color on the tables. We can send some of the church kids out to pick wildflowers."

"Can't we just go to Vegas and have Elvis marry us?" Nick countered, only half teasing. "I hear they even have drive-thru chapels that will do the dirty deed while you sit in your car."

Diana threw her pen across the table, Nick avoiding the impact with a deft tilt of his head. "Are you going to sit here and do this all day?" the Alliance leader challenged. "Because if you are, I can think of about 100 shitty jobs you could be out doing instead. And by shitty, I mean really shitty. I hear the sewers are backing up in Austin... I'm sure I could persuade the council to assign that task to you personally. Dirty deed, my foot!"

Terri tried to suppress her snort but didn't succeed. Bishop had been the same way before their wedding. *Why do the guys always act this way?*

Throwing up his hands in mock surrender, Nick said, "Okay, okay, you win. I know when I'm strategically outmatched. So we need flowers. What else?"

"General Owens has offered a variety of contributions from the military, including an honor guard, a flyover by a formation of fighter jets, and the marching band from Fort Hood," Terri continued.

"A flyover?" Nick said, shaking his head. "I don't think that's a good public relations move. The price of fuel has been going up all over the Alliance, and I'm hearing a lot of bitching. Wasting jet fuel on something like us getting hitched doesn't seem like an appropriate allocation of resources."

Before anyone could respond, there was a knock on the door.

"What now?" Diana grumbled before acknowledging the interruption.

An assistant poked his head through the opening, "Ma'am, I just received word from General Owens at Bliss, there's a situation developing out there that requires your attention."

"And this can't wait?" Diana responded, the annoyance thick in her tone.

"No, ma'am. The general was very clear. He needs to speak with you on the radio immediately."

Shaking her head in disgust, Diana glanced at Nick and Terri. "I'm sorry. Let me quickly take care of this. Believe me; I do not want to be wearing combat fatigues when I walk down the aisle. I'll be right back."

As she rose to exit her office, the aide looked at Nick and continued, "Sir, the general also requested your presence, if at all possible. He said to tell you, and I quote, 'It's concerning a potential N-level event.'"

Nick's face blanched stark white, the big man rising quickly to follow Diana. Almost as an afterthought, the ex-operator turned to Terri and said, "I don't know how long before we're back. Aren't you glad you retired from public service?"

Terri smiled politely, but Nick and Diana were both gone before she could answer. In reality, she was indeed glad to be out of the leadership game. She couldn't count the number of times such a message had interrupted her day back when she was part of the Alliance's government.

And it was never good news.

It seemed like there was always some potential disaster, threat, outbreak, or problem to deal with. No, she was glad her biggest problem today was getting Nick to participate in the wedding preparations.

Smirking, she thought, "And that might be the biggest problem I've ever faced."

She decided to check in on Hunter, her son just down the hall in the courthouse's nursery. After seeing he was sleeping comfortably, Terri then thought some fresh air would help clear her head.

She stepped out onto the front steps, scanning the hustle and bustle of downtown Alpha, Texas.

A comparison to just a short time ago was inevitable. Escaped prisoners had taken over half of the town, the remainder belonging to a church. Diana had become the congregation's leader, eventually winning what had become a civil war to control the town.

Alpha was a much different place now. Shops were open. So were the schools. Pedestrians walked without fear along the sidewalks, a few automobiles and trucks plying the blacktop streets.

But by far the most common mode of transportation was the bicycle.

Terri would have never guessed so many of the two-wheelers existed before the collapse. Now, it was common to see women peddling back from the market with the handlebar baskets full of goods. Child seats, luggage racks, and even small trailers were valuable commodities to the post-apocalyptic family.

When she was growing up, the image of a young boy towing a Red Flyer wagon was the symbol of iconic Americana. Now, all means of non-motorized transportation were a necessity.

Gasoline and diesel were being refined, but the supply was still extremely limited. So far, Diana and the Alliance brain trust had only managed to jumpstart a single, large refinery along the Texas coast. That, and a smaller unit in Midland Station, were trying to supply a region of over 10 million survivors. It wasn't enough.

With supply and demand playing their age-old game, gas and diesel were far too expensive for casual consumption.

With a bike, a cyclist could travel over twice as fast as walking. With baskets, makeshift saddle bags, and an assortment of creative carryalls hauling cargo, peddling made sense. And, unlike horses, there is no need to feed a bicycle.

"We'll probably be a healthier society for the effort," Terri observed, watching an elderly couple peddling down the street.

Nick appeared at her side, startling the young mother. The big man's capability to move so quietly had always amazed her.

"Terri, I'm so sorry, but we're going to have to go to Fort Bliss. Something's come up."

"Is everything okay?"

"I'm not sure. General Owens has come across information, that if accurate, it isn't good news. But facts are few and far between right now. You know how these things go. It's probably nothing, but he wants Diana and me over there on the base - post haste."

"I'm sorry, Nick," Terri replied. "I know Diana and you wanted to finalize the arrangements right away, but I can come back to town next week."

Diana then appeared, her disappointment at the delay painted all over her face. After apologizing and hugging Terri, she turned to Nick and said, "Let's get going before our general has a kitten. This must be serious, because I've never heard him so adamant that we get over there."

"Any idea what the threat is?" Terri asked out of curiosity.

"No, not really," Diana replied, shaking her head. "The general didn't want to talk about it over the radio."

"Good luck, you two, and say hello to everyone over at Bliss. That hospital saved my bacon more than once," Terri smiled. "I guess I'll take Hunter back to the ranch a day early. I'll drive back next week, and we can finish then."

Diana couldn't get accustomed to the military personnel treating her like some sort of visiting dignitary. She'd been a pilot in the Navy... and understood respect and discipline, but every time she stepped foot on a base or fort, it was as if a king had arrived.

"You are just like the president to them," Nick had stated, noting her discomfort. "All of these men were raised in a society where civilian authority controls the military. You're the ultimate elected official in the Alliance, so you'd might as well get used to it."

They entered the base's extensive headquarters building and were immediately shown to General Owen's office. After a quick greeting, the Alliance's top military commander showed them into a large conference room.

The general got right down to business, "We received a radio transmission from Washington a few hours ago. I'm not sure what it's all about, but my counterpart in the Pentagon was pissed to high heaven. Excuse my language, ma'am."

Nick shrugged, "So? Those guys haven't been happy since the Alliance was formed, and we inherited the military assets in Texas. I'm still not sure why you summoned us, General?"

Owens continued, "My ex-friend began the conversation with the question, 'What the fuck are you people doing in New Mexico? Why did you kill our people? Why do you want fissionable materials?' That's why I made the call to Alpha and requested your presence."

Nick whistled, "Ahhh... now I see. What the hell's going on?"

"I have no idea, sir. We have no operations in New Mexico. Nothing even close. Other than Bishop's report concerning his little adventure in the Land of Enchantment, I don't even have any Intel on the state of affairs over there."

Diana spoke up, "And when you informed your friend at the Pentagon of those facts, what did he say?"

"That's when he said, 'Yeah, right. Tell it to the president. He wants a private conversation... pronto. We're supposed to connect with Camp David on an encrypted link in just under two hours."

Navigating the entrance to their canyon home required all of Terri's attention, the large boulders and rock formations allowing just a wide enough lane for the pickup to squeeze through. Hunter, riding in the reverse-mounted car seat beside her, seemed to sense he was returning home.

"You're anxious to see your dad, aren't you big boy," she cooed at the smiling child. "Either that… or you think I'm going to feed you again."

The lad's eyes opened wide with excitement, his little arms moving with rapid motions that signaled glee. "Just like your father, you like the desert," she noted. "You can't take the country out of the boy."

Terri knew something was wrong with Bishop the moment she laid eyes on her husband. Having heard the truck's motor, he was walking from the bat cave to greet his family, but she could tell from the slump of his shoulders that something was troubling her mate.

After a quick hug and peck at the driver's door, Bishop moved around to unbuckle Hunter and raise his son in an embrace. "You've grown a bunch, big guy," the proud father noted. "What were they feeding you in Alpha?"

Hunter didn't answer the question, instead choosing to giggle and squirm against his father's chest. "He missed you," Terri stated. "When we turned into the canyon, he started smiling and looking around. I think he knew he was about to see you."

Holding Hunter with one arm, Bishop made to help Terri with her bags and boxes, but she stopped him cold. "What's wrong, Bishop?"

"Nothing. What do you mean?"

"Bishop?"

Her probe melted the façade he'd put on, a grimace crossing the Texan's face. "There was… we had a hail storm two nights ago. Look at the garden."

Terri set her belongings down, navigating around the last of the boulders so she could inspect the damaged plot. "Oh, goodness," she said, a mixture of sadness and sympathy filling her eyes. She went to her husband and reached for his hand. "I'm so very, very, sorry, my love. I know you worked so hard on that garden."

He sighed, squeezing her hand and lowering his head. "I

don't know what we're going to do," he confessed. I went hunting yesterday, and despite the rain, I didn't even see a rabbit. The garden was the best 'sure thing' between our little family and starvation."

Nodding, she understood his concern. "We can ask Diana for help... or Nick... or Pete. Hell, half of the Alliance owes you big time, Bishop. We'll be okay. We've got tons of friends."

"No," he barked, then was embarrassed at the harshness of his response. Softer, he added, "We can't burden our friends. Times are tough for everybody, and the last thing they need is us showing up with our hands out. We have to be able to make it on our own."

Terri smiled, her husband's pride and spirit part of the reason she loved him so. She decided to let him settle down and changed the subject. "Well, we're not going to figure this out standing here in the sun. Why don't you help me get my stuff inside the camper, and I can fill you in on all the latest while you play with Hunter. I'll make us supper in a bit."

"Sounds good," he replied, bouncing Hunter up and down. "My son and I have some catching up to do. I can't believe how much he's grown."

"No kidding. I've had to lug that little monster all over town the last few days. I'm going to have bigger muscles than you if he keeps putting on weight."

The family settled in, Terri unpacking while Bishop made up for lost time by playing peek-a-boo with Hunter. When she finally exited the bedroom, both of them were asleep on the couch.

Terri stood, gazing with admiration at her boys, enjoying the precious moment. Hunter was lying on his dad's chest, the top of the baby's head nuzzled against Bishop's neck.

Even in sleep, both of Bishop's arms were wrapped around the baby, holding him securely so he couldn't roll off. "You've always taken care of us, Bishop. I know you always will. As long as we're together, we'll be all right."

"The military guys have all the cool toys," Diana noted, entering Bliss's communications center.

"We get all the girls, too," Nick winked, walking along beside her.

"Not if you keep spouting that crap about going to Vegas and having Elvis perform the ceremony," she teased.

"Maybe that wasn't such a good idea..." he started to reply.

The couple approached a young enlisted man sitting at a console lined with radios, blinking lights, and digital meters. Seeing General Owens, the specialist nearly tripped over himself trying to stand and salute. "At ease," the general snapped, seemingly more worried about the expensive-looking hardware than being properly acknowledged.

Glancing at Diana, the radio operator said, "Ma'am, my counterpart at Camp David said the president will be on the air in three minutes. We are using an encoded, half-duplex shortwave, which means only one party can talk at a time. Furthermore, we are using an encryption device on both ends, so there is a delay. You should speak into this microphone. You push this button to talk, and make sure you let up when you've finished. Is there anything else I can help you with?"

"Are you leaving?" Diana asked, suddenly nervous about the equipment and operating it properly.

"He's not cleared for this communication," Owens replied.

"Ah. I see. Okay, I think I've got it."

Smiling, the specialist nodded in Owens's direction. "Ma'am, the general is familiar with this equipment as well. I'm sure you'll do just fine."

And with that, the soldier rose and looked at his superior, "With your permission, sir."

"Dismissed, and thank you, specialist."

Nick indicated Diana should sit in front of the microphone while he rolled over a chair for the general and himself.

A voice sounded through the speaker, "Bliss? This is Camp D. I have the president here. Everything ready on your end?"

Looking at Nick and receiving a nod to continue, Diana hesitated only a moment before pushing the mic's button. "This is Diana Brown from the Alliance. Good afternoon, Mr. President."

Nick had to tap her shoulder, motioning for her to let up on the button.

It was a few seconds before a familiar voice boomed across the airwaves. The president was clearly upset. "Miss Brown, I wish I could return your polite greeting, but that is beyond me right now. What the hell is the Alliance doing in New Mexico? Why have you attacked and killed our people?"

"Mr. President, I promise you, the Alliance had nothing to do with anything in New Mexico. General Owens assures me that there are no authorized operations there, and the council isn't aware of any activity on the civilian side. Trust me, sir, we've got our hands full on our own street."

The Alliance leaders were unsure if the pause that followed was due to a communications lag, or because the man on the other end was digesting Diana's statement.

"I want to believe you," a calmer voice sounded through the speaker. "But if not the Alliance, then who? Someone is going to answer for this outrage, believe me."

"It would help if we knew what was going on," Diana answered. "Honestly, sir, I have no idea what you're talking about."

"Of course. My apologies, Miss Brown," the president responded.

The U.S. leader then proceeded to provide a full five minutes of debriefing, describing the activity in Los Alamos, the missing nuclear materials, and the massive maze of earthworks.

"The last contact with our team on the ground has led my people to surmise that someone is indeed planning to turn the desert into a mini Garden of Eden. Whoever is behind all this… they now have over 80 pounds of very potent radioactive material."

It was Diana's turn to get angry. "And you didn't inform us of this?" she snapped into the microphone. "Someone is attempting to reroute the water that is the lifeblood of the Alliance's agricultural output, and you didn't let us know?"

"We just arrived at that conclusion a few hours ago, Miss Brown. And to be honest, the fact that it doesn't make any sense for you to cut your own throat is the only reason anyone in Washington is going to believe that the Alliance isn't involved in the nuclear theft."

The general moved closer, looking to Diana for permission to address the president. With her nod of approval, he pressed the button to talk. "Mr. President, this is General Owens. Sir, I can have a crack platoon of troops in Los Alamos in less than two hours, sir. We consider rogue nuclear materials as much of a threat to the Alliance as your people do to the United States."

"Normally, General, I would seriously consider your generous offer, but this situation is a bit more complex. Whoever is building those earthworks is organized, capable, and well-equipped. They have demonstrated both the proficiency and the will to execute violence, and shown a level of competence that is troubling. The message their leader gave to our people on the ground at Los Alamos was chilling, and given what little we know, my experts warn that they might just be able to pull off the nuclear threat."

Diana moved closer to the microphone, "What do you propose, Mr. President? I'm sure you can understand our concerns. Having what sounds like a terrorist in our neighborhood isn't acceptable. Cutting off the water that supplies our primary agricultural region isn't going to fly either. We can't just sit on our hands out here, sir."

A grunt came across the airwaves, but it was impossible for Diana to tell if it was sarcasm or amusement at her diplomatic understatement.

"Yes... yes, I suppose that would be somewhat of a concern for the Alliance. As far as the next step, we're analyzing various options at the moment. I would ask that you hold tight and let us handle our own problem."

That statement provided Diana the first hint of the president's position, and she didn't like it one bit. "I was hoping you would assure us that you were addressing the issue, Mr. President. The activity isn't taking place in our territory, so technically I have no authority to do anything. On the other hand, this is a direct threat against our national security, and we can't just stand by and let that happen."

"Your territory? Your national security? You speak as though Texas was officially a separate nation. The last time I checked, that status was informal... at best," came the gruff response.

Diana inhaled sharply, her temper about to explode. Only Nick's hand squeezing her shoulder stopped what was sure to have escalated into a diplomatic incident. The president's voice came back across the radio's speaker as she gathered herself.

"Miss Brown, if it were up to me, I would've granted Texas its independence years before the collapse. But I'm just the president, not a dictator. And not even an elected Commander in Chief at that. Senators and Congressmen up here think that our countrymen in the Lone Star State have gone too far. They believe strongly that we should shorten your leash and push all of this Alliance nonsense aside. So going back to our little issue in New Mexico, I would advise you not to send in military force. That would appear as though you were trying to expand the Alliance's territory, and I would be pressured to respond in kind. And if your actions didn't go as planned... if there was a disbursement of radioactive materials... that would be considered an act of war."

Diana didn't like being threatened or bullied. "I don't think you or the U.S. military is up for a conflict with us, sir. In the last two years, we've twice engaged in what can only be described as preliminary steps to civil war. A lot of men died in those skirmishes, Mr. President. We were lucky cooler heads prevailed. So I don't think either of us want to let the situation in New Mexico lead to another conflict."

"Things are different now, Miss Brown," came the steady voice from Washington. "Just like the Alliance, we're slowly recovering. If you move into New Mexico with military force, the optics here in Washington will be extremely unfavorable. Even if you went in and got right back out, it would still appear as though you were trying to squelch American citizens who were simply trying to better themselves. Now, please understand what I am trying to tell you. In a way, I wish our entire nation was addressing its problems like the people in New Mexico. We'd all be much better off. I am just saying we need to be aware of how this action might be perceived and used to further another political agenda."

"So what do you propose we do about this, Mr. President? We won't just stand by and let our people starve."

"Miss Brown, I am a man of action more than words. Now, I must ask that you trust me. We simply don't know enough to propose any action or recommend any solution – *at this time*. There is a tremendous void of facts, and until we figure out who and what we're dealing with, I'm not going to order more men into an unknown environment. We've already been surprised by these people twice, and I've got nothing but a body count and missing fissionable material to show for it."

Nick leaned in close, pushing the talk button. "Mr. President, this is Nick. Perhaps we can help with some Intel. I have teams that specialize in performing reconnaissance in just these types of situations."

Again, a pause from Camp David. "I'm aware of your SAINT teams, Nick. But the concern here is the warning issued by the people in New Mexico. If your people were discovered, it might result in a full bucket of radioactive hell being dumped on both of our heads."

"But the warning was for the U.S., not the Alliance, sir. I know I'm splitting hairs here, but we've got a lot at stake in all this. Probably more so than your side of the table."

"That's true," came the considered response from Camp David. "Let me talk it over with my people here. In the meantime, I ask for your commitment that you'll sit tight."

Diana shook her head, not wanting to make any such promise without more time to think. "Like you, Mr. President, I need to consult with my experts."

Something changed in the president's voice on the next transmission. "I see," he said in a monotone. "Could I ask for a private word with just Nick and Diana, please?"

It came across as just plain weird, the Alliance leaders exchanging puzzled looks. Shrugging her shoulders, Diana pushed to talk and responded, "I don't see why not, Mr. President."

General Owens mouthed the words, "Good luck," and then left the room.

"Okay, sir, it's just the two of us here at Bliss."

"From this point forward, I want you to know this is an unofficial, off the record conversation. Is that acceptable?"

Diana frowned at Nick, not knowing where in the hell the man on the other end of the microphone was going. Finally, she pushed to talk, and answered, "Of course, sir. Off the record."

"I can tell by the sound of your voices that you're inclined not to stay on the sidelines. I just wanted to assure you that this matter will get our best resources and full attention. You see, my own son may be a hostage. He was with the Special Forces team that got shot up. Furthermore, if you go in there and make things worse, I'm going to take it personally. I ask that you keep that in mind. We'll be in touch as soon as we know more."

And then the Camp David operator came on and simply said, "Transmission terminated."

They left Fort Bliss shortly after ending the call with the president, their mood somber and silent.

During the ride back to Alpha, Diana remained stoic, watching the arid landscape pass by with few words. Nick knew his passenger well enough to give her time to think it all through.

Fully understanding the dilemma, and not sure what he would do personally was one of those situations where the big ex-operator was glad he wasn't in charge.

On one hand, the Alliance commanded more than enough military capability to waltz right over and kick New Mexico's ass. Given the low population density, it wouldn't have taken much before the collapse, let alone after.

But there were always unintended consequences, even if such an action resulted in an overwhelming military victory. Just ask Presidents Bush and Obama. The words of Colin Powell echoed through the big man's mind. "If you break it, you own it."

The Alliance was stretched as it was, barely hanging on by the thinnest of threads. Restarting the economy was proving more complex than anyone had anticipated. It seemed like there was always some spare part, knowledge or expertise, or basic necessity that was missing or unavailable.

Yes, they were feeding the people – but just barely.

One of the most troubling aspects of the recovery was the mental condition of the population. Nick didn't know the numbers from pre-collapse society, but he'd heard several presentations in the council's chambers from medical experts who were concerned about the overall health of the people.

Depression, schizophrenia, bi-polar disorders, and substance abuse were being encountered in epic proportions. Just recently, Sheriff Watts had informed the council that bathtub booze was now one of his department's single largest issues. The lawman recounted issues of alcohol poisoning and drunken driving, while critical rations of potatoes, corn, and sugar were being hijacked by bootleggers.

And then there was the physical health of the population at large. Tuberculosis, pneumonia, and a host of other diseases pummeled the citizens of the Alliance. The bill for months of malnutrition, lack of medical care, and living in what essentially amounted to a war zone, was coming due. Lack of sewage treatment and insect control contributed to the problem as they were practically non-existent in many parts of the territory.

It all added up to frustratingly slow progress, and in some cases, regression.

Lugging the military away from its already overwhelming responsibilities and transferring soldiers to New Mexico would have so many negative consequences. No matter how well the council handled the public relations of such a campaign, the people would worry. Critics would decry the move, some sure to point out not only the questionable application of limited resources, but also the potential of war with the U.S.

Which led to a SAINT team... or some other semi-diplomatic outreach. Something small scale and reasonably quiet. The thought prompted Nick to grunt.

"What's funny?" Diana asked from the passenger seat. "Tell me. I need some comic relief about now."

"I was just thinking about sending Grim into New Mexico. With that guy along, you could hardly call it a *diplomatic* mission."

Diana laughed, but her levity was short. "I know what you mean, but then again, the president is right. We don't know what is going on. If we are going to commit military resources over there, they need to be our absolute best."

"Too bad Bishop is retired. Terri and he would be the perfect solution."

"That's out of the question. I'm sure Grim and you, or some of the other men, could accomplish the same. They've got Hunter and are trying to start a new life. Both of them have done enough already."

Chapter 6

The toymaker hadn't slept well, dreams of black helicopters and fast-roping assault troops ascending onto his roof keeping him awake.

As with most mornings, he would gladly trade his best toy for a jar of coffee. Even though it had been well over a year ago since he had used that last spoonful of instant, he still craved java. He fantasized for a moment about life after the project was completed, and the crops were being harvested. Maybe they could barter for some coffee. Perhaps there would be enough that someone would open a coffee shop. That was about the only thing he missed from his previous life in L.A.

Still, the locals had provided him with a strong tea. He couldn't pronounce the name but had heard it was one of the few things the Navajo had done better than the traditional American community.

He opened the microwave and extracted the steaming cup, taking a quick sip. "God bless solar panels and inverters," he whispered, anticipating the caffeine rush.

The drink was bitter enough, and obviously contained chicory along with who knew what else. He'd been drinking it for months, and so far it hadn't killed him.

He padded barefoot to the front porch, intending to honor tradition and offer his Apache friends something hot to drink. He knew they wouldn't accept, but it made him feel better to extend the courtesy.

Opening the door, he was surprised to find his security detail had grown significantly in size. Rather than the typical two or three individuals outside, he counted a least a dozen armed men. He could smell the smoke from their cooking fire.

"Hey, am I missing the barbecue? What's the special occasion?" he asked no one in particular.

Apache Jack strolled over, his only greeting a curt nod.

"Why so many new faces?" Hack asked, his gaze sweeping the property.

"The Jicarilla fear the whites will send more soldiers, Grandfather. They always do."

Hack grimaced, "Yes, you're right. I didn't sleep well last night, worried about the exact same thing. I have to go to White Sands today. There's something there I need."

"There is a big powwow today. The elders were hoping you would attend. Word is already spreading around the reservations. The meeting will be this evening at the Santa Domingo pueblo, and all of the tribes will be present."

The toymaker was surprised by the news, such meetings being rare. "What's going on?"

"It is a council of war," the tall warrior continued. "The largest anyone can remember. Even the Ute are sending a chief."

Hack was taken aback by the words his friend was using, and the reaction had nothing to do with the Ute. "We can't go to war against the U.S. military. That would be suicide. We don't have armor, or aircraft, or even large stockpiles of ammunition. They would crush us in a matter of days."

It was obvious the Apache didn't agree with Hack's perspective. "From the drifters I've spoken to, the U.S. Army isn't what it used to be. We've all heard tales of riots and strife back east. There have been stories of civil war and great battles among brothers. And now you have the radioactive metal from Los Alamos to deter their aggression. Many feel like we can win this time... with your help."

"My help?" Hack barked. "How on earth would the tribes expect me to help them in a war? My toys can improve the hunting and help spot intruders, but they aren't going to do much against an organized military force. As far as the fission materials, they won't do much against an army. They're only a deterrent, not an offensive weapon."

"You are a man educated in the world of science. You can generate fuel from wood, Grandfather. You create electricity from steam. You showed us how to make ammunition and explosives. With your knowledge and wisdom, we are confident."

Hack could see where all of this was going, and he didn't like it. But this was neither the time nor the place for a debate. "I appreciate your confidence, my friend. I truly do. Let's just hope it doesn't come to that. Right now, my highest priority is to get to White Sands, and I believe it's important enough to use fuel and the dump truck. We need to take along a few extra men to lift something heavy."

Hack proceeded back inside, his mind digesting the Apache's words and hoping the same sentiment wasn't widespread.

Yes, he'd helped with technology and trinkets. Extracting methane gas from wood wasn't rocket science. Steam turbines had been around for a long, long time. The drones had started off as a hobby – nothing more.

Hack had designed warplanes for a living and knew enough about military capabilities to understand that his toys weren't going to win any wars. The sensors on his drones were primitive compared to the pentagon's models, the explosives he mixed from pool chemicals and other household items were nothing compared to what the military would bring to the battlefield.

The toymaker had no doubt the local tribesmen were brave. Many were exceptionally skilled hunters and woodsmen. More than a few had served in the Armed Forces.

But fighting off the occasional rogue band of marauders was an entirely different world than combat with the regular Army and Air Force. It would be asymmetric warfare at an extreme level.

"The North Vietnamese did it with some success," he mumbled to himself as he looked for his sandals. "There have been countless guerrilla campaigns throughout history," he continued, finally finding his shoes. "But if the U.S. isn't happy about our little irrigation project, they won't send in an occupational force, they'll just come in and return the rivers to their original course."

But why?

Hack had heard the stories, too. With the exception of a few large cities under the military's control, the United States of America didn't exist anymore. So why would Washington, or anybody else for that matter, care?

There had been rumors of a few regional governments being formed. There was the Alliance down in Texas, the Co-op in the Midwest, and the Mountaineers up in Wyoming and Idaho. Hack had his doubts about any of them actually being as organized or well-run as what some of the nomads had claimed.

So why would Washington send in military assets to check on his project? It didn't make any sense.

What did resonate with the ex-engineer was negotiating from a position of strength. All of the old sayings rotated through Hack's mind, such as, "A bird in the hand is worth two in the bush."

His brother's favorite had been, "It's better to ask forgiveness than permission."

But the adage that really best described his thinking was, "Possession is 9/10s of the law."

Hack knew their best defense was to finish the project. After that, as soon as possible, they needed to start raising crops. That's when they'd be in the strongest posture to ward off any potential outside influences.

He mentally checked off the options such progress would allow. They could barter with food and water. The local tribes would gain confidence and swagger. The nearly worthless desert would become the new breadbasket of the region. People would flock to the territory. They would attract professional, hardworking people with the skills necessary to improve their society and raise the standard of living. People who could help them build a new country... and do it right this time.

"Maybe Washington realizes this," he considered. "Maybe they don't want any competition. Maybe they have some vision of keeping the Union whole?"

Hack was finally ready, walking outside to see his Apache friend waiting next to an idling dump truck, six men with rifles climbing into the bed.

Looking at the sky, the Native observed, "Looks like an excellent day for a road trip, Grandfather."

Bishop torqued on the bolt, his arms knotted from strain and slick with sweat.

It didn't move.

"You scum-sucking, bag of ass dander, I'm going to fix you, once and for all," he growled at the rusted connector.

The wannabe repairman climbed down the windmill's tower, pausing at the bottom rung, using his shirt to wipe the perspiration from his brow.

Grumbling all the way to the pickup, he ignored Terri and Hunter, his family resting on the tailgate, legs swinging in the air.

First, he swallowed a quick drink of water, the cold liquid doing little to improve his mood.

"What's wrong, Bishop?" Terri asked, already knowing the answer, but hopeful that giving her husband a chance to talk about it would make him feel better.

"Nothing," he mumbled, distracted as he dug in the truck's bed, looking for a particular tool.

Producing a 5-foot length of steel pipe, the Texan snarled, "This will fix your sorry ass," and proceeded back toward the malfunctioning water pump.

He ascended again, the fourth such trip just this morning, Terri and Hunter watching from the "box seats" below.

Bishop first connected the end wrench to the offending bolt and then gingerly slid the pipe over the tool's handle for leverage.

Again, the sinew and cords rose across his back as the Texan tried to break loose the stubborn bolt using the leverage provided by the extension.

Without warning, the pipe surrendered all its resistance, and Bishop lost his balance. He started to fall, his right hand making a desperate grab for the tower's cross member. He caught it, swaying in the air while the pipe banged and pinged its way down the steel rungs and then thudded onto the desert sand below.

Using the momentum of the fall to his advantage, Bishop grabbed hold with both hands and performed a chin-up, swinging his leg over the ladder's rung while scrambling to a safe perch.

"Are you okay?" Terri yelled from the truck, already moving toward the windmill with Hunter in the crook of her arm.

"Yeah, I'm fine," sounded Bishop, his tone indicating a barely contained rage.

Retreating down the steps again, Bishop recovered the pipe and took a few, deep breaths. Back up he climbed, a look of determination dominating the rancher's face.

An inspection of the stubborn bolt elicited another grimace.

Without a word, Bishop descended the ladder yet again. He skipped the bottom two rungs, his boots kicking up a small puff of sand as he landed hard on the surface.

Then without warning, he raised the pipe and swung it at the tower's support like a baseball slugger trying to knock one out of the park.

Terri began retreating with her child, backing away as Bishop began a tirade of low, menacing curses and strikes.

"You oozing sack of whore pus!"

Whack!

"You worthless, maggot-sucking dickwhistle!"

Thwack!

So animated was Bishop's attack, the third strike actually missed the tower, the pipe flying from his hands and soaring across the desert floor.

Terri had never seen such fury in her husband's eyes when he pivoted and began marching back toward the truck. Definitely wanting to stay out of his way, she and a concerned-looking Hunter backed off to give him space.

A moment later, he was pulling the "big rifle" from the cab and glaring at the windmill with murder in his eye.

"What are you doing?" she yelled, pulling Hunter close and covering the child's ears.

"I'm going to put that son of a bitch out of its misery, that's what!"

"Bishop! Stop! It's just a machine. You can't kill it."

"Oh yeah? Watch me."

Terri, mumbling something about Don Quixote, scurried toward the far side of the truck as Bishop raised the .308 to his shoulder and took aim at the doomed pump. But then he hesitated.

Maintaining his icy stare at the offending device, he lowered the rifle. "You're not worth the ammo," he spat. "I'll have to think of some nice, slow, painful way to bleed you."

Bishop spun, returning the firearm to the truck. Terri stayed back until she was positive the storm was over. She waited while he'd downed another guzzle of water, and then approached cautiously.

"What just happened, Bishop?"

"The bolt holding the sucker rod was rusted through. I sheared off the nut, clean as a whistle," he answered calmly.

"No, that's not what I'm talking about. I meant what happened after you came down the ladder... and began whipping and thrashing an inanimate object."

He smiled, a wee touch of guilt evident around his eyes. "I was just relieving a little frustration is all. Why?"

"You've been nothing but an old grouch since I got back from Alpha," Terri proclaimed defiantly, fists flying to her hipbones, signaling her displeasure and concern. "I know you're upset over the garden and the cows, but we've survived a lot, lot worse."

Bishop stared down at the ground, guilty as charged. "Sorry," he mumbled, hoping to avoid further scolding. "If I was taking it out on you, I didn't mean to."

She stepped close, reaching up to touch his face. Softer this time, "What's the matter, Bishop? This isn't like you to get down in the dumps or lose your temper like that."

The Texan made eye contact with his wife – but only for a moment before his gaze returned to his boots. "I don't know... I guess... I just feel like a failure," he stammered. "I put a lot of pressure on you to resign from the council so we could be together here at the ranch. I wanted that so badly. Now, I can't seem to make a go of it. Everything I touch turns to shit."

Brushing his cheek gently, she responded, "It will work out, I promise. It's not like you're a lazy bones. You're working hard every day. Things will come around. They always do."

Her words put a smile on his face, but it was short-lived. "I appreciate your faith in me. I truly do. But my hard work and your optimism aren't going to put food on the table. We went hungry for a long time, and I don't intend on letting that happen again."

Terri grinned, determined to cheer up her husband. She stepped back and then performed a perfect pirouette, gracefully extending her arms wide. "I don't know. Without all that sugar and carbs in our diet, I'm pretty happy with my girlish figure. It's one of the few post-apocalyptic benefits I can brag about."

"You've always had a great shape," Bishop replied. "You're the most beautiful woman I've ever seen."

Despite his words, it was obvious from the expression on her husband's face that her approach didn't have the desired effect.

71

Upping the ante, she again moved close, tracing her fingers across his chest in a seductive manner. "And a certain Texan I'm rather fond of isn't looking too bad either," she cooed.

Bishop took her hand, squeezing gently and looking deep into her eyes. "I appreciate what you're trying to do. Really, I do. My issue isn't with you... or Hunter... or our lives together. No man could ask for more. My problem is with me and my ability to provide for my family."

Terri hesitated, trying to decide how best to address her husband's fears. Finally, she said, "There are other ways to earn a living besides ranching, my love. Meraton and Alpha are full of men who don't raise cattle or gardens."

"But they have skills... or know a trade or craft. The only way I've ever earned money is with a firearm or a branding iron. I think I've pressed my luck living by the gun. By my way of thinking, I've done enough fighting for any two lifetimes. I'm sick of the killing and violence and risk, besides being damn lucky to be standing here with a beautiful woman who loves me. It's my turn to chill and live an ordinary life."

"That doesn't necessarily mean you need to learn all the verses to *Home on the Range*," Terri said. "You've got a bat cave full of ammo in there. Why don't you start seriously reloading and take the bullets to the Meraton market to sell? Or you could work on repairing guns for people. There's more than one way to earn a buck."

"Sell my ammo?" Bishop replied, his expression suddenly resembling that of a scolded puppy. "Umm... err... I don't know things had gotten *that* bad."

Terri shook her head in frustration, tempted to launch into her own temper fit. Instead, she brightened and said, "I've got an idea. You need a new part for your windmill and a break from your chores, Why don't we drive into Meraton tonight and stay at the Manor? You know how calming the garden... err... the grounds are there, and we can visit with Pete and our other friends. It'll make you feel better. What do you say?"

Bishop rubbed his chin, not sure about his wife's suggestion.

Terri pressed, "I picked up a new bathing suit in Alpha." Then, with her eyebrows moving up and down, she added, "It's white. It's sheer. The pool will be nice and cool, and then later I can show you a few other articles of clothing I found while I was in town. They're even more revealing."

The Texan grinned, bending down to kiss her forehead. "You're rewarding bad behavior, you know. I'm not sure we're setting a good example for Hunter."

"Well... if you don't want to see my new swimwear and

pajamas, we don't have to go."

"Oh, no," Bishop answered quickly, trying to recover. "I think you're right. An evening out on the town might just help my grouchy, old self."

"Then it's a date," Terri cheered. "Let's head to the camper and get packed up."

The first thing Bishop noted as they entered Meraton was the number of cars and pickups. "Is the market still open this late?" he asked Terri, glancing at the sunset in the rearview mirror.

"No, I don't think so. But it's been quite a while since we were here. Maybe they're having some sort of celebration or holiday?"

"I sure hope there's a room at the inn. I hate sleeping on straw with the horses."

The next surprise came in finding a parking space.

The lot behind the Manor was full of carriages, horse teams, wagons, and motor vehicles. "This reminds me of the pre-collapse days," Bishop complained. "I wonder what's going on?"

There was a handful of people in the Manor's lobby, many of them seeming to know Terri. While the small crowd gathered to "Oooh," and "Aww," at Hunter, Bishop made his way to the front desk.

"I'd like a room, please," the Texan announced. "With a king bed over in the new section."

"I'm sorry, sir," responded the woman behind the counter with a name tag identifying her as Wauneta. "All of those are occupied. I can give you a double or two twins."

"Fine. I'll take the double."

"Sure enough, Mr. Bishop," Wauneta replied. "That will be $10, per night. How many nights will you be staying?"

"What?" Bishop replied, surprised that there was a fee. "Did you say ten bucks per night?"

"Yes, sir," came the pleasant response. "I'm giving you the Alliance government discount, even though your wife no longer is formally part of the council."

"But... but when did the rooms start costing anything?" Bishop asked, digging for his wallet.

A look of understanding came over the new proprietor's face. "We have expenses, sir. It's all part and parcel of the recovery, I suppose. I'm trying to keep the price low, but the cleaning ladies just asked for a raise, and the cost of pool supplies, gardener, detergent for the linens, and everything else just keeps going up and up."

"I suppose," Bishop replied, digging a Hamilton from his billfold. With a grimace, he noted there were only a few green bills left.

Next came the registration form – another surprise.

"I guess the world is recovering," he mumbled, reaching for a pencil.

Terri appeared at his side, "Whatcha doing?"

"Did you know they're charging for rooms now? We have to pay $10 per night."

Shrugging, Terri responded, "Makes sense. I saw a lot of this in Alpha during my last visit. There is less and less barter, and more folks wanting currency. People have to make a living. It's progress, I suppose."

"I should've held onto the bank robber's gold," Bishop grunted. "I wonder what Nick did with it anyway?" he queried, only half teasing.

"They moved it to Austin a long time ago. They're using it... and other unclaimed treasure... to back the Alliance's new currency."

Bishop frowned while they waited for a key. "But we're using the old U.S. currency. I don't understand?"

Terri grinned, "Paper money wears out pretty quickly. Diana showed me some designs for the Alliance's bills that they'll start minting in a few months. They need the gold to give people faith in the new currency."

"Speaking of new money, I'm going to have to sell some of my ammo tomorrow in the market. The only bills I had were what we brought with us when we bugged out from Houston, and that wasn't much."

Terri, worried the topic would lower Bishop's spirits again, quickly changed the subject. "I've arranged for a babysitter to watch Hunter once he's asleep. He's pretty pumped up seeing all these new faces, so it will be a bit. Why don't you go visit Pete while I give him a bath and put him down. I'll come get you when it's time to go swimming," she said with a wink.

"Sounds like a plan."

"And no carousing, hard liquor, or brawling," she teased.

"And no wearing a thin, white bikini to Pete's," he responded with a grin.

After carrying their bags to the room and making sure Terri had everything she needed, Bishop strolled through the gardens, making his way to Main Street for the short walk to Pete's Place.

The next thing that struck the Texan as odd was the lack of

firearms. Six months ago, it would have been unusual to see a man walking down the street without some sort of long gun. Now, the M4 slung over his shoulder seemed out of place.

As he progressed the few blocks to the berg's famous watering hole, the Texan noted that all of the storefronts seemed occupied and sported goods in the windows. That hadn't been the case just a short time ago. There was even new construction going on, some of the market's booths being converted to more permanent structures, complete with pergolas and neatly lettered signs.

Bicycles and pedestrians were everywhere, people out and about despite the market having been closed hours ago.

And there were cops.

At the next corner, Bishop observed a police car, complete with two uniformed deputies idling nearby. It appeared as though the law enforcement presence was welcome, many of the pedestrians exchanging friendly nods and greetings with the officers.

They, however, didn't smile when they spied Bishop's rifle.

"Good afternoon," one of the deputies said, stepping purposely into Bishop's path.

"And to you, deputy," the Texan replied, not really sure why he'd drawn their attention.

"What brings you to Meraton, this evening, sir?" asked the second lawman, now joining his partner.

For a split-second, Bishop started to tell the man it was none of his business, but he reconsidered. "My wife and I are in town for the market and a little relaxation."

"In town from where?"

The question hit Bishop the wrong way, but again he checked his temper. *They're only doing their jobs*, he thought.

"I've got a small place south and west of here," Bishop responded nicely.

The fact that Bishop claimed to be a citizen of the Alliance seemed to help with the two officers' attitude, but only a little. "While it's technically not illegal, there's no need for that weapon, sir. Meraton has law and order, and we're trying to discourage citizens from openly displaying their firearms in public."

"At least shoulder-fired weapons," added the other lawman.

"I see," Bishop nodded. "The last time I was in town, that wasn't the case. I appreciate you two gentlemen letting me know. Next time I'll leave it back at the room."

"Are you staying at the Manor, sir?"

That did it, Bishop's temper going from a slow simmer to medium boil. Technically, he was a sworn Texas Ranger, even though the honorary award had been mostly for public morale and ceremony. But that didn't matter. It didn't make a difference if he was a king or a pawn, the two lawmen were crossing the line. "This is becoming intrusive, guys. Where I'm staying is none of your business. Now is there anything else before I continue on my way?"

"Let's see some ID, please," came the command, both deputies now becoming agitated.

"ID? Are you shitting me? Did I just wake up on another planet or something? I haven't had any ID since the world went to hell in a handbasket. You do know we had an apocalypse – right? I'm positive I wasn't just dreaming about the collapse of society."

"The Alliance will accept expired identification created before the event, although we highly recommend every citizen procure new documentation in Alpha or any of the other government centers."

Shaking his head, Bishop responded, "And how much does new documentation cost?"

"A driver's license is $10, sir. An ID card is $5. Our orders are to issue a warning to operators of motorized vehicles and a strong suggestion to all others. In a few more months, we'll start issuing citations that will carry a $50 fine."

"Orders? And who might have issued those stupid-ass orders?"

"Sheriff Watts, sir. By order of the council."

Bishop felt like his head was about to explode. Yes, he'd been secluded at the ranch for several months, but had everything really changed so much, so quickly? "Well, why don't you get on your radio and ask the good sheriff to come down here and ask me for my fucking ID personally? And while you're at it, you might want to advise him to bring a bunch of reinforcements. This is ridiculous, gentlemen. I know the man personally, and I ain't buying this line of crap for one second. Better yet, let's get Diana down here and let her ask me for my ID."

They didn't like his response, not one bit. Both of their postures snapped stiff as if they were expecting trouble. "There's no need to get aggressive, sir," one of the cops stated while the other moved to flank Bishop's position. The tactically-thinking officer's hand dropped closer to his sidearm.

"You've not even begun to see aggressive, pal. While I appreciate the job you're trying to do, there's a limit to..." Bishop began. But he never got a chance to finish.

"Well, Lord have mercy, look what the cat dragged into town," a booming voice rang out from across the street.

The Texan looked up to see Pete crossing the pavement.

"Pete!" Bishop smiled, seeming to forget about the two officers. "Damn, it's good to see you."

Meraton's barkeep, mayor, and council representative hustled the last few steps, accepting Bishop's extended hand and pumping it vigorously. "How the hell are you?" he grinned. "What are you doing here? You brought that beautiful wife of yours along, didn't you?"

The two cops stood by, mildly surprised that the stranger was receiving such a warm greeting from one of the Alliance's leading citizens.

"I was just having a friendly discussion with the local law enforcement," Bishop answered, nodding toward the two officers. "Things certainly have changed in Meraton since I was here last."

Pete turned toward the two deputies and said, "Do you know who this man is?"

"No," responded the senior of the two, "We were just coming to that."

Pete, noting the small crowd of gawkers that had gathered, shook his head. Wanting to avoid a public spectacle, he stepped close to the lawman and lowered his voice, "Have you ever heard of Bishop and Terri?"

"Of course I have," the cop answered. "Who hasn't?"

"Then you should introduce yourselves and be polite. Officers, may I introduce Bishop," Pete said, pointing toward the Texan.

The two deputies didn't seem all that impressed. "Councilman, we're just following orders. This man claims to be a citizen but is carrying a long gun and refuses to show any identification or cooperate with us."

Pete sighed, "It's okay, guys. I'll vouch for him. He's one of the white hats and has served the Alliance well."

The two officers didn't like it but backed down. With a curt, "Have a good day," they moved off, casually strolling back toward their patrol car.

Pete and Bishop continued on toward the bar, the local politician nodding and exchanging greetings as they passed through the gathered citizens of Meraton. When they were finally out of earshot, the mayor turned and teased his old friend, "Please tell me you weren't about to start a fight with the local authorities?"

"Those guys were getting under my skin pretty quick," Bishop responded honestly. "They had more than a toe over the line."

"They've been given a nearly impossible job. We want law and order, yet everyone wants to protect personal liberty. If you had been a vagabond looking for trouble, most folks would be glad they had crossed that line."

"What's all this bullshit about ID cards and driver's licenses?"

"New rules and laws. The people want order and civilization. They demand we make the Alliance a safer place to live, and the only way the council could address those concerns was to bring back some of the bureaucracy of the old times."

Bishop rubbed his chin, deep in thought. "I can't argue that, but it seems like it's all happening so quickly. I'd think trying to get things back to where they were in a big rush would open up the door to a lot of mistakes."

"I don't disagree," Pete responded, "But three weeks ago some drunk drove his pickup into a crowd of people up in Midland Station. Killed eight folks, including two children, who were waiting in line for shaved ice. It ends up the driver had walked away from prison after the collapse. He'd been serving 20 years for a string of DUIs and vehicular homicide. No one knew."

Bishop cringed, "Ouch. That sucks."

"As word of the Alliance's recovery spreads around, we've got every crook, con, nomad, carpetbagger, and criminal making their way to Texas. Some of them think it's still every man for himself, like most of the country. Others think things are business as normal… complete recovery back to the way things were, and that there are banks to rob and wealthy homes to burglarize. We've got bathtub gin factories putting out poison liquor that has already killed dozens and dozens of folks. We've got meth labs opening up all around south Dallas. Sexually transmitted diseases are near epidemic levels. Hell, I've talked to women who would've never even considered prostituting themselves, but found sex for food was their only choice to survive."

Bishop shook his head, remembering some of the situations Terri and he had encountered on their bugout.

Pete went on, "So the people want cops. They want big, mean, nasty police officers who can deal with everything from a marauding band of scroungers to a pack of rabid dogs. They want the streets cleaned up, and they want to go to bed at night without a shotgun sharing their pillow. That equates to having driver's licenses to pay the officer's salaries and to help them maintain order. We have identification cards for the same reasons. The council couldn't come up with any other solution."

"Next thing you know, I'll be paying property taxes again and having to fill out all those complex forms in April," Bishop said.

"That's already in the works, I'm sorry to say. Government isn't free. We're going to try and keep it as streamlined and minimal as possible, but maintaining rule of law is very, very expensive. We are going to implement a sales tax next month."

They arrived at Pete's Place, the sound of the crowd drifting out to the sidewalk. "Sounds like business is strong, my old friend," Bishop commented, happy to change the subject.

"We've expanded the place a bit. I had to hire a few employees as well."

Pete opened the door, a cloud of smoke and laughter escaping through the opening. The place was packed, filled with the noise of people interacting with each other while enjoying a libation.

Holding out his hand, Pete said, "Why don't you let me keep your rifle behind the bar? I trust you with my life, Bishop, but we have a lot of new faces in town, and they don't know you from Adam, or Attila the Hun, or Pol Pot."

Nodding his understanding, Bishop handed his carbine over. He didn't like it. Felt naked without it. But it was Pete's establishment, and the last thing he wanted to do was hurt their friendship.

While Bishop's eyes adjusted to the low light and air thick with pipe and cigar smoke, Pete went on ahead, working his way through the crowded room and exchanging pleasantries with his customers.

"What'll ya have?" came a voice from behind the bar.

Bishop looked up to see a familiar face. "Butter? What? Shit, fire, and cornbread, son! What are you doing tending bar?"

"Mr. Bishop? Well, I'll be. It's good to see you, sir!" responded Terri's former bodyguard. "Is Miss Terri in town with you?"

"Yes, she is, and I know she'll be absolutely thrilled to see you. I'll have a cold beer, please."

Pete appeared beside his helper, nodding toward the lacquer colored liquid Butter was pouring. "I've got three micro-breweries in operation now. One here in Meraton, one outside of Dallas, and a third just opening up between Austin and San Antonio."

"Wow, Pete, that's great. Soon you'll be a chain," Bishop responded, genuinely pleased his friend was doing well.

Butter spoke up, his voice full of pride. "Mr. Nick is training me to become a member of a SAINT team. I'm working here part time until I'm ready to go on an operation."

"You'll do great," Bishop said, sipping his beer. "It looks like the whole town is just growing like a weed."

Pete nodded, "There are two new restaurants opening up, and they're going to serve my wine. We've got a new cigar factory and a gunsmith as well. Things are really looking up."

"I hear they're opening an ammunition factory over by

Houston," Butter added.

"And a new gasoline refinery in Beaumont is supposed to come online soon," Pete continued. "The council has been working really hard on that project. With fuel at $20 per gallon, a lot of people haven't been able to drive or can't move to find work. That'll all change pretty soon and make the recovery even stronger."

"And then we'll have traffic jams," Bishop mumbled, his mind visualizing Main Street and honking cars.

"How's the ranch doing?" Pete asked.

The question, combined with the shock and awe he was experiencing in Meraton, bottomed out Bishop's already low mood. "Not so good," he replied honestly.

Pete, with decades of bartender savvy, detected the cloud behind Bishop's eyes instantly. "Bishop, you know you've got friends all over the Alliance. If there's anything I… or anyone else can do, don't be too proud to ask."

Bishop managed a "Thank you, Pete," before Butter's face lit up in absolute delight. "Miss Terri!"

All heads turned to see the new arrival, Bishop's wife sashaying into the establishment like a refreshing, autumn breeze.

She was wearing a simple black skirt, complete with sleeveless, snow white blouse that accented her smooth, tan skin. Bishop had never seen her look so beautiful.

In a heartbeat, there were a dozen people crowding her, the throng wanting to say hello, and most receiving hugs. Bishop was sure a couple of the friendlier cowboys didn't even know his wife but were merely jumping at the chance to embrace a gorgeous woman.

Even Pete and Butter abandoned their posts from behind the bar, a situation that no one other than Bishop and his empty glass seemed to notice. Given his frame of mind, the complaint, "Can't a man get a refill around here?" formed in his throat, but he quelled the words at the last moment.

And then she was beside him at the bar, the smell of his wife's hair and skin making it all better. "Hi cowboy," she cooed, "come here often?"

"No, but now that I know a stunning woman like you frequents this establishment, I'll be here all the time."

"Buy a girl a drink?" she winked.

"Barkeep!" Bishop barked, doing his best Western twang. "Whatever the lady desires."

Butter grinned, catching on to the game. "We've got some pretty good white wine, ma'am. Or something stronger if you're in the mood."

"Wine sounds great, Butter," she smiled.

Bishop could see the twinkle in his wife's eye, a sure sign Terri was enjoying all of the attention and social interaction. Even seated at the bar beside her husband, a constant stream of well-wishers made their way to her stool, many of them wanting to discuss the issues of the day... or their own personal problems... or their concerns about mutual acquaintances. Bishop was amazed at how deftly his bride handled the social mayhem, more than once glad it was Terri... and not he that had achieved celebrity status.

The Texan was content just to watch, amazed at how gracefully she moved, spoke, and listened. *Wars have been started over women like you*, he thought. *I'm truly blessed*.

He loved to study her, always amazed at some new facet of her personality she would allow him to see. Bishop had long realized that Terri's attractiveness stemmed far deeper than just a pretty face and shapely figure. From day one, she'd been a looker, often turning men's heads whenever they were in public places. But now, despite weathering society's breakdown, childbirth, months with barely enough to eat, and mountains of stress, her beauty had blossomed and matured into something far more stirring.

She had developed an inner confidence and poise that radiated warmth and compassion. She could make a person feel good about himself with a mere glance or rip a man's soul to shreds with the wrath of her disapproval. Helen of Troy? *No*, Bishop thought. *Eye candy didn't get a woman into the same league, no matter how big of a war she started*.

There was a rare intellect within her, as sharp and pointed as any edged weapon, ready to be drawn and used at a moment's notice. But she rarely brandished this advantage... and never for personal gain.

Hatshepsut? Perhaps, considered the Texan, but so little was known of the Egyptian Pharaohs.

She's a hybrid, he decided. The foresight of Empress Suiko, the backbone of Maggie Thatcher, and the conniving appeal of Cleopatra.

A slight commotion at the end of the bar distracted Bishop from his admiration.

There was a large man raising his voice, often not a good mix with whiskey and a crowded bar. But Butter was there, already talking calmly to the big fellow, the two even exchanging a smile.

And then suddenly, everyone was gathering around the pair. "What's going on?" Terri asked, straining her neck to see over the throng of onlookers. Bishop pined for his rifle.

"No idea, but it must be pretty interesting. It's the first time since you came in that every male eye is looking someplace else."

Terri swatted her husband playfully on the arm. "Let's go see," she said, hopping down from her stool without waiting for a response.

"Come on, man, Pete doesn't mind. From Abilene to Marfa, I keep hearing about this unbelievably stout cowpoke who goes by the handle of 'Butter.' I drove down off of I-10 special just to meet ya."

"But I'm working," Butter replied innocently. "I'd be glad to give you a shot after my shift's done."

The crowd got into it then, a bolt of energy surging through the onlookers as they started voicing their support. "C'mon Butter, whoop his ass!"

Pete, evidently drawn by the commotion, appeared from the back room. "What's up?"

"This man wants to arm wrestle me, sir. I told him I was on the clock."

Rolling his eyes, Pete gave his employee permission. "Make it quick, Butter. It's a full house tonight, and I'm still trying to finish the books from yesterday."

It seemed like the entire bar was eager for the contest, a table in the middle of the room cleared so the two titans could do battle. Bishop nudged Terri, indicating Pete at the end of the bar taking bets, stuffing money into a cigar box that had magically appeared from under the counter.

The stranger had his supporters, several folks making wagers against the hometown favorite.

"I'm going to bet on Butter," Terri announced. "Give me some money."

"I'm not so sure that's a good idea," Bishop frowned. "That's a hefty sized gent he's facing, and I can tell he's no softy."

"He doesn't stand a chance against Butter," Terri beamed with confidence. "Give me five bucks, please."

Noting he'd been reaching for his wallet more tonight than in the last two years, Bishop humored his wife, producing the bill. Terri was almost giddy as they waited in line to make the wager.

And then it was time for the match, the two contestants removing their shirts and taking a seat.

Pete, after stashing the overflowing cigar box, was evidently the starter and referee. "Join hands in the middle of the table. Your ass must remain in the seat, or you're disqualified. Both feet must remain on the floor, or it's over. Understand?"

Terri clasped her hands together and yelled encouragement to her former bodyguard, "Go Butter! Take him down!"

Once the two large hams were joined, Pete cupped his palms around the gladiators' clasped hands and announced, "On the count of three."

As promised, Pete did the countdown and then withdrew his hold and stood back.

Bishop knew enough to understand that the secret to arm wrestling was in the wrist and that getting the initial jump on your opponent was key. Evidently, both contestants understood this as well as the two men immediately tried to surprise the other with a burst of tremendous power.

Within a few seconds, veins were protruding from both men's foreheads. The bar room was filled with shouts of support.

Bishop had to hand it to the stranger; the man had strength, technique, and grit. Butter, somewhat surprised that his foe had withstood his initial onslaught, was starting to look a little worried.

And then, with a growl and grunt from the straining newcomer, Butter's arm started losing ground. "Come on, Butter, quit playing with him," Terri shouted, going up on her tiptoes with excitement.

Sensing weakness, the stranger again let out a roar and moved Butter another inch toward defeat.

But the local favorite wasn't about to give up.

Sucking in a huge breath, Butter turned beet red as his face wrinkled with the strain. Slowly, his arm moved back to the starting position, and then bit by bit, he started taking the stranger down.

With what sounded like a howl of pure pain, the stranger fought off the assault, fighting his way back upright. The crowd noise doubled with both support and disappointment.

Back and forth the ball of trembling fist-flesh moved, neither man seeming to be able to finish off the other. "Come on, Butter! Hunter needs a new pair of shoes!" Terri yelled.

Again the big, blonde Texan made a go at his foe, Butter's eyes squinting shut as he groaned from deep within.

A loud crash sounded as the stranger's arm finally gave out, slamming into the table with enough force that Bishop thought the heavy wooden surface might actually split.

The crowd erupted in cheering, several people approaching both men to issue their congratulations and offer drinks.

"We won!" Terri shouted over the din, turning to hug Bishop and celebrate the triumph. He had to smile at his wife's reaction, so caught up in the victory that she almost forgot to collect her winnings.

The Texan watched as Butter and his opponent exchanged handshakes, both of them going on about how challenging the match had been, each man bragging about the other's strength.

At least he's a good loser, Bishop thought, watching the stranger congratulate the winner with a sincere smile and pat on the back. *I wonder if I would show as much sportsmanship.*

While he waited for Pete to pay out the winners, Bishop experienced a bout of introspection. I've been getting my ass kicked out at the ranch, just like that guy, he realized. And I'm definitely a sore loser. But is it the same?

Terri bounced over, flashing her winnings and then making a show of securing the money in her bra.

"Can I at least have my original five back?" Bishop asked, almost knowing what the response would be.

"Maybe," she grinned. "I might let you go hunting for it later."

A short time passed before Bishop leaned close and said, "I'm ready to go anytime you are."

A pained expression crossed Terri's face, "Why? The babysitter is just fine until midnight. Hunter was out. He's had a busy day."

"I don't know. I'm just not in the partying mood. So much has changed around here. I just can't seem to get comfortable."

Terri's brow indicated she was thinking hard, and then her frown disappeared with an idea. "It is a little smoky in here, but I don't want to go back to the room just yet. How about we take a walk?"

Bishop perked up immediately, "That's a great idea!"

He retrieved his rifle from behind the bar, noting a few of the patrons glance his way with odd expressions. *Has Meraton gone anti-gun?* he pondered. *Or am I just being overly sensitive?*

Terri, of course, had to make the rounds and say her goodbyes. Wanting to get away from what suddenly seemed like a room full of disapproving eyes, Bishop whispered, "I'll wait outside," in his wife's ear.

He shook Pete and Butter's hands, promising to see them both again before leaving town.

Wanting to comply with Meraton's new-found sensitivity concerning firearms, Bishop slung the carbine upside down across his back, a universal sign of peaceful intent. It seemed silly.

A few deep breaths of the fresh evening air helped Bishop. While he thought of Pete as a brother, the bar had seemed stuffy and close. *You're becoming an anti-social recluse*, he thought. *You need to get out more. You've been in Pete's a dozen times when it was that crowded, and it never bothered you before.*

And then Terri was beside him, reaching for his hand and pointing back toward the Manor. "Let's tour the gardens first. It's my favorite place on earth."

Bishop had to agree.

They strolled slowly, holding hands like high school lovers, Terri resting her head on his shoulder. Despite his best intent to salvage their date, Bishop couldn't help but tell his wife about the encounter with the deputies.

When he'd finished, Terri stopped and faced her husband. Looking up with an adoring expression, she said, "You've had a bad couple of days, young man. Now, what could a girl do to make life better again?"

"Do you really think that's all there is to it?" he asked. "Do you really think I'm just hitting a low spell?"

"What else could it be? You're not getting feverish, are you?" she teased, playfully feeling his forehead. "Unless you're sick, or tired of me, there's nothing else it could be. Starting a new business like the ranch is an ambitious undertaking, even before humanity hit bottom."

"Tired of you? Now that's just silly. Hunter and you are the only things that make me feel better. Now stop being a goose."

She chuckled and then became serious again. "What do you think it is?"

Bishop wasn't ready to answer that, not just yet. With an arm around her shoulder, he resumed walking, thinking through his response. After another half block, he said, "When I worked at the gun store, I remember talking to a guy who called himself a prepper. He stored food, ammo, and all kinds of supplies, preparing for the apocalypse. He was convinced there would be an EMP attack, or a super-volcano, or asteroid strike, and then society would come to a screeching halt."

"Yeah, I remember there were television shows about people who thought that way. What did they call their movement... self-reliance?"

Bishop nodded, "Something like that. I think there were all kinds of names and labels. Anyway, I've often thought about that man since his beliefs became reality. I've wondered how he fared, and if his preparations had been enough. I don't even remember his name, but the encounter stuck with me."

"Go on."

"Well, one of the things I recall thinking at the time was that he actually seemed to be okay with the thought of society failing. He didn't come right out and say it, but his choice of words and attitude sure led me to believe he'd actually be just fine if it all went to hell. This guy wasn't some nut job or radical, as I recall. He came across as an ordinary enough gent... just an average Joe who was comfortable with doomsday being scheduled for next Monday."

"Really? That's almost kind of scary. Why would anyone

want all of the hunger and violence and uncertainty? How many times did we almost die? How many millions perished? The amount of suffering we've witnessed is enough nightmare material to last a lifetime."

"No. No, it wasn't that he *wanted* all that. He wasn't a masochist or sadist. It was more like he looked forward to a simpler lifestyle... like he felt the world had gotten entirely too complex, and that the hassle of not having modern conveniences would be offset by a less complicated existence."

"Still seems weird to me. Humans are pre-wired to advance, progress, explore, and invent. It's in our DNA to try and make things better. If everybody thought like your friend, we'd still be living in caves. That was a pretty simple existence... and a shorter lifespan, too."

Bishop nodded as if he understood his wife's reply, but then he stopped and faced her. "Those are all fair questions asked from a reasonable perspective. But here's the real scary part – now, today, I understand his attitude. I get where he was coming from."

"What? What the hell are you talking about, Bishop? Now *you're* scaring me."

Shaking his head, the Texan looked down at the pavement. "I know it sounds bad... completely illogical. But I can't help it. Before the recovery, when it was every man for himself, I felt like I had more control over our destiny. The only rules I had to follow were based on my own humanity. The only regulations I had to be concerned with came from the barrel of a gun."

Terri's face made it clear she wasn't following, so Bishop continued. "Did you ever think about the lure of the Old West? Why there was such a romantic draw surrounding all of those cowboy books and movies?"

She pondered the questions for a moment and then nodded. "I suppose. Free range, unrestricted travel. No mortgages or taxes or authority looking over your shoulder. Opportunity. Self-reliance. I get it, but it's a tainted image created by Hollywood producers and authors. They didn't dwell on the loneliness or lack of purpose. Those old horse opera movies didn't point out that a small cut becoming infected could kill a man in a matter of days, or that drinking bad water could cause a fate worse than death."

"Yes, you're absolutely correct. But the people back in those days knew all about the risks, and they still pushed west. Many of them could have left at any time and gone back east. But few did."

"That's all fine and dandy for the strapping young man like you, a guy who's good with a gun and has the reflexes of a cat.

86

But what about the older folks? What about the widows and young children? Think about Hunter's future in the world you describe."

Bishop frowned, "I know. You're right. My brain keeps telling me I'm being stupid and short-sighted. But my gut doesn't like being interrogated by policemen in Meraton or being told I have to keep a piece of paper on my person at all times. I've gotten accustomed to unrestricted freedom, and going back to the way things were is extremely hard for me to digest."

"Why? It doesn't seem like such a big deal to me," she responded. "Having to carry identification seems like a reasonable trade for not having to watch your back every moment of every day. Answering some nosey cop's questions sure beats having a shootout every ten minutes on Main Street. There are trade-offs for progress, my love. Always has been, always will be."

"I suppose, but you have to admit that over-regulation and dependence played a substantial role in the downfall. I know there was a combination of facilitators that landed us where we are. But if every citizen had been like that guy from the gun store, would we have fallen so quickly and landed so hard?"

"Oh, believe me, I understand where you're coming from. When I was on the council, it seemed like we faced this issue every single day. But... we're social animals, my love. We need interaction with others of our kind. Even the pioneers depicted in your romantic movies had goals... destinations... better places they were trying to reach. It's only human nature. Complete anarchy doesn't work. The physically strong will always prey on the weak. Doesn't the man with the slightly slower gun deserve the right to live as much as the quickest draw? Maybe he's a physician and is more interested in healing than fighting. Don't we need his kind to make it all work? Should he be subservient to a lesser intellect just because of physical strength or slower reflexes? Which of our two fictional characters, the doctor or the gunfighter, is going to improve everyone's quality of life?"

Bishop shook his head, admiring how skillfully his wife had just framed the debate. But she was taking his remarks out of context, and he couldn't let it go. "By my way of thinking, people would naturally protect the doctor from the gunslinger out of common sense. I don't see why we need government rules and regulations to enforce core values on society. It leads to a slippery slope... one we just traveled, and I don't know about you, but I didn't like the journey."

Terri stopped walking, turning to face her husband, a twinkle of mischief in her eyes, "And that is why I love you so much, my husband. If everyone was like you, then governance could be a much less intrusive exercise. If there were nothing but clear-thinking, well-intended people on the planet, we probably wouldn't need authority or elections. But that's not the case, and you know it."

She then softened, balancing on her tiptoes to kiss his cheek. "I'm sorry you're feeling like a fish out of water. All of us are going to have to make painful adjustments as the recovery moves forward. We really have no choice, though. There's no stopping it."

"I suppose. As usual, you're right. I'll do my best to stop being an old hermit-grouch."

They continued their stroll, eventually ending at the Manor's pool.

Again, Bishop felt the pangs of disappointment. There were a dozen people splashing and lounging around the crystal clear oasis. The chorus of laughter and low conversations made it obvious that any submerged romantic encounter was out of the question. So was any public display of Terri's new swimwear.

"See what I mean?" Bishop protested. "This recovery thing is entirely overrated. We had to sit at the bar in Pete's because there were no empty tables. I couldn't even find a parking spot on the street. We couldn't get a king-size bed. I had to use money. And now the pool is crowded. Is there any way we can initiate another collapse?"

Terri smiled and then lowered her voice to a sultry tone. "How about I go shoo away the babysitter and change into my new PJs? I'm sure I can take your mind far, far away from the troubles of this nasty, old world."

"Can I have my five bucks back?"

The comment drew a playful swat, and then she was strutting toward their room with an exaggerated swagger of her hips. Casting a coy glance over her shoulder, she said, "Only if you're good. Really good."

Chapter 7

With Hunter on his arm, Bishop headed to the market early, the Texan in a much better mental place.

Determined to have a good day, he left the carbine in the hotel room, opting to tuck a .45 caliber pistol inside his belt. He even left his shirt out to cover the iron's beefy grip.

One on one time with Hunter was always a joy. That... and the opportunity to let Terri sleep in had made shopping for the windmill's replacement bolt all the more palatable. But the highlight of the morning was having his five dollars back.

By noon, they were checked-out and driving back to the ranch. Terri had found a second-hand potty training book, spending most of the trip reading the work to Hunter in the backseat.

"He's just now wanting to walk, isn't it a bit early for potty training?"

"Yes, but they aren't printing books anymore, so I wanted to pick it up while I could," she replied. "Besides that acorn might not fall from your tree, dear. He might be the sort of lad who benefits from hearing something more than once," Terri teased.

Bishop was just about to turn into the ranch's long lane when he abruptly stopped the truck. "What the hell?" he groaned.

Terri followed his gaze to a small cloud of dust rising in the distance. Whatever it was, it was on their property. "Is someone at the camper?" she asked.

"Sure looks like a car is driving on our lane. Were you expecting company?" he asked, reaching for the carbine.

"No. I have no idea who it could be."

Recalling their recent experience with having a pickup shot out from under them, Terri reacted immediately. Unstrapping Hunter, she was out of the cab and slinging her rifle just a few seconds slower than Bishop.

"At least we won't have to walk very far if they shoot up the truck," Bishop said, his eyes never leaving the approaching billow of dust. "But our insurance is going to skyrocket if we have another claim," he added sarcastically.

Despite the seriousness of the situation, Terri actually smiled. "I'm glad to hear you're back with that delightful cornball sense of humor, my love. I was worried there for a while."

A dark colored SUV soon came into view, the vehicle slowly meandering along the ranch's crooked, unpaved lane. "At worst, there's only one carload of them," Bishop commented. "Hardly seems like a fair fight."

"Why are you assuming there's going to be a gunfight?" Terri asked. "That seems a bit pessimistic."

"Why did you grab your rifle, Little Miss Optimist?"

"Good point."

"It's probably just Avon calling, or some guy trying to sell us a satellite dish," Bishop commented, glancing at their surroundings in case a retreat became necessary.

"If it's a salesman, I want to do the shooting," Terri replied with a smirk.

Bishop was scanning the approaching vehicle through his optic when it suddenly stopped 200 meters away. He exhaled with relief when Nick exited the driver's door and waved.

"Shit," Bishop sighed. "So much for a running gun battle with rustlers or looters. It's only Nick."

"And Diana," Terri added, nodding as the Alliance's leader climbed out of the passenger side. "You almost shot our friends who apparently dropped in for a spot of tea."

A short time later, everyone was gathered in the camper's main saloon. "So you guys have been off partying in Meraton?" Nick teased. "So much for all of this, 'I can't leave the ranch, there's too much work to be done,' bellyaching I've been hearing."

"So who's running the show in Alpha since your fiancé is out here in the middle of nowhere?" Bishop countered with a grin.

Terri sensed right away it wasn't a social call, Diana's attempt to mask her stress just a little too transparent. Interrupting the boy's playful banter, she asked, "What's wrong, girlfriend?"

Diana produced a folder almost an inch thick. "We've got a problem," came the worried response. "While I've tried to respect your retirement and leave Bishop and you alone to start anew, we became aware of a situation yesterday that threatens everything we've worked for. I hate to do it, but I need advice... from both of you."

After exchanging troubled glances with her husband, Terri responded, "What's going on, Diana? You know Bishop and I would do anything for Nick and you... and the Alliance as well."

Thirty minutes later, the two visitors had relayed what they knew of the activity in New Mexico, as well as the conversation with the president.

Bishop grunted, "That sounds about like the Colonel... err, I mean the president. He's not going to do squat until he knows who the players are. Back when I worked with him at HBR, he always played it the exact same way."

"There's a certain amount of wisdom in that," Nick agreed. "On the other hand, we can't just sit back and let someone cut off our water or nuke our territory."

Terri looked at her husband, "How much do you think the involvement of the Colonel's son has to do with this?"

"I'm not quite sure. I never met any of his family other than David and Samantha after their plane crashed. I knew the guy was an operator... a PJ... but other than that, the Colonel didn't talk about personal matters at all."

"It has to play a role," Diana added. "There's no way it can't impact his decision-making."

Nick looked at his hosts, the big man's expression growing dark. "Diana and I have come to the conclusion that we need to send in a SAINT team to gather information."

"Risky," Bishop said immediately. "If that team is discovered, it may light the fuse for a nuclear event. Like you both said, the U.S. would blame us for that and who knows where it all goes from there."

"But we don't have any choice," Diana countered. "We can't just sit around and twiddle our thumbs. The U.S. has very little motivation to address what's being done to the rivers, and with the president's son potentially being held, that just adds to the conundrum."

"We wanted our independence, and now we've got it," Terri added. "Is there any other option?"

"Even if you discount the nuclear threat, a military campaign is the last resort," Nick stated. "The manpower that we inherited is being stretched to the limit as it is. While we've made significant progress in the recovery, people are still anxious and jittery. The general population wouldn't take an invasion of New Mexico lightly."

"Terri and you were on the run the last time war threatened our fledgling little democracy. The people got so keyed up, the Alliance was on the verge of revolt. We may be stronger now, but so are they, and every citizen knows it," Diana added.

"Pick your best team and send them in," Bishop concluded. "You're both right. We can't wait for the Colonel to take action. Besides, he's going to be looking out for his best interests, not ours."

Nick nodded, "I hate to ask, but would you be willing to lead a team?"

Bishop's response was fast and sure, "Of course I would, but we both know I'm not the right man for this job. There's too much riding on this. It has to be you in command and making the judgment calls in the field. You're the only one who can make decisions that will impact the entire Alliance."

Looking at Diana, Nick shrugged his shoulders. "See, I told you he'd say that. And he's right."

Diana didn't like it but wasn't going to reopen what had evidently been a long debate with her fiancé. "Would you at least go with him?" she asked Bishop, almost pleading.

Again, Bishop answered from his heart. "Yes, I would go if he asks me. You know I'd follow Nick through the gates of hell… but I'm not the best option for him or the team. We both are used to running our own show. There could be too many cooks in the kitchen if things got rough. Besides, I've been away for a long time now. It would take me a while to get back up to speed with all of the latest tactics and equipment. I'd just get in the way and slow the team down."

Terri, sensing her friend's discomfort at the prospect of Nick going into the field, reached across to place a comforting hand on Diana's arm. "I could come up to Alpha and stay with you while he's gone."

Nick tried to lighten the mood, "It's only a scouting mission. It's not like we're going over there with guns blazing. I'll have Grim and Kevin along. They're the best we have."

Diana looked at her future husband and said, "You're still short a man. Cory's leg won't be healed for another month or more."

"What about Butter?" Bishop asked. "You won't find anyone stronger this side of the Pecos. And he's got the right mindset for this type of mission."

Nick nodded. "I was going to wait another few weeks before assigning him to a team, but you're right. He's ready."

As their guests stood to leave, Bishop hugged Diana and shook Nick's hand. "Good luck, brother. In a way, I wish I was going with you. But Grim and Kevin are the best. Let me know if there's anything I can do to help."

"Will do."

And then they were gone, Bishop and Terri standing in front of the camper and waving goodbye to their friends.

Once Nick's SUV was out of sight, Terri turned to her husband and said, "I thought I'd never hear myself say this, but in a way, I wish you were going with Nick. It doesn't get any more critical than this."

Bishop nodded his agreement, "I know, but I'm no spring chicken anymore, hun. I'd just slow them down or get in the way. There are better men in the Alliance for this type of job."

Terri turned to enter the camper, but a change in Bishop's voice stopped her.

"Hey… wait a minute… I just realized what you said about wishing I'd go with Nick. Are you trying to get rid of me? Time to trade me in for a newer model? Well, let me tell you something, young lady. There were plenty of girls at the Meraton market that were giving me the eye. A couple of them were hotties!"

Terri spun quickly, swooping low to pick up a handful of small rocks. "Let's see how fast you can run, Mr. Spring Chicken," she ordered, doing a pretty good job of pretending to be mad while cocking her arm to launch a projectile.

"Oh shit," Bishop said, ducking under the first missile.

Terri already had another round locked and loaded. "Go on now... let's see how well you hobble around, old man."

Bishop tried the traditional hands-up, don't shoot position, but it was clear from the mischievous look on his wife's face that she wasn't going to hold her fire. He started backing away.

Again, Terri's arm let loose with a stone. It missed, but Bishop decided it was way too close.

Unable to hold it any longer, Terri started laughing. "You look like you still move pretty well to me, my love. And no, I don't have any plans to trade you in. Hunter is way, way too attached to you."

But Bishop didn't come any closer. Terri was still holding the rocks.

"Oh, no, I'm not suckering for that tactic," he said, pointing at the projectiles. "Your weapon is still loaded."

Snapping her finger in an "aww shucks," motion, she said, "Dang it, you caught me," and dropped the rocks.

Before they hit the ground, Bishop was moving. In a blur, Terri was over his shoulder, laughing, kicking, and hitting his back while filling the air with pretend protests. "You cad! Scoundrel! Scalawag! Put me down this instant!"

Bishop carried her to the pool formed by the natural spring and held her over the water, threatening to dump her in. Terri, in an effort to avoid a dunking, wrapped her arms around his neck and hung on for dear life. "Don't you dare," she threatened, trying to keep a straight face.

"Or what?" he grinned.

"Or I'll... I'll... I'll..."

Bishop jumped in.

The drive to White Sands Missile Range passed without event, nor were there any surprises once Hack's party entered the now-abandoned facility.

Hack and his Apache bodyguards hadn't been overly concerned. Multiple teams of Locusts had raided the base long ago.

Several months after the collapse, rumors had circulated that the contract and military personnel assigned to the remote facility were pulling up stakes and relocating to nearby Fort Bliss. National Guard armories had provided excellent booty for the scavengers, so a recently uninhibited Army base was a natural draw.

Before retiring from the Skunk Works, Hack had worked at the nation's largest military installation on two occasions. White Sands was absolutely the best place to test anything that flew, exploded, or used a guidance system to accomplish the mission. At the time, he'd been like a kid in a candy shop, anxious to see and learn everything.

Today, however, Hack wasn't interested in acquiring sophisticated equipment or advanced weapons. Other than batteries, always high on his priority list, the toymaker was after something much more primitive and mundane.

Balloons.

On one of his previous visits, the toymaker had noticed a large storage building full of weather balloons. "Those are left over from long ago," one of the base's personnel had informed the visiting engineer. "But you know the Army, they keep shit lying around forever. It's cheaper to build new storage sheds than to dispose of old hardware."

Hack wasn't after any old party balloons. Nor was he interested in the beautifully colored variety that lifted people into the sky in their straw basket gondolas.

No, the toymaker wanted high altitude, military-grade units that could reach heights of 15-25 miles above the earth's surface, and carry a reasonable payload along the way.

That payload, if necessary, could be a leaking container of radioactive dust.

Pleased with the accuracy of his memory, Hack pointed the dump truck's driver to the precise building where he remembered seeing the inflatable devices years ago.

An hour later, they were heading back north to Caldera country, several crates of silver-skinned, latex balloons in the back of the truck. And there was a bonus as well. Six large tanks of hydrogen had been discovered, along with yellowed instruction guides.

"We now have an Air Force," Hack informed his Apache friend. "As well as a strategic deterrent. It's shaping up to be a pretty good week."

Grim was griping again. "I was just getting used to trees... and grass... and green stuff," the contractor complained. "Now, not only do I have to behave myself because the top dog is leading the mission, but I'll be washing the sand out of my hair for a fucking week."

"I didn't think you bathed more than once a week anyway, Grim," Nick pushed back with a grin. "Last time we were on a job, it sure didn't seem like it."

Riding in the Humvee's back seat, Kevin was his usual, stoic self... perhaps a bit more reserved than usual since his dad was along. Butter, the FNG, or fucking new guy, didn't know what to make of any of it.

"Do they always go at each other like that?" the big ex-rancher leaned over and whispered to Kevin.

"No," replied the team's sharpshooter. "Normally, it's worse. But the day is young."

Kevin's statement confused Butter even more. Double checking the passing New Mexico landscape, he spied the fading light of dusk outside the windows. *What does he mean the day is young? It's almost dark out there.*

Grim, with a map spread across his lap while he monitored a handheld GPS, paused from his primary duties to interrupt the FNG's thoughts. "Ten minutes until we dismount," he said plainly. "And then we start earning our pay."

Nick guided the off-road vehicle across the rough terrain, looking for a larger than normal patch of scrub they had chosen from the old satellite photographs on file in the archives at Bliss. From the dated snapshots taken several miles above the earth, it had looked like the perfect place to stash the oversized SUV.

In addition to the limited, aged information from Bliss, General Owens had convinced the brass at the Pentagon to share what information was available from previous missions. Much to everyone's surprise, the Washington boys had sent what appeared to be a complete package, including video and still photographs.

"Let's go over it again," Nick started as the Humvee bounced across a small wash. "We'll dismount, cover our transport, and then wait for darkness before moving out. Grim and I will form a two-wide point. Butter will be in the middle, Kevin will cover us with that long-range tack driver from the rear. Any questions so far?"

There was none, the team having already heard the same instructions a dozen times before. But no one complained. It was just the way things were done.

"Our number one priority is to avoid contact. If we are

spotted, we egress immediately. The rally point is the Humvee. Make sure you can find your way back there in the dark."

The ex-Green Beret paused, a large berm with a steep downside requiring all of his attention. As soon as it was clear they weren't going to roll over or get stuck, Nick continued.

"We will be approximately 10 kilometers from where the PJ took the video. The area, even before the collapse, was sparsely populated. There are less than a dozen structures in the vicinity, and most of those appear to be outbuildings or storage sheds. I'll be surprised if we even hear a dog bark."

Again the briefing was paused, Grim pointing to a cluster of scrub and cactus off to the right. "That looks like our garage," he announced.

Nick nodded, altering their direction before continuing with his orders. "We will find a good place to set up tonight. Tomorrow, we'll stay put and observe the construction activities in the valley. We'll be running a cold camp – no fires. Tomorrow, we'll use the cover of darkness to move back to the Humvee and head back to Bliss. Any questions?"

"What exactly are we looking for, sir? I've never quite understood that part," Butter asked shyly.

Grim grunted, and for a moment, the FNG thought he'd asked another dumb question. But the more experienced man in the front seat bailed him out. "That's a good question, Butter. I'm not quite sure of the answer myself."

Nick shook his head, a smartass remark forming in his chest. But he let it go. That time was past. "We want to find out who is running the show around here. We want to gain an understanding of how organized they are, what communications methods are being used, and some general knowledge about the size and compilation of the local forces."

"Isn't this all Native American land?" Kevin asked. "Isn't it most likely that it's the Indian tribes?"

"Yes, it probably is, but we need to be positive. Quite frankly, from what we know, the recent activity in the area doesn't fit the Native profile. Why, all of a sudden, would they start rerouting rivers? Where did they get the knowledge and wherewithal to take nuclear materials from an armed escort? How in the hell did they catch the PJ's team, and why shoot it out with them? The council needs to know who and what we're dealing with."

"Who else do you think it could it be?" Kevin pressed.

"According to the eyewitnesses at Los Alamos, there was a white-haired, older Caucasian male in charge when they took down the Department of Energy team at the lab. For all we know, it might be some rogue military unit using the locals for slave labor. For sure, it's more than just the local tribes that are behind all this."

They arrived at the designated parking spot, finding a safe hiding place for the Humvee. Nick had insisted on using a civilian transport, on the off chance that the team was spotted crossing the desert. The locals seemed to be anti-military at the moment.

There was a hustle and bustle of activity, the SAINT team strapping on equipment, double-checking loads and weapons, all along helping each other.

As per routine, the three team members lined up, Nick passing along in front of each man, tugging on gear, asking fundamental questions, and looking into each man's eye to make sure there wasn't any problem. Butter, being the FNG, received the most attention.

Satisfied his men had the proper kit, and that they weren't going to rattle or squeak while walking to their destination, Nick summed it up one last time. "Our top priority is to avoid detection and contact. Even if we don't learn a single new fact, this mission will be deemed a success if we get in and get out without anyone knowing we're here. Next on the list of critical parameters is that we leave no one behind. These people aren't pussies, and they definitely don't shy away from a fight. If we are discovered, we shoot our way out if necessary. Is that clear?"

A chorus of "Yes, sir," sounded from the small group.

"Let's do it, gentlemen. The steaks are on me in Alpha tomorrow night. I'm looking forward to paying for four big meals. Move out."

The sun had disappeared behind the mountains when they finally formed up. Each man had a small piece of glow tape attached to the back of his pack and hat in order to maintain the unit's spacing and not get lost. Grim called them "cat eyes."

Grim and Nick took the lead, each man using night vision to plot the route, avoid dead ends, and make sure the column didn't stumble into an ambush.

The terrain was rocky and arid and supported little plant life. The predetermined path took them up a small mountain with no name, down into a valley and across a series of lower hills. Nick had pined for an easier access point, but it just didn't exist.

As they walked, the big man thought about how many times he'd set off on just such a mission. Unlike Hollywood movies and popular lore, the vast majority of Special Forces operations involved similar objectives. Combat wasn't nearly as common as the tasks of observing, scouting, and gathering hard intelligence.

If discovered, they would engage, and more often than not, would give more than take. Live to fight another day was common wisdom, but sometimes that required putting lead on target.

Like anyone responsible for the lives of others, Nick ran through all of the checklists... again and again. Butter was a worry, only because he was new. Grim was often impatient and trigger happy. Kevin was solid as a rock, but the kid was just 19 and often hesitated just a second too long.

While Nick was confident his team would give a proper accounting for itself if engaged, that wasn't his primary concern. They needed to be stealthy, calm, and patient. Body control and walking without sound were more important than accuracy with a carbine. *Had he spent enough time with Butter teaching the big kid how to step toe-to-heal and distribute his weight gradually?* Paying attention to their surroundings and noticing details was far more critical than target prioritization. *Had he drilled Kevin enough on suppressive fire tactics used to break contact?*

His mind then wandered to each team member's physical conditioning. No one was going to get any sleep for 36 hours. Kevin and Butter were unproven in that environment, Grim and he both getting a little long in the tooth for such joyrides. He knew the lack of sleep could have a tremendous impact on the human brain, affecting everything from judgment to disposition. How would his team react 20 hours from now? Would Butter go from mellow to lion? Would Grim start getting stupid? Would Kevin just fall asleep at the helm?

Like always, the retired Green Beret eventually reached a point where his mind ceased cycling on the negatives. "Run what ya brung," he mouthed silently. "It's done. We're here. Make the best of it. Do the job, and get these guys back home in one piece."

Up the mountain they climbed, their progress sluggish and fatiguing. Each man was carrying over 40 pounds of weapons and kit up the steep inclines and loose footing.

Nick was actually pleased by the rugged ground. People were like animals, they almost always took the path of least resistance. If his team was struggling, that meant the locals wouldn't frequent the area.

Nearer the crest, the foliage and landscape began to change. Elevations weren't as vertical, the desert scrub and low cacti turning into an undergrowth of vines accompanying a canopy of small trees. The hard sand that crunched under their boots was replaced with a soft carpet of pine needles and spongy ground.

And then they were descending.

One would think that the downhill leg would compensate for all of the pain and strain of going up, but that wasn't the case. While the punishment was directed at difference muscles, the heavy packs and need for noise discipline pushed the team members to their limits. The high altitude, with its lower oxygen levels, didn't help.

By the time their GPS indicated they had reached the halfway point, Nick's confidence and pride in his men was growing. No one had complained, fallen back, or imitated a thundering buffalo charging through a china store. The Alliance crew moved as well as any he'd ever led.

Crossing the valley was child's play compared to the hike up and down the hills. As anticipated, their speed over ground improved considerably.

At 3:20AM they finally arrived at the designated coordinates, less than 100 meters away from where the U.S. team had been ambushed.

After verifying they were alone and undetected, Nick called his men into a tight huddle. "Good job on the way in, guys. Nicely done. Now, I know everyone's tired. Hell, my legs feel like I've run a marathon. But now is not the time to get sloppy. Let me remind you that two Green Berets and a PJ were taken out not far from this very spot. We don't know if our foe has night vision, thermal, or some other type of early warning device. So I want everyone under thick cover. I don't care if you have to chisel out a cave, I want zero visibility from ground level, or above. They could have scouts in the trees for all we know. Is that clear?"

All of the heads nodded affirmatively.

"Nobody sleeps. Everybody is wide-eyed and bushy tailed. I'll make one last round to verify your hide before dawn. Do not shoot me. Stay frosty, and get it done. Go!"

Part of the burden of command was not only did Nick have to ensure his team was executing properly, but that he did the same.

He began looking around for a hide.

It was excellent terrain for concealment. Rocky outcroppings, intermixed with healthy patches of sizeable pines provided an abundance of nooks, crannies and ground cover, all serving to limit visibility.

After seeing the area first hand, Nick was more convinced than ever that the other side possessed some sort of sophisticated personnel detection equipment. U.S. Special Forces were as good as any fighting men on earth. The odds against detecting a competent team in these surroundings must have been astronomical. The fact that they had been taken out in less than two minutes was close to a miracle. Unless the other side had help.

Nick had used infrared, light amplification, laser beams, ground scanning radar, and a host of other methods over the span of his career with the teams.

But most of those technologies were deployed around fixed fortifications with consistent power supplies and clear fields of observation. Other than thermal and NVDs, little else worked in the open field, especially in rough terrain like they were operating in now.

It all led back to camouflage and the art of deception.

In Afghanistan, he'd come across Taliban fighters carrying thick wool mats. At first, everyone thought they were sleeping mats or some particular type of prayer rug. A captured prisoner had spilled the beans – they were a desperate attempt to defeat NATO's thermal imagers. An example of Islamic fundamentalist urban myth.

So how did the previous guys manage to get themselves caught, cornered, and overrun? None of it made any sense, but if things went well, he would soon learn the answer to those questions.

The big man found his hide, the combination of a downed tree limb forming a natural lean-to against a granite boulder. Working quickly with the saw blade side of his machete, Nick trimmed numerous smaller branches from a nearby sapling and within a few minutes, had excellent concealment from all angles.

After verifying his handiwork, it was time to check on his team.

Only Kevin seemed to be struggling. Nick pointed to a small indentation in the earth, "Why don't you lie prone and cover that little trench?"

"Because the last time I did that, the fire ants just about ate me alive. I want to be on rock or higher off the ground," Kevin whispered.

Nick spotted another good spot a minute later, a small groove between two outcroppings of rock. "You can fit in there just fine. It gives you excellent fields of fire, and you can get out in a hurry if need be. Let's cut some brush to stack in the opening, and then you can seal yourself in."

Butter was good, Nick having trouble finding the big man's hide. Grim, as expected for a man with his experience, had chosen an excellent position.

It was just an hour before daybreak when Nick settled back into his own makeshift hut, the operator taking a few minutes to drink and consume some nourishment. "Now the monotony kicks in," he whispered to no one. "And Lord, I pray it stays that way."

Chapter 8

Hack awoke and went about his usual routine, making his tea and padding around the cabin until the fog of sleep cleared from his brain.

While he waited on his water to heat via microwaves, he had to admit that despite all of the danger and activity, it was easier to climb out of bed these days.

"You've got a sense of purpose again," he told the bathroom mirror. "You're important to other people. Life, once again, has meaning."

Putting away his toothbrush, Hack reflected for a moment on his forced retirement. He'd never married, never had any interest in either sex. Airplanes, technology, and solving problems had been his love interest. When the powers that be at the Skunk Works had visited his office and informed him of the company's policy regarding "age separation," the engineer had thought it was a badly played joke.

Bitterness was hardly adequate to describe his feelings over the whole ordeal. There had been the typical parties, lunches, and all the other trimmings of an old man being sent out to pasture. He wouldn't have been surprised if one of the uppity-ups had pulled a gold watch out of his pocket.

And then he'd sat in his small condo for days, waiting to be called back into his former life. He was sure some project would require his skills... positive some problem would arise that only he could solve.

Nearly three months passed before it dawned that the phone wasn't going to ring. He spent the time drinking... at home... alone. The empty bottles of bourbon lined up on the kitchen counter were his scoreboard of misery. The hard liquor was winning.

He could still remember the day he'd looked in the mirror and said, "Solve your own problem, old man. Fix this, or you'll simply drink yourself into the grave, and no one will know or care."

He had money. He had time. Where did he want to go? What did he want to do?

One day he was walking to the liquor store to replenish his ever-dwindling supply. A poster in a travel store window caught his attention, the image displaying beautiful mountain scenery with emerald green foliage and smiling vacationers. "Come to the Land of Enchantment," the text read.

Hack studied the ad for almost five minutes. Smaller

images showed a Native American dance, skiing, hikers with backpacks, and the beautiful town of Santa Fe.

Everyone looked so happy. The countryside was appealing. The images weren't anything at all like he'd seen the few times he'd been assigned to projects in New Mexico.

Three days later, he backed his seldom-used sedan out of the driveway, the backseat occupied with a couple of small overnight bags. He had cash, a full tank, a folding map from the gas station, and a heart full of adventure. It had saved his life.

Now, today, he was important again. People came to him to solve problems, and he was making a difference. Even the danger was thrilling.

His usual trip to the front porch produced no surprises. The Apache were there, looking up to acknowledge his presence with a nod. "Anyone want a cup of tea?" he asked, more from habit that any anticipation of anyone accepting his offer.

No one responded.

Shrugging his shoulders, the inventor decided to go and check on their prisoner. He'd been stalling the Cochiti, the families of the fallen still wanting revenge. "He may become a valuable asset if we have to negotiate," he'd told the governor. "You never know the value of a hostage."

He found Grissom lying on his cot in the storage shed... a vigilante Jicarilla nearby. "Good morning," the toymaker greeted.

The sergeant only nodded an acknowledgement, the man understandably finding captivity less than agreeable. "How are you feeling?" Hack asked.

"I guess I'm okay... given the circumstances."

Realizing there wasn't going to be any meaningful conversation this morning, Hack turned to the guard. "Is he eating?"

"Yes, Grandfather."

Hack hung around for a moment, giving Grissom another chance to strike up a dialog. The sergeant merely closed his eyes, returning his head to the canvas surface of the cot.

Shrugging, Hack returned to the front porch and informed Apache Jack of the day's agenda. "I want to visit the project this afternoon after I get some new aerial pictures. But first on our itinerary is a visit to the mine."

Nodding his understanding, the tall warrior barked some orders to his comrades and then hurried to catch up with Hack.

"The Mescalero returned two metal hawks early this morning, Grandfather," the bodyguard reported. "One crashed and has a cracked motor mount, the other's camera isn't working."

Hack stopped mid-stride, a scowl crossing his face. "Damn

it! I told them to take it easy. My creations are only toys, not industrial strength tools. How many is that in for repair now?"

"Six."

Shaking his head, Hack continued toward what had originally been intended as the cabin's garage. Since the collapse, Hack had taken to calling it the "hangar."

Rolling up the door, he gazed in at a concrete floor now littered with drones, all in need of mending.

There was a variety of shapes and sizes present, the flyers scattered here and there, each with an attached sheet of paper describing its unique problem or failure.

"Have the Locusts delivered any more batteries lately?" Hack asked.

"Yes, they delivered a box of laptop computers while we were away in Los Alamos. Many of them looked like newer models."

The news uplifted Hack's mood, somewhat. Batteries were his largest single concern regarding his flying toys. They weren't making them anymore.

As his drones had become a daily factor in the life of the tribes, Hack had soon realized that batteries were going to be a problem. The latest, greatest cells produced just before the collapse could be charged and discharged 500-700 times. But those were rare.

On average, the toymaker's calculations predicted 400-500 cycles before the internal chemicals became tired and wouldn't hold a charge.

With the Valley Green project, hunting parties, scouting missions for the Locusts, and the security of the Caldera area, they were running over 20 flights per day. At that rate, their tiny Air Force wasn't going to last very long.

There was now an airport of sorts in every major pueblo around the Caldera. Hack had discovered that the local high school and college students were fast studies, many of the youth already adept at basic programming, computer usage, and other concepts required to utilize his inventions. They, with his tutelage, soon became competent pilots.

One of the primary uses was what the locals had started calling the "carrier pigeons," an apt nickname for the mail and message delivery between the villages.

Without cell phones or landlines, communication had been nearly nonexistent between the tribes. The first use of a drone to request emergency services had been to save a pregnant woman during a difficult delivery. Trained medical personnel of all sorts, whether you were looking for a Medicine Man, western doctor, or nurse, were rare. Both mother and child had survived.

Once everyone figured out the power of Hack's pigeon message service, a regular mail delivery of sorts had begun operations. Every morning, people would go to their pueblo's airport with addressed envelopes or to see if any new correspondence had arrived. Sometimes it took a few days, but the message would eventually be routed to the proper place.

Hack had spent countless weeks making new drones. With the Locusts delivering parts and components, he'd repurposed everything from lawn chair frames to tiny industrial motors. Circuit boards taken from cell phones, televisions, and even salvaged medical devices had been soldered in his workshop.

An electronics warehouse outside of Albuquerque had been a godsend. A radio repair shop in the suburbs of Taos a goldmine.

But frames, motors, and computer chipsets weren't the primary issue with keeping the drones airborne. Months ago, he'd listed batteries as the Locust's top priority.

He could manufacture, tool, carve or weld practically any other component required, except the fuel cells. And in order to lift even the smallest amount of cargo, the tiny flyers needed the latest in electrical storage technology. The scavenging teams had happened onto a few good finds, but Hack was concerned it wasn't enough. Laptop computer cells, home alarm systems, and even repurposed cells from cordless power tools had been implemented. Some of Hack's hacks had worked well, others, not so well.

Cell phones had excellent cameras, accurate GPS units, and usable transmitters. Small appliances ran on brushless DC motors. Hack was proud of his accomplishments. The Locusts weren't the only ones who could scavenge.

But batteries were still an issue, and at their current rate, Hack had estimated they would have to cut back on flights in less than six months. In a year, they would be grounded unless a new supply was discovered.

"I'll solve that problem when we come to it," he whispered, bypassing the bone yard and heading into the workshop to retrieve his latest, most sophisticated invention.

The Apache security detail watched with great interest as Hack returned a short time later, clad in a head-to-toe white suit. "He looks like an astronaut," one of the Indians commented.

Raising the face-shield, Hack turned to Jack and said, "We're off to the old mine. I need to work on those cases from Los Alamos."

For the first time since they'd been protecting his property, Hack noted a bit of hesitation in the Apache's demeanor. *He's scared of radiation poisoning*, the toymaker thought. *Good... he should be*.

The suit was clumsy, and Grandfather needed help entering the golf cart. A few moments later, they were heading up the mountain.

Hack wasn't really sure of the mine's original purpose. The narrow tunnel was barely wide enough for two men to pass, cut into the solid rock at the base of a 30-foot wall. Given the lack of a rail line, the toymaker assumed it had been excavated by a small-time outfit, probably over a hundred years ago. A real estate agent had actually discovered the overgrown entrance while surveying the property for a listing.

"Could have been silver, maybe turquoise… there's no way to know. Whatever they were after, I don't think they found it," the agent had reported.

The tunnel was only 30 feet deep, ending in a chamber no larger than Hack's bedroom. It was the perfect place to develop a nuclear deterrent.

With the heavy protective suit, a box of Sieverts badges, and a pair of lead-lined gloves, Hack was taking every precaution. He'd even rigged a small water tank and nozzle in order to douse his clothing after working with the deadly substance.

As the Apache approached the entrance, Hack noticed the posted guards were keeping their distance. He didn't blame them and was actually pleased his warnings were being heeded.

He entered the mine, carrying two large, battery powered lights salvaged from a Santa Fe office building. He found the protective cases for Los Alamos exactly where he'd left them, stacked neatly near the "spreaders" he'd fashioned in his machine shop.

Each of the cases contained nine pounds of Colbalt-60, shielded by three inches of layered tungsten polymers and lead. Hack had zero intention of opening any of the "caskets."

The deadly substance was, according to the documentation captured in Los Alamos, in the form of a finely granulated powder. Colbalt-60 was a synthetic by-product of nuclear reactors, this particular batch having been processed in Canada.

The plan to weaponize the radioactive powder was simple. He would rig an altimeter with enough explosives to disintegrate the cases and scatter the contents. Carried aloft by the weather balloons, his makeshift detonators would ignite once they reached an extreme height. The resulting explosion would create a poisonous cloud in the upper atmosphere. By the time gravity pulled the gamma-ray emitting particles to earth, the prevailing winds would have distributed the substance across a wide swath.

Hack knew his plan was fraught with peril. The

concentration, disbursement, and net effect of the contamination was subject to wind, humidity, soil conditions, and a host of other variables.

But like his Apache friends outside, he knew the average citizen was terrified of radiation. He hoped that fear would be enough to deter anyone from interfering with Valley Green.

Wishing he had the time and resources to test his explosives and detonators, Hack proceeded to rig each case with a shape charge he hoped would be sufficient to achieve his goals. In reality, he was probably placing more homemade explosive on each "bomb" than what was required, but better safe than sorry.

It was nervous work.

Hack was certain the government cases offered sufficient precaution against any leakage, the captured Geiger counter reaffirming his faith. But, if one of his spreaders were to accidently explode, it might breach the shielding, and that would result in the entire mine being contaminated.

His work was further complicated by the thick gloves and hot, non-breathing suit, and the constant need to check his dosage badge.

Twice, Hack had to exit the mine, rushing to pull off the restrictive head gear and drinking in both air and water.

After four hours, it was done, the Nations of the Caldera joining the elite club of global nuclear powers. At least that was how the toymaker hoped his trinkets were perceived.

He exited the cave after checking the entire area one last time with the Geiger counter. Next came two showers, one with his suit on, the other without.

After dressing, he waved at Jack, the Apache leader keeping well back.

"It's safe, my friend," Hack announced.

"Are you sure, Grandfather?"

"Yes, I'm sure. It's perfectly safe. Now, let me show you how my latest toys work. If something happens to me, you'll have to launch these weapons."

Nick couldn't believe his eyes.

They'd heard the first engine fire up just after dawn, a large bulldozer appearing from the tree line a short time later.

Soon after, another unusual sound echoed from the valley below - the whinny of horses. Lots of horses.

The Alliance team watched in amazement as dozens and dozens of wagons came bouncing and rolling into the valley below, their teamsters shaking the reigns to urge the beasts of burden.

Nick saw oxen, horses, and even mules pulling all sorts of wheeled contraptions. He even spotted a school bus "convertible," sporting a topless frame, its seats still intact and full of people.

Another massive team of stout-looking plow horses came into view, straining as they pulled against the flatbed trailer of an over-the-road semi. All of the makeshift wagons were filled to the brim with people, shovels, rakes, and baskets.

Supervisors wasted no time issuing instructions, and in short order there were thousands of workers shoveling, hauling, and raking dirt.

Astonished at the scene playing out below them, Nick's team stayed hidden, snapping pictures and trying to take notes and counts.

Butter scribbled a quick line that summed it up best, "This looks like those old movies showing slaves building the pyramids. It's on that scale."

Once they'd delivered their human cargo, the horses were put to work hauling, pulling, and assisting with a variety of other manual tasks. By mid-morning, Nick had counted five heavy, diesel-powered pieces of construction equipment supplementing the flesh and blood labor pool.

At 10:45 the supervisors began blowing whistles, motioning for all of the crews to move to the near side of the valley. From his elevated perch, Nick wondered if the workmen were being given a break.

Once the area was clear of occupants, another round of whistles and harsh shouts rose from below, and then the entire ground shook as a series of explosions rattled the New Mexico desert.

Huge, billowing clouds of dust and dirt rose into the air as tons of rock and sand rolled down from a hillside. The minute the fog of sand and soil settled, the heavy equipment teams rushed in and began working the blasted rubble.

The technology fascinated Grim. Logs, ropes, pulleys, and blocks were all being used to move earth and stone. He spied teams of well-coordinated men moving huge slabs of granite, while women with buckets of water lubricated the rollers and rope.

Nick was taking pictures when a new noise reached his ears. Glancing right and left, he couldn't identify the source. It sounded like some sort of jet engine.

Motion from Kevin's hide drew Nick's attention, his son trying to discreetly point skyward.

Nick followed the boy's finger, but still couldn't see what his son was trying to point out. Finally, the small drone moved and that drew the Green Beret's eye.

The big man watched as the quad-copter hovered above the activity down below. Slowly, so as not to draw attention, he moved his rifle's magnified optic into place in order to study the airborne contraption.

What he found was a sophisticated looking array of black boxes, wires, and lenses hanging from the flying machine's belly. Even the airframe itself was ominous, appearing as a giant, multi-legged insert with barbed stingers and claws of electronics.

"So that's how they found the Special Forces team," he whispered. "They're using drones. What a hell of an idea."

Much to the ex-operator's relief, this particular one didn't appear to be looking for them. Nick watched as it slowly moved up and down the valley, its lenses and sensors pointed at the workers below. "They're using it to map and control the irrigation project," he realized. "That's another piece of the puzzle solved."

Just as quickly as it had appeared, the drone whisked away, traveling back north along the route of construction. "Now I know which direction leads to your headquarters," Nick observed.

"No! No! No!" Hack snapped, his face twisted as if he were in pain. "They were supposed to blow the other side of the valley first!"

He flipped to another image downloaded from the drone, and then another. "This is just wrong! What were they thinking?"

The toymaker pivoted abruptly, snatching up a small stack of papers from a nearby countertop. Poking the top sheet emphatically with his finger, he pleaded to Apache Jack, "It's right here in the outline."

No comment came from the bodyguard, which seemed to infuriate the toymaker even more.

"Get my cart ready! Right now! I'm going down there and jerk a knot in somebody's tail."

A short time later Hack was driving his golf cart down the twisting mountain lane, his mounted security detail struggling to keep up.

"Grandfather! Please slow down. You won't have the pleasure of chewing on somebody's ass if you kill us both on the way to the site."

Hack did as suggested, inhaling deeply to calm his nerves.

They arrived at the head of the valley, Hack's frustration mounting again as he had to wait on a horse-drawn wagon of rocks that was blocking the way.

Finally they arrived at an elevated area bustling with activity. Hack was looking for a yellow hat.

As part of the system he'd devised, the toymaker had implemented a trick he'd once read about in high school. Before the advent of radios and cell phones, construction crews commonly wore color-coded hats. Yellow covers were the top management, red the mid-level foremen. Blue caps were specialists, like the explosive experts. Each of the yellow-tops involved with Valley Green had been issued a walkie-talkie radio.

The Apache watched with a smirk as the toymaker demanded the yellow hat call *all* of the field foremen to "the mound." The Native always enjoyed watching Grandfather rant and rave. It was an art form, the older man a master.

They soon began arriving, some walking, others riding bicycles, and two on horses.

Hack then proceeded to rip ass.

Nick noticed the odd pattern of movement below, his rifle optic focused on what seemed to be a meeting of the important minds. He sucked in a lung full of air when a man with snow-white hair appeared through the glass.

He watched with keen interest as the tall, bean-pole of a man waved his arms in wild, animated motions indicating either anger or frustration, or perhaps both. The pissed-off gentleman's description matched what the DOE team had described as the man in charge during the hijacking at Los Alamos.

"Well, now we know who the brain of this outfit is," Nick whispered, exchanging the view through his optic for an image on his camera.

The scolding below was soon concluded, Nick noticing that once he'd bled off his rage, Mr. White Hair seemed to be giving his troops a pep talk. "Good leadership skills," he whispered.

And then there was a scrambling of activity, the brain-trust disbursing and rushing off to execute the boss's orders.

Nick was fascinated with the wizard-like persona below, a level of genuine respect forming as he watched the Jefe issue orders and direct the workers. So intense was his study, he failed to notice what was happening at the base of the ridge where the Alliance team and he were hiding.

The first hint was the workers gathering on the far side. When the initial whistle warned of a pending explosion, Nick's reaction was immediate. "Oh shit!" the big man yelled. "Break cover! Now! Get the fuck off this ridge!"

Under strict orders to remain under cover no matter what, Grim and the guys were slow to react. When they saw their leader running away from the valley like he was being chased by demons, they wisely decided to follow.

The thought of being buried alive under tons of sand and rock motivated the team's feet, their legs pumping like pistons as they scrambled to put distance between themselves and the pending detonation.

Nick didn't hear the sound of the second whistle, his own breathing and pounding boots blocking the distant signal. He didn't have any problem at all hearing the blast.

A thunderous, deafening roar ripped across the New Mexico desert as a wall of rocks, sand, and soil was shot skyward over 100 feet into the air. The Alliance team didn't see the eruption, their backs turned to the event. But they felt it.

The ground shook under their feet, the upheaval so violent Nick lost his footing, rolling hard to the ground with the jarring impact. Grim was right behind him, the contractor managing to maintain his balance and slowing to help his comrade.

No sooner than Grim had extended a helping hand, a shower of rocks and dirt came raining from the sky.

Nick pulled Grim over his body, practically throwing the ex-contractor toward cover. They both were scrambling for the security of an overhang when rocks the size of car engines began raining from above.

The hailstorm of granite and grit lasted only a few seconds, but to Nick it seemed like it would never stop. His thoughts were of Kevin, the deadly shower more terrifying than any firefight the big man had ever endured.

A thick fog of dust blanketed the area, the disturbed soil making it difficult to breathe or see. Following Grim's lead, Nick quickly wrapped his shemagh around his face, the cotton cloth acting as an air filter as his eyes desperately searched for any sign of Kevin or Butter.

The soil-cloud was heavy and thick, settling enough for limited visibility in less than a minute. Nick exhaled with relief when Butter and Kevin's outlines appeared in the distance, both of them apparently unhurt.

"We just dodged one big-ass bullet," Nick commented to Grim. "That was way too fucking close."

"No shit," came the grumbled response as the contractor brushed the soil and dirt from his clothing and gear. "What now?"

Nick didn't answer immediately, choosing instead to survey his men and ponder their next step. "We know who the leader is," he said, thinking out loud. "But it would really help if we knew where their headquarters was located."

"You're in charge," Grim responded, rinsing his mouth of the grime with a pull from his Camelbak. "Lead on, oh fearless one."

Nick, ignoring Grim's sarcasm, scanned their surroundings and then pulled a map from his load vest. After a minute of deliberation, he pointed north. "I saw the drone fly off in that direction. That wizard-dude came from that way, too. Let's see if we can find out where their HQ is located, and then we can head home."

The team was soon moving out, staying to the thickest part of the forest to avoid detection. Nick knew traveling in broad daylight was dangerous, but now that he understood the technology being used by the locals, he judged the new objective worth the risk. No matter what kind of camera was hanging from a drone, it couldn't see through these trees.

They made good progress, traveling along the unexploded portion of the ridgeline that bordered the valley where all of the construction was taking place. Nick kept listening for a warning whistle, but none sounded.

Every half kilometer or so, Nick would halt the team and stalk to the ridge's edge in order to keep his bearings and spy on the workforce below. It was during the last such side trip that he spotted the wizard-boss riding in a golf cart, surrounded by several armed horsemen.

Nick followed their progress up the valley, using his magnified optic to track their movement. Without warning, the white-topped buggy made a sudden turn and entered a narrow opening in the forest that appeared to be some sort of logging lane or dirt path. The horsemen followed.

Returning to the team, Nick filled everyone in on what he'd seen. "We'll move on down the valley for another two clicks and then hold up for nightfall. Let's hope we can track those horses back to the outlaw's lair."

Feeling better about the day's progress, Hack was actually whistling as he plugged the golf cart's recharging cord into the

111

outlet.

Satisfied that his ride's batteries were being topped off, he then made for the drone that had returned from the construction site. Flashing a mischievous grin to his Apache friend, the toymaker's voice sounded full of teenage glee. "I want to see the video recording of the explosion," he informed the bodyguard. "That was one hell of a bang."

A few moments later, Hack was connecting the flying robot's memory to his computer, eager to see an airborne view of the devastation. "I haven't had this much fun since we flushed cherry bombs down the toilets in college," he confessed.

Motioned over by their leader, several members of the security force gathered over Hack's shoulder, apparently anxious to see the ridge obliterated.

The recording appeared, the hovering drone above the soon-to-be blasted ridge. Hack could make out the ant-like figures of the workers moving to the safety of the opposite side.

Pushing a button, he fast-forwarded the mundane images, watching as the squiggly lines and distorted images rolled across the computer's screen. "There, that's about right," he said, slowing the picture back to its intended speed.

Several puffs of what looked like smoke shot out from the ridge's wall, and then the entire formation of stone and rock seemed to rise into the air. So violent was the concussion, the drone's camera shook and rattled from the wave of air striking the tiny flyer.

It was the Apache leader who saw something odd. "Can you rewind the recording, Grandfather?"

"Sure," Hack replied with a grin, glad that he wasn't the only one who enjoyed a good detonation.

Hack's fingers manipulated the touchscreen and soon the video was playing for the second time. "Stop it right there!" the Apache ordered, his finger moving toward the display. "What's that? Or who is that?"

The toymaker saw what his friend was pointing at, three tiny human figures where no one should be. "What are those people doing up there?" he whispered, trying to order the computer to magnify that section of the image.

Eventually, Hack figured it out, and the video display zoomed in on the top of the ridge.

The picture was grainy, but what they saw was clear enough. Three men, running away, the outline of two rifles clear against the backdrop of brown desert. While it was impossible to be certain, Hack and the Apache both thought they were looking at soldiers.

After exchanging troubled looks with his protector, Hack

said, "Come on, I want to launch another drone and have it scout that area. Maybe they were killed in the explosion."

"I'll send some men to search that side of the ridge, and I'm going to double the patrols tonight," added the Apache.

"We'll find them," Hack replied with confidence. "There's really no place for them to go."

Chapter 9

The trail had been easy to follow, even in low light.

Accounting for the fact that horses were a common mode of transportation in the area, Nick didn't believe that golf carts were. In the end, it had been the tire tracks than put the Alliance team onto the cabin's lane.

Motioning his men close, Nick took his flashlight and held it a few inches from the ground. After the team had formed a tight huddle to block the torch, he poked a finger in the soil and then drew a ring around the middle.

I want to circle the property, he has saying.

They moved like ghosts through the New Mexico pine forest, Nick and Grim up front, one scouting ahead with their NVD, the other advancing slowly. Butter stayed ten meters behind them, Kevin bringing up the rear at a similar spacing.

The clear sky, combined with the high mountain star field allowed them to make safe progress at a good clip. They were one quarter of the way around Nick's circle when Grim's fist snapped into the air.

Everyone froze, the rest of the team going low and raising their weapons.

Nick waited and listened a good 20 seconds before moving forward to see what had stopped the point man cold.

Grim waited until his friend was close enough to make eye contact and then with minimum motion, the contractor pinched his fingers together and drew them through the air. A trip wire!

It took Nick only a moment to find the line, the length of wire stretched taut against Grim's shin. Another quarter of an inch, and the trap would have sprung.

Tracing the line with his eyes, Nick followed the barely-visible wire to a nearby stump. There, he found a section of pipe, someone having wrapped the small bomb with rusty nails and screws.

Chancing his flashlight, Nick illuminated the device, finding a simple trigger mechanism. After exchanging a "here goes," look with Grim, the team leader proceeded to disarm the booby-trap.

Happy to have both of his legs intact, Grim led the duo back to Butter's position where they then waved Kevin forward.

"The area is wired," Nick informed his team. "They're using pipe bombs and trip lines. We're going to back out the way we came in. Be careful, and make sure you follow Grim and me precisely. Close up our spacing to three paces, and try to use the same footfalls. Got it?"

The two junior members nodded their understanding, Nick noting Butter's eyes seemed a bit wider than before. *You wanted to be here*, he thought. *Deal with it*.

Nick backtracked over about 50 meters, again motioning his people in close. "We're still going to circle that property, but in a wider arch."

Their progress was slowed by an abundance of caution, but Nick was determined to scout what he deemed a critical location. If the Alliance was going to figure out a solution, every fact was important, even the smallest bit of knowledge might make the difference.

He was watching Grim's cat eye, the small glowing patch of tape bouncing and moving as the contractor progressed through the forest. In a blink, it disappeared.

Nick went low without thinking. A few seconds later, he could hear the patrol.

He estimated there were five or six of them, walking in a straight line less than 20 meters to the south. They evidently were pretty good, able to approach that close before Grim had picked them up.

It was the innocent rattle of someone's equipment that had given them away, other than the occasional tinkle that sounded like a far-distant cow bell, Nick was impressed with how quietly the patrol was moving.

The Alliance team let them pass, their path intersecting Grim's position by less than 15 feet. After waiting a minute to give their foe a head start, Nick went forward to his point man's position and said, "Follow them in."

Grim's eyes went wide at the order, such a bold maneuver fraught with peril. "They're amateurs," Nick reassured. "They won't post a rear guard. Go."

"I hope you're right," came the mouthed response, and then Grim was moving again.

Nick's logic was simple. The patrol would know where the booby-traps were located. Following in their footsteps would be the safest way to close on the objective.

For over 40 minutes, they tailed the local patrol, Grim struggling to maintain a safe distance while at the same time not losing his guides in the forest.

Twice the Alliance men got a fairly good look at the group in front of them. There were six males, all with long guns and small packs that appeared to contain ammunition and water. "They're all Indians," Grim observed after almost running into the back of their column. "They're wearing war paint... or whatever they call it."

"So are you," Nick replied, pointing at the streaks of camo-paint crossing his man's face.

"They move pretty good," continued the report. "They've wearing boots, just like ours. I always thought Indians wore moccasins?"

Nick nearly broke noise discipline by laughing at Grim's expression when he delivered the report. The ex-contractor seemed on edge about the discovery, like he was haunted by the notion of facing Native Americans.

"They don't take scalps anymore," Nick reassured.

"That's good to know," Grim mouthed.

"These tribes are headhunters. They want your entire brainpan."

There was enough light for Nick to see Grim nearly bought it, realizing a moment later that his team leader was messing with his mind. "Very fucking funny," the ex-contractor hissed.

At one point, the Alliance team watched as someone in the patrol decided he wanted a smoke. A match was struck, momentarily glowing like heat lightning, and then the red of a pipe's embers could be seen as the owner stoked the bowl. A few seconds later, Nick smelled the tobacco.

After taking their short break, the patrol resumed its pace, now having traveled to a point almost directly north of where Nick believed they would find the headquarters. And he was right.

Twenty minutes later, they made a sharp right turn and then held that course.

They crested a small rise a short time later, the Alliance men finding themselves looking down on the faint glow of electric lights gleaming through a cabin's windows. Nick called a halt, thinking they were close enough.

They watched the patrol continue into the compound, small pools of electric light allowing the team to track their progress as they moved closer to the complex.

It was Grim who found the notches.

"They've got the safe route marked around the booby-traps," he said. "See those cuts on the trees? They always pass between them."

It took Nick a bit to see what Grim was talking about, but then he was nodding. About shoulder high on two nearby trunks were what initially appeared as random bark damage, but after his man's observation, the ex-operator could spot the guides.

"Good, Grim. Very good. That will help."

Daybreak found the team fed and in reasonably concealed positions. They were approximately 600 meters north of the complex, peering down on three buildings that Nick guessed were a cabin, some sort of barn or workshop, and a garage.

In addition to the fixed structures, there was also a grouping of tents. *The security force is temporary*, Nick observed.

Into mid-morning, the Alliance men watched, photographed, and scribbled notes on the activity below. The horses were fed and watered, a cooking fire was rekindled, and the perimeter security changed shifts. Overall, it looked like any other military camp the ex-operator had scouted.

And Grim was right; the men they were surveilling were all Native Americans.

The discovery of the opposition's HQ had expanded the duration of the mission but was well worth it in the big man's mind.

While the Alliance leader pondered what he could do with such information, there was a change in the rhythm of movement below. Mr. White Hair appeared on the cabin's front porch, his arrival prompting a new level of alertness in the guards.

Nick watched as the apparent leader marched across the ground, one of the older security-types keeping step. The duo opened a side door of one of the outbuildings and went inside, only to reappear a short time later with two other men.

One of the newcomers was clearly part of the security force, his rifle and face paint making that determination easy. It was the second man now being led outside that puzzled Nick.

At first, Nick thought the unidentified person was very old or drunk. There was something off in his step, almost as if he was struggling to keep his balance. A few seconds later, the man half turned, and Nick could see his hands were bound. A prisoner?

And then he knew. It was one of the U.S. team members. They weren't all dead like Washington believed.

Fuck, Nick thought. That changes everything.

His previous thoughts of a helo-born assault, surgical ground invasion, or even a smart-bomb taking out the enemy HQ, were now far more complicated with the appearance of the prisoner.

Nick couldn't tell which member of the previous team had survived, but knew if it was the president's son, the entire situation might easily spiral out of control.

The guards returned the captive to the interior after letting him walk the perimeter of the building for 30 minutes. It reminded Nick of something he'd read about maximum security prisons, and how the inmates received a half hour of outdoor time each day.

After that, things seemed to settle into a routine below, and that presented Nick with his own problem.

His men were exhausted, perhaps not so much physically, but mentally. They hadn't rested, and despite his training and conditioning, Nick himself was feeling the effects of sleep deprivation.

He was just about to order a rotating shift of two hours shuteye for each of his team when the White Wizard's flowing mane reappeared.

Carrying a coffee cup, he proceeded toward the garage with purpose in his step. Nick noted a few of the idling security men wandering closer, obviously curious about what the boss was doing.

The Alliance team's angle didn't allow them to see inside the garage after the rolling door was pulled open, but that didn't matter much.

Again the easily identifiable hair appeared, this time holding something larger in his arms.

It became clear a few moments later that it was a drone.

With a small crowd of onlookers gathered around, the flying robot shot skyward. Nick followed the machine's progress as it rose, his own curiosity piqued. That soon changed however when the drone flew directly at the Alliance team's position, and then hovered above them.

"Oh, shit," Grim heard his boss say. That was never a good sign.

Hack's deductive reasoning was causing him to experience bouts of paranoia.

When his flying eyes hadn't found the intruders around what was left of the east ridge, he'd begun to worry. The Apache entourage had returned empty handed, and that had fueled the toymaker's stress even further.

They had flown infrared equipped drones throughout the night, but still no sign of the three men clearly depicted in the video.

That left only three options, the least likely being they were buried in the hundreds of tons of rubble that had been blasted from the cliff. Given their position and speed from the video recording, Hack wasn't prepared to accept that explanation.

The second possibility was that they had escaped.

Again, the toymaker found that option unlikely. They would have spotted a motorized vehicle with drones. Any sort of helicopter extraction would have been reported by the picket line of listening posts the tribes had established around the territory. There was no way men could travel on foot beyond the scope of their searches. It was across open desert, and distances were too great, no matter how well conditioned those individuals might be.

That left the third alternative, which meant the strangers were still in the area and hiding in the forest.

They'd launched twice the normal number of "patrol drones," Hack devising an expanding search grid centered on the last known position of the quarry. Most of those flyers had been loaded-out with thermal imagers.

The infrared cameras he'd modified to fit on the drones weren't exactly high-resolution devices. Mostly, they'd been scavenged from German luxury cars equipped with IR as a nighttime driving safety feature.

His best unit was hacked from the internals of a military infrared optic normally mounted on a rifle. That jewel had been found in a desk drawer at a New Mexico National Guard armory, packaged to be sent in for repairs. Hack had fixed the malfunctioning device in less than an hour.

Infrared could detect varying levels of radiated heat, but the technology couldn't see through solid objects, like the forest canopy, rock, or building walls. As a matter of fact, it couldn't even see through window glass.

What little sleep he managed had been filled with nightmares of vengeful soldiers kicking in the bedroom door and spraying his mattress with bullets.

When dawn finally broke, he was more determined than ever to find the intruders so he could put this incident behind him and continue with more strategic projects.

Evidently, the Apache were a little paranoid as well. As Hack had his tea, he was surprised to hear that no one had bothered to check on their prisoner. "If they somehow know he's alive, that's going to be where they go first," he chided the security team.

After finding their captive still secure in the storage room, Hack wanted to test an adjustment he'd made on his best infrared sensor.

"I'll just fly it long enough to scan around here and test my enhancements," he informed Apache Jack.

After watching the metal hawk launch, Hack had guided it north of the cabin, into an area he knew was void of human life. Less than a mile from his home, heat signatures equaling 99 degrees displayed on the viewer.

Turning to the Apache, he asked, "Do you have men up on the mountain?"

"No, Grandfather. The only patrol is toward the south."

In a lightning flash of logic, it all made sense to Hack. Of course, they would be spying on his cabin. That's where the prisoner was. He was the one who'd issued the threat in Los Alamos.

The toymaker's first instinct was to turn and run. The thought that the enemy was so close to his abode nearly drove the man to panic. "There they are!" he snapped to the Apache, trying to point to the tablet's screen and the forest at the same time.

The bodyguard's eyes grew wide for a split second, and then he was shouting commands to the surrounding warriors.

Nick knew instantly they'd been detected.

Raising his rifle, he centered on the hovering flying machine let loose with several shots. One of them must have connected as the device went crazy, jerking and wobbling before starting a death spiral toward the earth. The big man didn't hang around to watch the impact. It was time to move.

The Alliance team was up and hustling in seconds, Nick shouting orders the entire time.

"They have horses," he barked at his crew. Head into the thickest woods, or they'll run us down in no time.

A few moments later, the scream and whinny of excited horses sounded from below.

Grim assumed his normal position on point, the contractor fighting the urge to run like the wind. The forest was booby-trapped. It took time to find the markers on the trees.

Nick realized the dilemma at the same moment, his commander's mind weighing the options. He estimated there were 30-40 armed men in the camp below. They weren't unskilled. Their supply line was shorter. They had reinforcements close by. The odds were too long to stand and fight.

But he could slow them down.

"Kevin! Drop back and give them a few rounds. Make them think about it."

The boy did just that, slowing his jog to a walk as his head pivoted trying to find a suitable sniping position.

Nick watched his son duck behind a small mound of stones, the barrel of his long distance rifle protruding from behind the mini-fortress.

"Grim, I'm staying back with Kevin. You go on ahead with Butter. Move 1,000 meters straight north and then wait on us. We're going to be coming in a hurry, so disable any wires along the way, clear?"

"Roger that," came the response, and then the other half of the Alliance team disappeared into the foliage.

Nick took up a position slightly behind and off angle to his son. From there, he could discourage any flanking maneuver while watching Kevin's back.

For a minute, Nick thought the pursuers had given up already. There was no movement, noise, or any sign of the hunters.

Kevin saw them first, the report of his weapon shattering the otherwise quiet mountainside. Nick followed his son's aim and saw a semi-hidden horseman fall from his mount.

Again, the sniper rifle fired, this shot answered with the howl of a wounded man.

Damn he's good, Nick thought, judging it over 700 meters to where his son's rounds were impacting.

The big man kept scanning downhill but knew Kevin's superior optic would allow him to see any target well before his naked eye.

A minute passed, and then another.

Movement drew Nick's attention, a man running bent at the waist, trying to reach the guy Kevin had knocked off the horse. A third shot rang out, this time Nick saw the target rise up and clutch his gut before falling to the ground.

"Let's go, Kevin. That ought to slow them down a little."

And then they were moving, heading straight north, praying Grim had disabled any trip wires.

Their speed over ground was good, and Nick couldn't detect any pursuit. An old infantry adage popped into the big man's mind – if it's going well, you're probably walking into an ambush.

At that moment, Kevin pulled up short. The terrain had changed.

They found themselves at the edge of a high mountain prairie, a beautiful creek running through the middle of the open spaces. While the postcard perfect scene would have normally been inspirational, it was a big problem for the hunted.

Crossing any open space was a worry. It was a natural barrier for those trying to escape, and Nick knew full well that the locals would be aware of the field's existence.

"Shit," he mumbled, looking left and right across the thigh-high grass and flowers.

They stayed put for a bit, watching for any sign of the hunters... or the other members of their team. Grim must have crossed the field, but with his head start, the locals probably hadn't had time to get into position.

The sound of shouted orders and human voices came from behind, Nick knowing he had to act soon or they'd be pinned against the open space.

"You go first," he ordered Kevin. "Run like the wind. Once you reach the other side, cover my crossing."

"Yes, sir," the kid responded as he launched himself out of

the tree line.

Kevin was less than halfway across when the riders broke from cover, their battle cries and firing weapons sending a bolt of fear through Nick's soul.

In a flash, his carbine was at the shoulder, spitting round after round into the charging horsemen. Kevin, wisely, kept running.

Again and again, Nick poured lead into the men trying to kill his son. An animal went down, another rider knocked from his mount.

Somehow the big man's mind managed to calculate the distances and speeds involved in the pursuit, his fatherly instincts concluding that Kevin wasn't going to make it. The carbine's bolt locked back empty just as the third hunter fell. There were still seven or eight left.

The meadow's grass was evidently thicker than it looked, Kevin seemingly taking forever to cross. His stride was more of a bounding motion, uneven and slow. Worse yet, the vines and thick grass didn't seem to slow the horses at all.

The fresh magazine was out of Nick's vest and slammed home in a flash, his hand moving in a blur as he palmed the release and forward assist in the same motion. But it wasn't going to be enough. They were going to run Kevin down before he reached the other side.

With a war cry of his own, born of pure desperation, Nick charged from his cover. Like the riders, his accuracy suffered, the pumping of his legs throwing off any semblance of aim. His goal was distraction.

But the riders were focused, either not hearing or not caring about Nick's exposure. With murderous howls of bloodlust, they continued to rumble directly at the fleeing boy.

And then Kevin pulled up lame, hobbled two steps, and went down.

The fury that surged through Nick's veins was unlike anything he'd ever felt. He'd seen his son shot before, the boy taking a round in the Alpha courthouse, but this was different.

With his attempt at distraction failing, Nick changed tactics, taking a knee and hoping for accuracy.

Evidently, the horsemen thought Kevin was dead, the lead rider changing directions and now charging directly toward Nick's exposed position.

Nick made them pay.

One screaming warrior flew backward off his steed, a cloud of red mist hanging in the air were the man's head had been a moment before.

Another took a round to his shoulder, dropping his rifle and clutching the wound.

When the riders were 50 yards away, Nick dropped prone, his weapon continuing its steady cadence of death.

The big man rolled away at the last moment, the hammering hooves of the lead rider missing his head by mere inches. Twisting around, he continued to send high-velocity pain into the backs of the passing riders.

The war party reigned up their mounts just over 100 meters away, the leader barking orders as they all dismounted.

"Now we're going to fight the old-fashioned way," Nick growled, inserting a fresh box of pain pills into his weapon. "Come on in boys, I'll bleed out every one of you fuckers. Right here, right now."

The hunters went low, using the grass and weeds as cover, trying to advance on Nick's position.

The Alliance leader wasn't stupid enough to remain still. Thinking of his down man... his son... Nick began backing toward Kevin's last known position.

But Kevin wasn't there.

With a quick sweep, Nick knew he was at the spot where his son had gone down, the depressed grass a sure sign. He spotted the blood on the second glance, and then a trail leading toward the distant tree line. "At least he's still alive," the father whispered in relief.

With his barrel sweeping the ever-deeper weed line, Nick followed the bent grass and blood. He came across Kevin's crawling form 20 steps later.

Thinking to help his son scramble into the woods, Nick reached down with a helping hand. "Come on, I'll be your crutch."

"No, dad! It's too bad. Go on. Get away!"

Nick assessed Kevin's leg and grimaced. The bullet had struck the boy right below the knee and striking bone. The yellow-white stub of a compound fracture was protruding from the exit wound. Blood pumped from the hole.

As a Green Beret, the father had seen more than his share of combat wounds. Instinctively, he knew Kevin would survive the injury – if it could be treated quickly.

Nick flung his carbine around to his back, bending to lift his wounded man into a fireman's carry and hustle to the cover of the pine thicket. He was just about to pull Kevin over his shoulder when his son's eyes went wide, a warning forming in his throat.

They came from three directions at once, appearing out of the grass like ghosts.

Nick was hit in the upper thigh and chest with the first salvo, his body armor stopping only the second round.

With the speed of a striking snake, Nick pulled his knife and stepped into the closest attacker, driving the blade up and into the man's chin.

The ear-shattering blast of Kevin's sniper rifle shattered the prairie as the prone boy managed a shot.

Something heavy hit Nick's arm as another man's shoulder slammed into the team leader's hip.

A confusing hurricane of swirling bodies, flashing steel, and the pointblank discharges erupted on the prairie. Nick registered a scream of agony, but couldn't tell if it came from his own throat or someone else's.

His knife found flesh again. He stumbled on a body. His fist crushed into something solid. A stream of blood droplets flew through the air in a slow motion arch, beautiful and translucent, glistening in the high sun. His vision was limited by a grey tunnel around the edges. The grass was no longer green but stained the dark purple of a bruise. The smell of copper overrode the sweet bouquet of wildflowers.

The world went dark and silent.

Chapter 10

Someone was carrying him, and that struck Nick as funny. Nobody had ever been able to manage his girth before. It must be an angel. Maybe Gabriel himself. *I hear he is pretty strong for a fellow with wings*, Nick thought.

And then there was light without passage of time, and finally, Diana's face.

I'm dead, he thought. I'm seeing the ones I love. Where's Kevin?

It was the pain that changed the big man's mind and forced his tormented brain to swim to the surface.

Again, he was gazing into Diana's worried face. "Nick!" sang her wonderful voice. "Oh, Nick... I've been so... how are you? Are you in pain?"

It all came rushing back, the chase, the horsemen and their screaming cries of war. "Kevin! Where's Kevin?" he croaked.

Diana didn't answer, "You're in the hospital at Fort Bliss. Butter carried you out."

"Answer me, damn it," he grumbled. "Where's my son?"

Her expression said it all. Looking down, she mumbled, "We don't know. Grim and Butter couldn't find him. They fought off the men who hurt you, but they couldn't find Kevin."

Nick looked around the room, seeking a first-hand account. But only Diana was there. "Where is Grim? Where's Butter?"

"Grim's in the brig, cooling his jets. He was going all over the base, demanding he be given troops and transport to go back after Kevin. He lost his temper and beat the shit out of two MPs, and they... umm... detained him for a while."

"And Butter?"

"He's in a room two doors down. He's okay, but he hurt his back carrying you off the mountain. They're checking the x-rays right now."

Nick tried to rise, thinking Grim's reaction was the only one that made any sense. Rivers of pain changed the big man's mind.

"And me?"

"You're not in any shape to do anything but lay there and recover. They dug two bullets out of you. You've got 90 staples in your body. You've lost a lot of blood, and the docs are worried about a concussion. You didn't have a heartbeat when Grim and Butter drove you up to the emergency room."

She took Nick's hand in hers, tenderly squeezing her reassurance. And then it all came welling to the surface, tears streaming down Diana's cheeks as sobs racked her body.

"I'm here," Nick tried to comfort in a soft tone. "I'll be all right. We'll find Kevin. It'll be okay."

"Oh, God, Nick!" she wept, letting it all out. "I thought I'd lost Kevin and you both. I haven't slept for two days."

Kevin thought the man examining his leg was one of the weirdest individuals he'd ever laid eyes on. *If this dude walked in claiming to be Merlin, I'd buy his story.*

"His injury is beyond me," Hack said over his shoulder to the hovering Apache. "We need to send for a real doctor."

"Why, Grandfather? Why bother? My men want to watch him scream as they peel away his skin bit by bit. Why fix what we're only going to kill?"

Hack shook his head, motioning his friend outside. "We gathered valuable information from the first prisoner. This one is younger and doesn't wear the patches of the U.S. military. His equipment is different. His weapon is not standard issue, and he wears no rank or insignia."

"Let me have him, and I promise he'll tell us anything you want to know... before his brain seizes out from the pain."

"Well, now that's the problem, isn't it?" Hack replied, his patience growing thin. "I don't know exactly what to ask him. At least not just yet. Besides, I'm still convinced there's value in keeping hostages."

"It didn't keep them away this time, Grandfather. They still came. My men still died."

Hack shook his head in disagreement, "I don't think so, my friend. I don't think this group was regular Army... at least not anymore. Even their ammunition was different. The rounds we pulled out of that kid's sniper rifle had been reloaded. The U.S. Army doesn't do that."

The Apache didn't back down. "I still want him. I'll wait until you're finished, and then I want him."

Hack stared at his friend for a moment, almost as if he was making a difficult decision. "Look, I know you're wondering if I value Indian life as much as my own kind. Let me be absolutely clear, right here, right now; I'm trying to do everything in my power to save Native lives. You are the only people on earth who have never judged me by my appearance, only by my heart. But that is just a kid in there, and he may know valuable information that can save lives... red and white. Do you understand?"

There was a hesitation, but finally the Apache nodded his agreement.

Hack extended a hand and placed it gently on the Native's shoulder. "Now, I'm going to send for a doctor."

Hack scribbled a note on a small piece of paper and then stuffed the message into a plastic tube. A few minutes later one of the toymaker's drones blasted into the air, rushing away on plastic propellers to deliver its cargo.

Hack returned to the prisoner, smiling with good news. "I've convinced my Apache friends to leave you in my care for the moment. Your outfit hurt them badly, and they want revenge. What is your name?"

"Kevin."

"Okay, Kevin, that's a start. Can you tell me your full name, rank, and serial number, please?"

The captive's eyebrows knotted, almost as if he didn't understand the question. "I don't have a rank or a serial number. I'm not in any army, ours or theirs."

It was Hack's turn to be puzzled. "Okay. Maybe that's a good place to start. Could you define ours and theirs for me?"

In the younger man's mind, it was a strange question. *Maybe he's testing me*, Kevin thought. *Maybe he's trying to see if I'll tell the truth*.

"Theirs is the U.S. Army. My dad used to be a sergeant in that Army. Ours is the ADF, or Alliance Defense Forces. I'm not in either."

Hack rubbed his chin in thought. He'd heard of the Alliance in Texas, but there had been only wisps of information and rumor, little of which he believed.

"So by using the word, 'ours,' I assume you are from Texas?"

"Yes, that's right."

"And what were your friends and you doing, sneaking around our territory?"

"Gathering information, that's all. Really."

"Why?" the toymaker frowned.

Kevin thought long and hard before answering. He'd heard his father complain several times about the lack of funding and training the council gave for the SAINT teams. One of his favorite examples being a SERE (Survival, Evasion, Resistance, and Escape) course. "If any of those guys are ever captured, they won't know how to handle it," he'd argued with Diana.

"I don't think I should answer that," Kevin replied honestly. "But I will say that we didn't want to hurt anybody or anything. Those were our instructions."

Hack took a minute to digest the answer, a sadness filling

127

the older man's eyes. "Do you know anything about our desert army ants, Kevin?"

An hour later, Hack emerged from the storage room, his entire perspective of the world having been changed by a young man with the busted leg.

Waving over his Apache friend, the toymaker said, "You're not going to believe what I've just learned. But I'm fairly confident what that kid just told me is true."

The Native didn't respond, but Hack didn't seem to care.

"I need a drink," he announced, moving with purpose toward the cabin. "I'll be right back."

Knowing the Apache wouldn't accept even if he offered, Hack poured himself a shot of bourbon. Swilling the brown liquor around, he downed the two-fingers in a single swallow. The burning sensation surprised him.... It had been how long? Four years? Five?

He eyed the bottle, thinking of another, but then dismissed the urge. He wasn't going to do anyone any good intoxicated.

Returning to the front porch, Hack motioned for the Apache to join him on the swing. After the two were seated, he began repeating Kevin's story.

"Those rumors we've heard of the Texans organizing and forming some sort of government? Well, according to our young friend, all that is true, plus more."

Hack continued, relaying how the Alliance had learned of the Valley Green Project, and that had been the primary reason why a team had been sent in to spy.

"And you believe him?"

"I do. I verified certain facts with our other prisoner, who would have no reason to lie about Texas."

The Apache shrugged, "So what does this mean to the people and the project, Grandfather?"

"Now that's the question of the day," the toymaker replied. "On one hand, it seems we've made two powerful enemies. On the other, I wonder if there is a way to play them against each other."

Their conversation was interrupted by the arrival of a man on horseback, the lone rider allowed to pass through the security perimeter without much fuss.

"Welcome, Doctor," Hack called from the front porch. "I have an interesting case for you today."

The president pushed back from the table, his appetite lacking. That seemed to happen a lot these days.

While the news of his son being seen alive had provided a great measure of relief, the actions of the Alliance in discovering that fact were troubling.

Diana and her council had taken it upon themselves to send in a team. They had managed to mess things up even further, and the information coming out of Fort Bliss was fueling a growing movement of hostility against the Alliance.

The president now had people, important individuals he depended on to govern, pushing him hard to "Knock those cocky Texans on their asses."

He had tried to warn them. He'd made things as clear as possible over the radio. He'd even played the trump card of his son being held captive.

And yet, they had still gone rumbling into U.S. territory with armed men, hell bent on securing their precious "national security." That little tidbit had not been received well with the men running the rest of the country, and in a way, the president couldn't blame them.

Despite the near-destruction of the city of Washington, the inner-circle of political power brokers had managed to survive mostly intact. It was amazing.

Few legislators had lived through the uprising and riots. Despite the heroic efforts of the Capital Police and the Secret Service, the vast majority of Congressmen had perished. How was it that with half of the city burning out of control, nearly all phone lines and common forms of communications failing… how was it that the partisan dynamo of backroom dealers and behind the scenes titans had managed to survive? The Colonel often wondered if any of these power mongers had defied the odds by negotiating deals with Lucifer himself.

The president could feel the vibrations of trouble brewing. Like a seasoned captain could sense the health of the ship's engines through the deck under his feet, he knew turmoil, strife, and backlash were about to rear their ugly heads. War was the inevitable result.

He'd never had any political aspirations whatsoever, let alone any objectives of sitting in the Oval Office. Not once did he visualize a future of kissing babies, shaking hands, or of giving an acceptance speech in front of an enthusiastic crowd of supporters.

His boyhood dreams had been of soldiering, defending the flag, preserving the American way, and strolling across the battlefield like a victorious Audie Murphy or John Wayne.

Military service was everything he'd hoped, at least until promotions and the recognition of his politically astute mind had taken him away from the core of Uncle Sam's Army. They sent him to Washington for reasons unknown. He reported as ordered, arriving as an exceptionally bright, freshly minted young colonel.

He could remember those days clearly, the excitement and sense of purpose associated with working in the nation's capital. Better still, everyone knew the path to achieve the Mount Olympus of military careers lead through the Pentagon.

The bowels of the political machine that was the U.S. federal government required a steady diet of fresh meat. Light colonels were a dime a dozen at the Pentagon, essentially the main course for a very hungry beast. They were consumed in quantity, chewed up and swallowed by the all-powerful triad of elected officials, the military industrial complex, and the enormous amounts of money that flowed through the system.

The gifted military phenomenon was thrust into a grinder that had long ago forgotten the men and women who actually did the fighting. Contracts, purchase orders, grants, and procurement commitments were all that mattered to the vast majority of the people he interacted with. No one seemed to care about the 18-year-old private being asked to carry a weapon into battle. There was no consideration of the young sailor who would be charged with making the missile system function properly, his life and ship depending on the technology purchased to assist him.

The Colonel was fine with all of that. Men were greedy. Corporations existed for profit. Senators and Congressmen won votes by bringing jobs and federal dollars back home. No, the political aspect was to be expected, and while he found the breadth of the carnage somewhat surprising, it wasn't his primary issue.

No, what began to eat at the young officer's core was the fact that his superiors seemed more than happy to play along. These were the men he had admired, valiant leaders and brilliant military minds giving inspiration to the young officer. Until he began to work at the Pentagon.

He watched senior officers sell their souls for the promise of a corner office after retirement. He witnessed reports being faked and test results being altered in order to keep the pipeline of money flowing in the right direction.

All the while, no one seemed the least bit concerned about the citizens who had volunteered to serve and protect their country. No one had the common soldier's best interest at heart, and it poisoned the Colonel's soul.

Within three months, he had requested transfer. Within six, he considered resigning.

And now... now he was the man behind the curtain, pulling levers and pushing the buttons of that very same machine. He was now in charge of the beast that consumed men. It was his finger on the big trigger, and he despised it.

The hatred and bigotry against the Alliance was just such a charade. Like those officers before, the truth was being twisted, manipulated and ignored. There was a cadence in the air – a march toward war.

Like the overpriced, underperforming weapons systems of before, the president knew none of the insiders cared one bit about the men and women who would die if conflict came. No one addressed the suffering that would occur on both sides. That was far away from Washington. Any battle would occur in the Southwest, and wasn't that mostly wasteland anyway?

Rising from his lunch, the president left the dining room and decided on a stroll to help him think. The cigar he retrieved from his desk on the way out would do its part in helping clear his mind.

He needed a solution to the growing problem in New Mexico, the dilemma both complex and a political hot potato.

Strolling through the perfectly manicured grounds of Camp David, the Commander in Chief realized this wasn't the first time he'd been taxed with the burden of a pending civil war.

His thoughts returned to a time when the Independents threatened to tear the country apart. Massive numbers of troops and equipment had chosen to follow their leadership, and it had almost spelled the destruction of what little remained of the nation.

How had they avoided that?

Grunting, the president thought about his old employee... and now friend. He visualized Bishop toiling on that patch of desert scrub he called a ranch. The image of his former contractor wearing a western hat, sweat-soaked shirt and worn work gloves actually brought a smile to the chief executive's face.

"What a waste," he grumbled. "One of the best shooters I've ever seen, and he wants to spend his days chasing cows around a worthless pit of sand and rock."

"Sir?" Agent Powell asked, another Secret Service man and he stepping closer to the POTUS as they continued to shadow him.

"I'm sorry, Powell. I was just thinking aloud about an old friend of ours. You remember Bishop, don't you?"

A scowl crossed the agent's face, his hand subconsciously moving to rub his jaw where the Texan had landed a particularly hard right hook. "Yes, sir, I remember him."

"I know you don't like my comrade down in Texas, Powell, but you have to admit, there's never a dull moment when he's around."

"Are you asking my opinion, sir?"

The president thought he knew, but what the hell. "Yes, I am."

"That man is out of control, sir. He is a danger to anyone around him, and I'm surprised someone hasn't killed him before now."

Chuckling, the Commander in Chief thought to have a little fun with his bodyguard. "It seems he's a hard man to kill, wouldn't you say?"

"He's lucky, sir. That's all there is to it. The man is a loose cannon, and that kind always end up in the same place – a 6x3 farm with a headstone for an address, with lots of their friends residing nearby."

"Oh, I'll admit Bishop is a cowboy. No doubt about that. But sometimes the world needs men who act on passion and honor alone. He's bailed me out more than once."

"Yes, sir," Powell replied, thinking he'd said too much already.

The three men continued their stroll, the president puffing on his stogie, apparently admiring the landscape.

With an abrupt motion that surprised his escorts, the president turned and looked at Powell. "Yes, sometimes the world needs a cowboy. I need to talk with Miss Brown. Someone hook up a call... or transmission... or whatever you call it."

"Yes, sir."

And then the chief executive hesitated. "No, never mind. Belay that. There's something more important right this second. Where are my grandchildren? It's time to have a talk with them about their father."

Bishop was helping his wife with the laundry, the hot tub's spring-fed water providing a handy place to clean their wardrobes.

Terri had procured a new type of soap during her last visit to Alpha, the mushy, yellow substance having come from the core of a cactus common to the area. Who knew?

It didn't smell bad, but its bubble yield was disappointing – a fact that made Terri's face wrinkle. "The real test is *your* son's dirty underpants. I look forward to the day when somebody starts making disposable diapers again. Washing out these cloth rags just plain sucks."

Bishop grinned at his wife's complaint, thinking of comparing her remarks to a recent encounter he'd experienced with the windmill pump, but decided against it. Then, he just couldn't hold it any more.

"I thought you had friends in high places? You need to set the record straight with Diana and the council, help them realize the error in their priorities. To hell with antibiotics, insulin, law and order, and electricity for all... we need diapers!"

His response was a splash of water, the airborne wave catching him across the face. *I hope that was from the rinse tub*, he thought. *Still, it was better than a rock.*

Peace again returned to the desert, Bishop deciding there was wisdom in silence while he twisted each item, wringing out the excess water, and then hanging the article on a nearby line.

Trying to scrub the stain from one of Hunter's better efforts, Terri held the swath of cloth up to the sunlight to see if the new detergent was the equal to her son's bodily functions. "Not bad," she noted.

Smiling at his wife, readying to make a smartass remark, Bishop's face flashed to serious. "Company," he warned, dropping a damp shirt and moving for the nearby rifle.

Terri turned, shielding her eyes from the bright sun. She could see the trail of dust rising up from what could only be a car driving across the ranch. "Before you ask, no, I wasn't expecting the Avon lady."

The couple, now both armed, watched as the pickup approached their home. "I hope that's not bad news from Nick's venture into New Mexico," Bishop said.

"I hope so, too," Terri responded, glancing over at Hunter napping in his stroller, and moving to put herself between the visitors and her child.

The Texans watched as the truck rolled to a stop, both doors opening to reveal a young man and woman. Shielding his eyes from the sun, Bishop ventured, "Teenagers? Maybe they were out for a joyride and got lost?"

"With the price of gas?" Terri responded. "Better not be."

And then Terri recognized David and Samantha, the Colonel's grandchildren. Bishop was right behind her.

The reunion was joyous, hugs, handshakes and observations of, "My, look how you've both grown!"

Hunter received the same comments.

133

During it all, Bishop knew why the now-president's grandchildren were in Alpha.

Remaining polite, and genuinely thrilled to see both teens doing so well, Bishop let the conversation go on about Meraton, David's flying, his sister's studies, and the general well-being of their grandpa.

Bishop and David reminisced about Bones, the stripped down Humvee the Texan had stolen from the Columbian drug dealers and used to procure medical devices to save the Colonel.

The celebration moved inside, Terri pouring cold water, and offering the visitors what little they had in the way of snacks.

Both kids, after a knowing look at each other, declined. "Actually, we're here on business... sort of. Our father has been taken prisoner, and the whole situation is getting out of hand. We came to ask both of you to help Sam and me," David admitted, looking Bishop straight in the eye.

"You don't say," Bishop replied, skepticism written all over his face. "And what kind of shit storm does the Colonel want to pull us into now?"

"Actually, grandpa forbade us to come here. We're probably going to be in trouble when we go back. We kind of... err... borrowed an airplane," Sam confessed.

The Texan started to scold the two youths, but once glance from Terri stopped him short.

"It must be pretty serious," she said in a sympathetic voice. "What's going on?"

"Well, it's more than just our dad," Sam pleaded. "A friend of yours... Kevin? Right before we left, grandpa was reading the reports and told us that a guy named Kevin had been taken prisoner as well."

Bishop looked at Terri, asking the unspoken question of, "Have you heard of any of this?"

She responded, "Diana wouldn't let me stay with her while Nick was gone. She said she was a big girl, and that I had a family to take care of. This is the first I have heard of this."

The frustration of finding out their friends were in trouble via such a remote, unlikely source, didn't sit well with Bishop. While he appreciated Nick and Diana respecting their privacy, it seemed they'd taken it too far.

Turning to his wife, Bishop said, "Why don't you pack some things? I think we're going to be gone for a while."

Nodding, Terri flashed a smile of worry. "I was hoping you'd say that."

"So you're going to help our dad?" Sam asked.

"Maybe. If I can, but no promises. Now I want you two little

134

plane thieves to get your butts back to Camp David before the Colonel has the entire U.S. military out looking for you. The last thing I need right now is to have some jerk trump up charges that we kidnapped you, and given my past experience with being a wanted man, I wouldn't put it past them."

Hugs, handshakes, and goodbyes went quickly, Bishop and Terri obviously worried about their friends.

Twenty minutes after the kids had left, the couple were pulling out as well, the truck's bed filled with hastily gathered belongings.

"I didn't finish the laundry," Terri remembered as they turned onto the paved road leading to Alpha. "I guess it'll still be there when we get back."

"One can certainly hope not," Bishop grinned, accelerating the pickup. "Fort Bliss or bust," he added.

Being back at the base hospital brought back a flood of memories for both Bishop and Terri. They had rushed to Bliss at full speed, the partial information delivered by David and Samantha making the trip seem like they were driving forever.

They passed through the MPs guarding Nick's ward without incident, walking quickly down the long, sterile hall while glancing at the room numbers. Diana's voice drifting through the corridor told the couple they were close.

A few moments later, Terri's smiling face peeked in the door. "Some people will do anything to avoid getting hitched," she teased, entering the room.

Bishop was right behind her, carrying Hunter on his shoulder.

In a flash, Diana was up and in Terri's arms, the two women shaking with the release of emotion as both broke down crying. Bishop and Hunter moved to the bedside, the Texan mumbling, "You okay, big guy? You look like shit."

Nodding, Nick's gaze centered on Hunter, his eyes growing cloudy with moisture. "Spend all the time you can with him," the former Special Forces operator whispered. "You never know when they'll be taken away."

"What the hell has happened to the Army?" Grim demanded. "Has the whole world lost its fucking honor? We do *not* leave anyone behind. Nowhere, no how, no way. I only asked for a couple of Blackhawks and two rifle squads. Butter and I would have taken care of the rest. And what did I get? First, a nice young LT tried to blow hot air up my skirt, telling me he was confident the authorities would address the matter. Then a captain refused to let me see General Owens personally, informing me that I should use the established chain of command. When I let that little pipsqueak fucker in on the fact that I was no longer a subscriber to Mother Green's hierarchy, he tried to shoo me away to the Office of Civilian Affairs. And that's when I finally got pissed."

Bishop sat across from his friend, expressionless, letting the man rant until he was out of breath. Experience had taught the Texan that might take a while.

Rattling the chains that secured his wrists to the heavy table, Grim continued his tirade. "And now look at me. Chained like a common fucking criminal. I'm telling you, Bishop, somebody from the Alliance council needs to come over to this base and kick some ass."

Bishop sighed, a smirk forming on his lips. "You put two MPs in the infirmary, Grim. According to the major that let me in here, it took another four men to settle your ass down. You broke three windows, smashed two chairs, and destroyed a bookshelf during the... err... ongoing discussion."

"And a partridge in a fucking pear tree," Grim responded, rolling his eyes. "I was a little upset. They wouldn't let me go back in after Kevin."

The Texan studied his former teammate, knowing exactly why Grim had reacted with such outrage. The man was convinced he'd messed up and gotten his commander shot up and Kevin captured. With Butter in the hospital, Grim was the last man standing, and the guilt, deserved or imagined, was eating him up inside.

Bishop understood. He'd been there. It was as debilitating as any bullet's wound, the closest the Texan had ever come to ending his own life.

"A *little* upset? Really?" Bishop replied, shaking his head. "Let's go through it, Grim. From the top. How did you insert?"

An hour later, Bishop stood and stretched. He stepped to the door, hit the electric buzzer, and asked that the prisoner's shackles be removed. The MP had strict orders to do as Bishop asked... and instantly produced a key.

"That's it? I'm free?"

"No," Bishop responded gently. "It just occurred to me that

those chains were unnecessary. Now, keep going, what happened when Butter and you heard the gunfire?"

Grim's mind returned to the skirmish in New Mexico, the pain leaking from the man's soul and filling the small room. "When the first shot rang out, I knew instantly where they'd gotten hit. Butter and I were 200 meters beyond that little pasture, waiting on Nick and Kevin to catch up. I even told Butter it was the perfect place for an ambush when we were crossing that same open space."

"Go on."

"Well, it was obvious Nick and the kid were in trouble. There was a lot of small arms fire, screaming and shouting. We were tearing ass to get back and help."

"What kind of terrain were you in?" Bishop asked, already knowing the answer from his interview with Butter, and well aware it was a key point during the encounter.

"Oh, shit, it was nasty stuff. Some sort of vines with briars were just everywhere. Even the trees were a pain in the ass, low branches snagging everything from our hats to our slings. Between tripping on the undergrowth and navigating through the limbs, it seemed like it was taking forever to get back there. It was like one of those nightmares… you know… the ones where the alligator is chasing your ass and you can't run. Your feet won't move fast enough."

Bishop didn't say anything, waiting on Grim to continue without prompting.

"We hit the edge of the wood line right as the shooting stopped. The grass was chest high there. I could see movement about 50 meters in, but I couldn't tell what was happening. Butter and I charged in, hoping our guys were still alive."

Again, Grim's thoughts drifted from the room, his conscious mind wandering back to that fateful encounter. The rugged, seen-it-all contractor quickly brushed a tear from his cheek. "We slogged through to the location where the fight had occurred. Five of them had Nick down. I thought he was dead. One was going through his pockets, the other trying to wrestle his watch off his wrist. Butter and I tore into their asses…. We hit 'em with everything we had."

Bishop knew Grim was telling the truth, Butter having already relayed a nearly identical story. The Texan also knew Grim had to get it all off of his chest.

"It was CQB (Close Quarters Battle) out the ass in those weeds. Every combatant had time to fire his weapon about once, and I don't think any of us hit a damn thing but air. And then it degraded into hand to hand," the contractor confessed with a low, monotone voice.

"Other than Nick, I'd never, ever, seen a big man move like Butter. He took out three of those fuckers just 'wham, bam, thank ya, ma'am.' I know he snapped that one dude's neck with his bare hands."

This is where the story finally differed from Butter's version. According to the team's newest member, it was Grim who stacked up the corpses at his feet. *It doesn't matter*, Bishop thought. *At least not right now.*

"And where was Kevin?"

"I guess they'd carried him off before we got there. I looked around. All around. Under the bodies... around the weeds... in case he had crawled off. I called out, shouted his name a dozen times. I swear I did! But the kid wasn't there. During the fight, one of the guys we were taking down had yelled for help. I couldn't understand the words, but it was pretty clear he was hoping for reinforcements."

"How long did you look?"

Grim's answer was full of pain. "Not fucking long enough, that's for certain."

"Why did you stop looking?"

"Butter checked Nick's pulse and found the big man was still pumping blood. We heard horses and other voices getting closer from three different sides. The next thing I know, Butter is lifting Nick onto his shoulders right when bullets start whizzing past our heads. We got the hell out of Dodge City."

Again, Grim grew quiet, his voice barely audible. "I kept thinking we'd find someplace to take care of Nick's wounds and then go back for the kid, but those assholes chased us all the way down the mountain. At one point, I had a chance to assess the boss's status, and I knew right away we had to get him back to Bliss pronto. To be honest, I'm surprised he's still drawing air."

"It sounds like you made the right calls, brother," Bishop said. "I haven't heard a single thing I would have done differently. So why all the anger and frustration?"

Grim ignored the question, his mind still trying to justify his actions. "You know, I kept thinking about the prisoner we saw at their HQ. Kevin said he thought the guy was a PJ, said the guy was wearing Air Force camo. Anyway, I kept telling myself that they wouldn't kill Kevin outright. I kept saying that if the enemy had kept the PJ alive, no way would they kill the kid. Do you think that's true, Bishop?"

The pleading in the man's voice tugged at Bishop's heart. "Probably. I would have hoped for the same thing in your shoes."

"That's why I want to go back in," Grim stated, some of his old swagger coming back. "We have to go get that kid. He's one helluva shot and a good trooper to boot."

In his pocket, Bishop carried Grim's release orders, signed by the base commander personally. "I'll let him go on your recommendation, Bishop," General Owens had stated. "But if he goes busting up my facility again, I'm going to throw the book at him."

Bishop studied the man across from him, still undecided if Grim was ready to walk out of jail. "You know it's not your fault – right?"

"What's not my fault? What are you talking about?"

"Oh, come on, man. We both know exactly what I'm trying to say. You've been blaming yourself for Kevin's capture all along. But that's wrong. You made all the right calls, and the shit still hit the fan. Nick doesn't blame you, and Butter doesn't blame you. And I'll bet my next paycheck that Kevin doesn't put it on you either. So why are you still carrying this load of crap on your shoulders?"

Grim started to protest, his finger stabbing in Bishop's direction. But no words came out. Then he clenched his fists, fury and rage coiling in his arms.

"Because he trusted me!" Grim blurted, eyes watering with emotion. "Because the kid always thought I would be there... and I wasn't.... I failed him, Bishop. Do you know what it's like to have someone trust you? Do you know how it feels to let them down? He looked up to me, man."

Bishop didn't answer, watching as Grim buried his face in his hands and lost control like a man possessed; gut-wrenching, demonic moans afflicting him until the emotion bled out.

Ten minutes passed, neither of them saying a word while Grim struggled to regain control. Finally, Bishop decided the torrent of feelings had subsided, the worst of it having been expelled from his friend's soul.

Reaching into his pocket, Bishop produced the orders granting Grim his freedom and dropping all charges. Sliding the documents across the table, Bishop's voice was stern. "Go home. I want you to eat, bathe, sleep, and then repeat. You've not had any shut-eye for over 48 hours. You smell like a pig's ass. Go back to Alpha and get well. In a few days, I'll send for you. We'll get Kevin back, one way or the other. That's an order."

A second passed before the contractor realized what Bishop had just said. "You're coming out of retirement? You are coming back to the teams?"

Bishop didn't respond, instead rising to his feet and pressing the buzzer.

When the MP opened the door, the Texan pointed to Grim and said, "He has new orders from General Owens. I vouch for their authenticity. Clean him up and get him a ride back to Alpha."

"Yes, sir."

"You can't get in," Nick managed between sips on the straw. "They're using drones, patrols, trip wires, and lookouts. They'd be onto you in a New York minute."

"What about inserting by helicopter? Maybe we could drop a couple of teams into a remote area... storm the cabin and set the prisoners free."

Nick, despite his injuries, waved off the idea. "There are so many problems with that strategy, I can't even begin to list them all. How are you going to repel without having a bird or two shot out of the sky? Besides, you go buzzing around their territory with anything bigger than a hang glider, and they'll kill those hostages outright and fade away into the woods. Hell, if I were them, I would have already moved the captives just to be safe. Who knows where they are now?"

Bishop stood and moved to the window, gazing out over the desert terrain that defined Fort Bliss. "There has to be a way," he mumbled to the glass. "There's always a way."

"Believe me when I tell you that I've been lying here with nothing better to do but come up with an idea to get my son back home. Who knows what they're doing to him? It's maddening. And if I thought there was a snowball's chance in hell that you could pull off a rescue, I'd be begging you to go. Hell, not even the Commander in Chief of the United States has got a plan."

Diana and Terri picked that moment to stop in, the two women thick as thieves since Bishop and his wife had arrived from the ranch.

Terri caught her husband's eye and motioned for him to join her in the hall.

Hooking arms with her mate, Terri guided Bishop a few steps away where they could talk in private. "I have a favor to ask, my love."

"Sure. Anything."

"Diana and I have been hatching a plot."

"Oh, shit. I'm in trouble. I can tell already."

Terri grinned, "Yes, you are, but that's not the favor. I want your word that you'll hear us out before throwing a shit-fit."

"And when you're done, then I can pitch a bitch?" he asked, not liking where this was going one bit.

"Yes, you can stomp around, cuss, and flail all you want."

Bishop's scowl deepened, "And it's not going to do me one

bit of good – is it?"

Terri grew serious, "If there is a hole in our scheme, then yes, we need to listen, learn, and fix it. But that's not going to be the issue."

"And what is?"

"Just hear us out, Bishop. Give our plan the benefit of your professional experience and knowledge. But please leave emotions out of it, at least at first. Okay?"

The Texan nodded his agreement, but still didn't like it. He'd been on enough missions to recognize a tiger trap when he saw one.

They reentered Nick's room, Terri closing the door behind them.

Nick flashed Bishop a look that asked, "What the hell is going on?"

Diana, evidently, had just finished the same conversation with Nick, the big man's apprehension still visible beneath the bruises and cuts that covered his face.

"Let's get started," Diana began, using a voice that sounded like she was presiding over a council meeting. "Terri and I have been listening to you two and everyone else from the president to Grim trying to come up with a solution to this multi-tiered problem we face in New Mexico. So far, the only thing that has surfaced is frustration. Do either of you disagree with that general assessment?"

Nick started to protest, "These things always take a while to come together. Military ops are complex and...."

Diana cut him off, "Nick, you promised."

"Sorry," he mumbled, retreating back to silence.

She continued, "Terri and I strongly believe that a diplomatic solution is the only option."

Bishop inhaled, readying to comment, but a curt glance from Terri cut him off.

Diana continued, "The outline of the plan is simple, the Alliance needs to establish formal relations with the people in New Mexico. We need an ambassador and an open line of communications."

Terri took over, "I'm convinced that if we can talk openly with our neighbors to the west, we can negotiate acceptable agreements and end this whole crisis. Job one is to circumvent the confrontational lines all sides have drawn in the sand, and make them see the value in working together for a common solution."

Bishop couldn't hold it anymore, "So what do you propose? We just drive into their reservation, hop out, press the flesh and introduce ourselves? I can hear it now, 'Hi, we're from the government, and we're here to help you folks out. Never mind that we have hundreds of years of bad blood between us, you can trust *us*, fellas.'"

Terri's eyes became daggers, thrown at her husband. "No. That's not what we propose. And if you're through jumping to conclusions, I'd be happy to explain it to you."

Bishop backed down, but just barely. His bad feeling was quickly turning into a full-blown stomachache.

"Unfortunately, emotions on all sides are running far too high for something so simple. Shooting and spying on each other tends to do that. They would probably take the envoy prisoner and add to their growing collection of hostages," Terri said.

"But, if we can earn just a little bit of trust and open a dialog, I'm positive they could be persuaded to see things our way," Diana added.

Nick took a deep breath, "Okay, so far I can't disagree with anything you've said, but how do you get the Alliance's foot in the door?"

The two women exchanged knowing glances, and then Terri giggled, "We call this plan, Operation Sacagawea. We thought since you guys are always using all those military terms and phrases, we'd sink to your level and give it an official sounding, secret code-word name."

Bishop was clueless. Ignoring the jab, he asked, "What in the world are you two talking about? A sack of... what did you say?"

"Actually, my love," Terri replied, "It's *who* in the world is Sacagawea. *She* was a person, but I'm not surprised you don't recognize the name. I am betting the United States Army didn't bring up her name at their war college," she retorted, rolling her eyes to emphasize her point.

Bishop looked at Nick, but his friend didn't understand either. "Okay. Fill the big lug and me in on this woman."

Terri sighed, preparing to relay a story that was hurtful. "When I was traveling all over Texas with Betty, I used to have these guilt trips every now and then. I always felt like such a terrible mother, hauling Hunter around the countryside, taking chances and not spending as much time with him as possible."

She paused for a moment, needing to gather herself, but then pushed on. "We were in Dallas attending some meeting with the local Army guys when Betty spied a book in the commander's office. She asked if she could borrow it to read while we were traveling. It recounted the story of Lewis and Clark, the famous explorers."

"Everyone knows that story from elementary school," Bishop acknowledged. "But what do they have to do with this

Sacaga-whoever-she-is?"

"Betty was trying to make me feel better about dragging Hunter around and putting him in what could be dangerous situations. She read to me about Sacagawea, a member of the Shoshone tribe who traveled with that famous expedition," Terri explained.

"She was the wife of one of the mountain men Lewis and Clark hired on as part of their party to be a guide. She is known as the woman who walked 1,000 miles with a baby on her back," Diana added.

Terri continued, "Captain Lewis gave her a lot of credit for their success."

"I remember that name now," Bishop said. "Wasn't she an interpreter? Didn't she speak French as well as the language of several local tribes?"

"Yes, that was originally the justification for her being part of the journey," Terri smiled. "But years later, Captain Clark explained her role differently. He gave her and her infant credit for keeping them from being killed or ambushed by the Natives. It seems that the tribesmen believed in the explorers' peaceful intent due to the inclusion of the young mother and her newborn as part of the entourage. War parties didn't generally travel with women and children."

It all became crystal clear to Bishop in that moment, the Texan standing abruptly and shaking his head. "No. I know where you're going with this, and I can't agree. Those were completely different times and circumstances. We don't know how the people in New Mexico will react. They may eat babies for all we know."

Terri shut him down, "Bishop, you promised. It's not time to rant and rave… not just yet. Hear us out."

Bishop paced toward the window, turning his back on the room. Terri could tell he was pissed. A blind person could see it, but she continued laying out the plan. "Once we make contact and establish trust with their leadership, I'll drop the hammer and make them see the negative consequences of rerouting the rivers and stealing nuclear materials."

"Let's say for a moment you did pull this off… that somehow you managed to gain access to Mr. White Hair. How are you going to make him see the light? What is this hammer you intend to use?"

For the next 20 minutes, Terri and Diana took turns explaining the finer points of Operation Sacagawea.

When they'd finished, Nick was shaking his head, amazed at the plot. "Brilliant," he admitted. "I have to admit, it's genius. I'm glad you two are on our side."

Everyone stared at Bishop, the Texan never having returned from his stance at the window.

"Bishop?" Terri chanced. "I know you've been listening."

The Texan turned, nodding his head. "Yes, I promised I would. Is it my turn?"

"Yes," Terri nodded, lowering her gaze and preparing for the firestorm.

"So, let me see if I understand the basics of this plan. You want me to agree to take my wife and firstborn son into a known hostile environment without backup or a brigade of shooters. Did I get that right?" he asked, no attempt to disguise the frustration in his voice. "What makes you think I'd agree to such madness?"

"Precedent," Terri reminded him. "You did this before. When you were being framed for that massacre, we packed up the camper and headed into the badlands."

"Yes," Bishop shot back, "and I almost lost my wife and child. I may be an old dog, but I can be taught new tricks, and that was an episode I don't want to repeat, thank you very much."

"But why did we risk it in the first place?" Terri countered. "We knew it was dangerous before we packed up and left. Do you remember why?"

"Freedom," Bishop responded. "To keep me from having a face to face, up close and personal introduction to a firing squad… or the hangman's noose."

Terri rose from her seat, moving to confront her husband. "It was more than that, and you damn well know it. We went on the dodge because of the Alliance. If you had been convicted and shot, it would have been a black eye on everything we were trying to accomplish. Having one of the council's leading citizens labeled a butcher would have undermined everything we'd accomplished. That's why we bugged out. That's why we put our lives on the line."

"Maybe. So?"

"So… so, now the Alliance's future is on that line again. Our future and quality of life all hang in the balance. Yours, mine… and Hunter's, too. So does Kevin's, and the same for the Colonel's son. This is the time when good people step up and don't hold anything back. We're those people, Bishop. Like it or not, that's who we are."

"Why us?" Bishop pushed back. "Haven't we already done our part? Haven't we put it all on the line enough times? Our luck isn't going to hold out forever, hun. We've come way too close to the reaper's embrace, and one of these days he's not going to let us go."

"Because we're the only ones who can pull this off, my love," she gently reasoned. "This is a critical point in time. An

144

intersection of needs and capabilities, and our family is the perfect fit."

Bishop looked around the room, desperately seeking support from his friends. He found none, but after considering it for a moment, he should have expected that response.

Nick was no doubt troubled by mental images of a wounded Kevin being tortured, abused, or even killed. Diana's primary purpose in life, the Alliance, was being threatened like never before.

Was he being selfish?

He had to admit, the plan was creative - one of the most insightful pieces of strategic thinking he'd ever heard. But what about Hunter? A week from now, would Bishop be the one lying in the hospital bed having nightmares about someone harming his son? Would he be attending his wife's funeral? Would Terri be mourning him at his?

Terri, sensing her mate's silent deliberations… came closer, looking up with eyes full of love and purpose. "We've always said as long as we're together, all is well. I won't press on this if you're not 100% sure. You're more important to me than any old Alliance… more important than anything else. But please keep in mind, we'll be together, and we're unbeatable as a team. It's up to you, my love. We can head back to the ranch and that nasty old windmill this afternoon, and you'll never hear another word about this."

Bishop turned away, finding the view out the window a reprise from all the eyes that were waiting for his decision. His brain was reminding him of how much he desperately wanted to go home, his heart knowing Terri's plan was the right move.

He thought about the windmill, the garden, and his little speech about only knowing how to make money using his rifle. Maybe he wasn't cut out to be a rancher. Was living by the gun his destiny?

The Texan mulled, weighed, debated, and pondered. Go with your heart, he concluded. That's where Terri lives, and she's right. As long as we're together.

Finally, with a deep sigh, he turned back, smiled, and nodded. "I'm in. How much does this gig pay, anyway?"

Chapter 11

The top sergeant clicked off the M4's safety while shouting, "Going hot!"

Bishop moved his hands to protect his ears, watching as the non-commissioned officer (NCO) took aim.

The sergeant's rifle spit and barked, carefully aimed rounds whacking and pinging into the old truck's sheet metal. The Texan grinned, thinking the man was having way too much fun.

The ancient Ford had been acquired in El Paso. Sporting a faded paint job, rusting fenders, and miss-matched rims, the workhorse had definitely seen better days. In reality, the holes being punched into the bed and hood didn't degrade the rattletrap's appearance all that much. Even the two holes in the front windshield were hardly noticeable.

"Safe!" called the sergeant, removing the magazine while admiring his handiwork. "Sure looks like the owner of this old beast has seen his fair share of trouble, sir."

"Yup," Bishop replied. "Now, what about the radiator?"

"My guys in the motor pool will use a file to wear down one of the cooling hoses. You'll be leaking the entire drive across the border. While we can't execute with great precision, I can get pretty close in predicting when the engine will overheat. We'll throw an extra milk jug of water in the back, just in case she steams up before you get to the departure point. Just pour in a little coolant, and she'll hobble along another few miles."

Bishop understood, his college girlfriend's old Chevy suffering from the same affliction.

One of the base's pickups arrived, Terri hopping from the passenger door, brightening Bishop's mood instantly. His wife darted to the vehicle's bed, lifting two black trash bags of some unknown content and ambling toward their new ride.

"Whatcha got there?" he asked, nodding toward the bags.

"Our luggage," she said with a sweet smile. "This being a hobo couple on the run is kind of fun. There's an old, worn-out car seat still in the back of that truck. Can you get it for me?"

Bishop did as instructed, retrieving Hunter's new car-throne. Shaking his head at the stained cloth and worn plastic, he had to wonder about the device's safety rating.

"Are you sure this is okay for him to ride in?" he asked, eyeing the relic with suspicion. "Better not try driving through Alpha with that contraption. Lord knows Officer Dudley Do-Right would write us a ticket for that thing."

Laughing, Terri said, "Hunter's not going to be in it very

long. Even at that, we're going to be driving across the desert, not through Manhattan *or* Alpha. Unless you're worried about a collision with an armadillo, I think he'll be just fine."

"Good point."

"Hey, look what I found," Terri said, holding out a worn-looking sheet of paper.

He unfolded the yellowish parchment, shaking his head at the old wanted poster showing his face. For a brief second, it brought back memories of a bad time.

"The Army printed up thousands of those," Terri said. "They posted them on telephone poles and bulletin boards all over West Texas. I don't know where they got that picture of you, but I have to say you were a cute outlaw."

"Dashing," Bishop countered, refolding the poster with a smirk. "Outlaws are dashing."

"Seriously, read the bottom line. It will help sell our cover."

"Last seen heading west toward New Mexico," the Texan read aloud.

"I read one time that a lot of the crooks in the Old West considered it a badge of honor to be immortalized on a wanted poster. I figured it wouldn't hurt to have it along. Just another little piece of evidence to back up our story."

His wife's comment brought Bishop's thoughts back to what had been troubling him most since the decision to implement Operation Sacawagea.

In all of their jouneys and adventures since the collapse, he'd been able to bring along the tools of his trade. He'd always had night vision, plenty of ammo, body armor, and other kit-based assets that gave him peace of mind, and had often bailed their asses out of a bad spot.

But not this time.

Terri's plan had them as refugees, one of the many wandering families that crisscrossed the badlands in search of a better place. Bishop, being a wanted man, would help dispel any natural suspicions in New Mexico.

Such people didn't pack three rifles or fancy thermal imagers. They didn't sleep in a camper or bring along five days worth of MREs. Their child didn't ride in the lastest model car seat, and they most likely weren't pulling along Gucci luggage through the mountains of New Mexico.

The deception was critical. For the plan to work, the couple had to sell anyone they encountered on the fact that they weren't a threat. That initial impression, including Hunter's presence, would hopefully avoid their being shot on sight. They had to look and act the part, down to the minor details.

Terri sensed her husband's thoughts as he buckled in the

well-worn car seat. She leaned close and sniffed his body. "Not too bad yet," she pronounced. "Another day or two, and you'll be nice and... errr... outdoorsey... nice and...."

"Ripe," he finished for her.

With a grin, Bishop reached up and twirled a tress of her unwashed hair around his finger. "And you'll be just as fresh as a daisy."

"Look, I don't like ignoring my hygiene any more than the next person, but Bonnie and Clyde wouldn't have the time or resources to bathe. They would be on the run and low on assets. This is a small price to pay."

Then a cloud formed behind the Texan's eyes. "Are you sure this is the right move? This whole ordeal doesn't seem to be going the Alliance's way."

"No one's come up with a better option," she replied, noticing her husband was staring at Hunter's car seat. "You're worried about our boy, aren't you?"

"Yes. I was just thinking this operation should be nicknamed 'Fathers and Sons.' New Mexico seems to have an appetite for both lately."

Terri had to think about it for a second, realizing the Colonel's son, Nick's son, and the two fathers were all embroiled in the conflict. With a smile, she said, "That's why I'm going along. We need a mother involved to provide much needed balance... set things straight."

Grinning at Terri's bravado, he said, "And a damn fine looking mother at that."

She leaned close, pretending to approach for a kiss, but then stopped at the last second, sniffing about his person with a teasing frown.

Bishop rubbed his unshaven stubble and then wrapped his arms around her waist, yanking her tight against his chest. "How about a little 'savage catches wench' role playing, slave girl?"

Laughing, Terri stared him down. "Not in your wildest dreams, cowboy. You ain't getting near me until this mission is over, when you don't smell like a goat."

Even poor Hunter looked like a rag-muffin. Terri, shopping at a secondhand market in El Paso, had found a pair of grass-stained, threadbare overalls and scuffed up shoes. Bishop had immediately taken to calling his son, "the little sod farmer."

After one last round of double-checking the contents of their getaway truck, it was time to initiate Operation Sacagewra.

Diana was there for the send off, as was General Owens. Nick, still bedridden, sent his best.

"I forgot to ask," Terri said, getting into the truck, "Does this thing have air conditioning?"

"Well, it does, but it uses a little different 'technology' than what we're used to."

"Oh?"

"Yeah, it's called 60-2 AC."

"What's that?"

"You go 60 miles per hour and roll down 2 windows."

"Ha, ha, ha," Terri smirked, and then turned to Hunter sitting between them. "Your dad's humor *stinks*."

And then they were off.

Bishop turned north, heading off into the vast, empty expanses of Fort Bliss, which consisted mostly of desert criss-crossed by tank trails and small berms.

"How did all these paths get here?" Terri asked, curious as usual.

"This is where they train and exercise those big battle tanks back at the base. This area, combined with White Sands, is the largest range in North America."

They continued bouncing and jolting across the desert, sometimes finding trails and paths, other times crossing open ground. It had been determined that outlaws wouldn't be using paved roads, but instead would try and avoid law enforcement at all costs. Bishop kept hoping the old junker had a spare tire, or two, the rough terrain sure to overwhelm their rubber before they had reached their destination.

"I'm not going to have any fillings left in my teeth," Terri complained after one particularly nasty stretch.

"You don't have any fillings in your teeth," Bishop responded, his arms covered in sweat from fighting the wheel. "You've never even had a cavity that I know of."

"See, I told you so," she teased.

After four hours of rock'n'roll desert touring, Terri demanded a break. After changing Hunter and doing her best to wash out his cloth diaper, Terri needed a visit to the facilities. Digging around in their meager belongings, she began growling over not finding what she was after. Bishop tossed her an old copy of *The Army Times* and dropped the proverbial bomb. "Here you go, my love. This is our toilet paper. Save the gun porn if you can," he teased.

"Seriously?"

"Yup. Desperados wouldn't have Charmin' or wetwipes," he reminded her. "But where are my manners? Can I dig the shovel out of the back of the truck for you, sweetie?"

"No," she snapped, turning to stomp into the desert.

"Watch out for the rattlesnakes," he added, half expecting a missile to come flying his way.

Bishop turned to a now happier Hunter and said, "And your mother thinks she is that Saca-whoever. Let me tell you, son, those women in the old days had no complaints about using a catalog for TP."

Terri returned a short time later, unbitten and undeterred. "Ready?"

"And able."

"Are we there yet?"

Bishop judged they were close to the area where the truck was supposed to "break down." He'd been watching the dashboard temperature gauge for the last hour, the red needle inching slowly toward the danger zone. As far as he could tell, that was about the only functioning piece of equipment in the entire cab.

A few bumpy miles later, the couple detected steam rising from the hood. "Damn that radiator," Bishop complained, going into character.

They stopped in the late afternoon shadows of some unknown mountain range, Bishop instinctively scanning to see if the hills had eyes. It seemed strange to *want* someone aware of their presence.

Bishop opened the hood, pretending to be upset, cursing the engine, his luck, and the Ford Motor Company in a loud voice.

Terri, on the other hand, made a show of playing with Hunter while daddy fixed the truck.

"We're not going anywhere in this piece of junk," Bishop yelled back to Terri. "It looks like we'll be spending the night here. I'll set up the tent."

An hour later, they had shelter and a fire, Terri unwrapping some salted beef she'd procured in El Paso, Bishop finding a patch of purslane and using his knife to harvest a handful of the tasty green leaves. Hunter would be dining on rice and small bits of beef.

Throughout it all, the family tried to fulfill their theatrical roles, just in case they were being observed.

"Will we be able to see the drones?" Terri whispered,

worried someone might even be close enough to hear normal conversation.

"I doubt it, although Nick did claim to have shot one of them down."

The campfire proved therapeutic, it's licking flames and crackling embers helping settle the couple's nerves. They even relaxed enough to sing Hunter a few songs.

Terri announced she was turning in, the youngster's yawning reaffirming the notion.

"I'm going to lower the fire and then circle the camp once. I'll be in the hammock."

"Is that a good idea? To patrol?" Terri inquired.

Bishop shrugged, "If I was on the dodge and trying to avoid the authorities, I'd remain pretty diligent. I don't think it's out of character."

Terri nodded, "If you say so. Being a desert thespian is harder than I thought."

Twenty minutes later, Bishop returned, scanning the campsite one last time before turning in. He'd rigged his survival net with paracord, stretching the mesh tight between the truck and a nearby boulder. It wasn't as high off the ground as he preferred, but it was better than crowding his wife and son inside the 2-man tent. Body odor and snoring aside, it was tight in there.

Another length of cord was stretched taut above his hammock, a black, plastic leaf bag draped over the higher line. While the Texan didn't figure on any rain in the forecast, dew wasn't unheard of in the desert. Waking up with damp clothes in the middle of the night wasn't a recipe for a well-rested bandit.

He'd also taken the precaution of heating a pile of baseball-sized rocks near the fire. If it became too cold, he could stack them under his suspended bunk and keep nice and toasty warm.

He rolled into the net, resting his rifle across his chest. He did his best to sleep, but every sound of the night had the Texan gripping that weapon.

Dawn found Bishop already up, rekindling the fire and heating water for coffee.

Terri's head appeared from the tent's flap, rubbing her eyes and sniffing the air. "Where did you get the coffee, Mr. Bandito?"

"I stole it in the last town we passed through."

"Did you happen to pocket any eggs while on that crime spree?"

"As a matter of fact," Bishop smiled, producing a handful of white ovals.

"And that's why I love you," she grinned.

Mother and son soon joined dad for breakfast. While they ate eggs and home-fried bread, Terri questioned their meal.

"Should we be splurging like this? I mean, would crooks have coffee and eggs?"

"Those of us on the wrong side of the law have to eat, too," Bishop replied. "Maybe that's why were on the run – we robbed a grocery store."

"Well, Mr. Gangster, the next time you knock off a market, would you please remember to get some toilet paper?" she teased, eyeing the nearest berm.

"Don't pay any attention to the drones," Bishop said as she went over the rise.

Terri paused, her eyes going to the sky. "Pervert drones… that's all a girl needs," she mumbled, continuing on.

As Terri picked up around the camp, Bishop went for the academy award fussing over the truck. He did everything typical of a stranded motorist, starting the engine, kicking a fender, and issuing a string of creative cursing.

"Well, the truck's shot, my love. I guess we better start walking before the sun gets too high."

"I was afraid you were going to say that," Terri winked.

An hour later, they had everything packed, Hunter not sure what to make of the makeshift papoose Terri crafted out of apparent scrap cloth gathered from their luggage.

In reality, the couple had spent a significant amount of time carefully preparing their hiking equipment.

"Ounces equal pounds, and pounds equal pain," Bishop reminded his soon-to-be walking partner. "Since you will have Hunter most of the time, I'll have to carry the majority of our water and sleeping gear. We'll eat off the land as much as possible. The only special food we'll need is for the baby."

Terri glanced at the nearby mountains, the road ahead daunting. "How far?" she asked as if having second thoughts.

Bishop followed her gaze, "Actually, right on the other side of that rise we'll be in pine forest. According to Nick, it's quite the beautiful place if you're not dodging drones and war parties."

"We've got someone out in the desert," the young Cochiti reported, his eyes studying the laptop computer's display. "Looks like two adults and a child," he added, puzzled by the family's arrival.

An older man appeared over his shoulder, the announcement unwelcome given the turmoil of the last few days. "Rewind the recording. I want to see it all."

Ten minutes later, the two Natives had studied the video thoroughly. "It looks like their truck broke down," observed the senior man.

"Could be some sort of trick?"

"Maybe, but who brings along a baby if it's a military probe?"

"I still think we should let Grandfather know. I can ride up to the cabin with the drone's video card. Grandfather will know what to do."

"Launch another flyer before you go. Let's keep an eye on them… just in case."

An hour later, Hack pushed back from the table and turned to the Apache. "In the video, it looks like a nomadic family to me. The man's got a long gun, but their equipment is anything but military issue. What do you think?"

Apache Jack was skeptical. "Even if you're right, we should send out some men and chase them away. We've seen our share of thieves, beggars, and other scum. Or we could just kill him and turn the woman and child over to one of the tribes. Better safe than sorry."

Hack considered his friend's words. He was probably right, the logical course of action being to dispatch the intruders and get on with the hundreds of checklist items that consumed his day. But there was more to it than that.

At one point in time, he'd had high hopes of the project attracting people from far and wide. He'd envisioned engineers, doctors, scientists, and other skilled professionals joining the tribes, lured by an abundance of food and water.

Part of that dream was still alive, but now, with the Alliance in the picture and Washington no doubt sore over the loss of the radioactive metal, it was going to be difficult to separate the refugee-wheat from the contributor-chaff.

Hack believed human talent was the key to not only rebuilding, but creating a better place to live – an environment where the residents of New Mexico could thrive and instill the positive values of Native American society. They could build a new country, and do it right this time.

When he'd first arrived, Hack had been appalled at the region's poverty. Like most visitors, his vision of Native Americans had been warped and distorted by a lack of knowledge and Hollywood's inaccurate depiction. He'd expected to encounter the noble red man, steeped in tradition, one with nature, and unconcerned with many of the traditional values that were so important to the euro-whites.

Indians, he believed, weren't all wrapped up in material possessions, greed, corruption, politics, or many of the negative aspects of western society. He anticipated a refreshing change from the rat race that had been his life in L.A. He hoped for neighbors more accepting of his exotic appearance and behavior.

What he found were third-world economic conditions, mismanagement of resources, and many of the locals living in absolute squalor.

His first reaction had been to shrug it off, justifying the tribe's conditions with the typical list of excuses and stereotypes. The Indians didn't care about earthly wealth or possessions. They were lazy. They were caught in a cycle of generational poverty and now suffered from an addiction to government handouts and support. Drug and alcohol abuse, inspired by low levels of self-esteem, were to blame.

Always a keen observer, Hack had watched, read, and listened to the local news and gossip. He'd visited ceremonial dances, powwows, and other local events. He'd tried his best to integrate into his surroundings.

The first hint that he, as well as most of American society, had it all wrong occurred while he'd been on a rare road trip to Albuquerque. A shipment of parts for his toys had arrived, but the parcel delivery truck had been unable to locate his cabin.

It was an especially hot day, the temperature rising as Hack wound his way down the mountain and into the lower altitudes of the desert. He passed a car that was pulled to the side of the road, one of the tires shredded beyond repair.

A short distance later, he spotted a woman walking, a toddler on her arm and another small child at her side. There wasn't a town or pueblo for miles, and the radio had warned of a 100 degree plus day. Hack pulled up next to her.

"Do you need a ride?" he asked, trying to smile nicely.

Despite the heavy-looking child and long walk ahead of her, the already-perspiring Native didn't immediately accept. Without a word, she studied him for several moments before nodding. "If you would be so kind," she answered, reaching for the door handle.

"Where are you headed?"

"I'm going to visit my aunt," she replied. "It's her birthday."

After a quick exchange, the traveler provided Hack an idea where the relative lived, and he was happy to deliver her. "Well, hop in. I'm going that direction and can swing by to drop you off."

A few times during the drive, Hack tried to strike up a conversation to pass the time. His efforts were met with polite, but short answers. He wrote it off to the woman being upset about her car and wary of a stranger.

Turning into the pueblo, Hack noticed every residence had

an identical cardboard and wood crate sitting at the curb. There were dozens and dozens of the containers, all of them covered with dust and road grime. Weeds grew around the eyesores, some of the sides and fronts eaten with insect holes.

"What's up with the big boxes?" he inquired, winding his way through the narrow, dirt streets.

Her initial response was a grunt, followed by a vague and sketchy explanation, "The BIA (Bureau of Indian Affairs) sent each resident a clothes dryer. A big truck came and dropped one off at each house."

"Really?" Hack replied, thinking such an event would be welcome and not understanding her negative tone.

"The people don't know what to do with them. The trash haulers can't take them away, so they just sit in their yards."

"Why not use them?" he asked innocently.

"They're gas powered, and the pueblo has never been plumbed for natural gas."

Hack could believe it. He'd spent his entire career working with government contracts. Sometimes the bureaucracy simply messed up.

"Why didn't the tribe's governor ask the BIA to swap them out with electric dryers?"

She frowned, obviously frustrated by the entire affair. "Because the tribe requested them."

Hack shook his head, clearly not understanding. "The tribe requested gas dryers? Why would they do that?"

"Well, not exactly. A government man from Housing and Urban Development visited the pueblo. He wrote a letter to the governor suggesting that the local businesses would attract more tourists if the area's visual appeal was improved. One of the items he pointed out was the fact that the residents dry their clothes outside in the sun. When there was grant money available at the BIA, the tribe asked for a way to dry the laundry inside. They sent the dryers."

"So, why not just swap them out?"

"That was considered, but electric dryers require 240-volt electrical outlets. Most of these homes are older, and barely support 120 volt, so it wouldn't have done any good."

Hack pulled up in front of the aunt's house, his passenger thanking him graciously for the ride.

"Before you go, I'm curious about the dryers. So why didn't someone send them back and reallocate the funds for some other improvements?"

"It was too late," she said sadly. "The crates had been sitting outside for several weeks, and the manufacturer refused to take them back."

Hack could understand her bitterness. "And let me guess. The local trash trucks can't haul them away?"

She nodded and then proceeded to thicken the plot even further. "You got it," she answered, "so some of the people got together and contacted a scrap dealer in Santa Fe, just to get the ugly boxes out of the pueblo. But the BIA said we couldn't do that. They said that the dryers were government property, and the equipment had something called a 'five-year depreciation schedule.'"

"I'm sorry," Hack said. "I hate stories like that. Maybe the people could convert them to bookshelves or coffee tables," he added, trying to lighten her mood.

She looked at him with sad eyes. "There's no room inside anymore. As part of the grant money, the tribe agreed to pass a rule eliminating clotheslines and outside drying. My aunt's home is already quite small. Now it is full of wet clothing."

Hack didn't know what to say.

His passenger gathered her well-behaved children, thanked him for the ride, and proceeded to walk toward the modest home. Almost as an afterthought, she returned to the car window, asking, "Would you like some bread? My aunt has made bread in her oven since I was a little girl. Every weekend, she would sit outside on her porch and sell the loaves to tourists. But now, not many tourists come because of the ugly boxes, and she always has more than we can eat."

Smiling, Hack said, "I'd love to buy some bread. How much is it?"

"No money," she replied, a flash of insult behind her eyes. "You were kind to my children and me. I don't have any money, but I can repay you with bread."

His experience that day had stuck with Hack. As he began to sell his toys in Santa Fe, he became friends with the other artists and craftsmen, most of whom were Natives. Tragedies, such as the gas dryers, were common.

Over time, he came to accept that the locals were a people out of sync with their surroundings, being squeezed from all directions by the overwhelming force of society as a whole.

Hack thought about the Apache's suggestion for a moment, finally shaking his head. "Go check them out. If they resist at all, then do what you think is necessary. If you detect any hint of foul play, bring them to me. With the funerals, additional security, and extra patrols, the project is falling behind schedule. Not everyone passing through Native lands is up to no good. Don't invest a lot of manpower in this. We've got work to do."

"Yes, Grandfather."

Hack watched his bodyguard head off to issue orders, and

then turned back to the video monitor. His attention, however, was elsewhere.

Chapter 12

Terri was never so happy to see flat terrain in her life.

The climb up the mountain would have been bad enough on its own, but Hunter's makeshift pouch wasn't exactly a product of scientific design and years of field testing. It was off balance, ate into her shoulders, and her child hated the contraption.

Soaked in sweat, legs burning with fire, and with a fussy, constantly wiggling boy riding poorly on her back, Terri finally gave in to her body's protests and conceded that she needed a break. "Bishop," she panted, "Sacagawea, I'm not. I need a break. A good, long one. Hunter is in agreement, which means you're out-voted."

Her husband nodded, indicating a strand of trees just ahead. "The sun's getting hot, even at this altitude. The shade will feel good."

They found the cluster of pines surrounded with a nice, soft carpet of old needles. Interspaced between the trunks were table-sized rocks, a few covered with a plush layer of cushy moss. It was truly an oasis for Terri's tortured body.

After helping her unload Hunter, the Texan began a routine Terri had watched him perform a hundred times. He scouted their surroundings, watching and listening with an intensity that reminded her of a wild animal stalking prey.

Only after he was sure their location was safe did he unload his own heavy pack, stretching and rolling his shoulders. "Now that was a hike," he proclaimed with a cheery voice. "Can you believe people actually did this shit for fun and recreation before the collapse?"

"They must have been sadistic," Terri replied, rubbing her sore legs. "Either that, or I'm completely out of shape. That was painful. Are we done climbing?"

"Yup. It's downhill from here. I'm going to poke around ahead for a bit. Do you have your pistol handy?"

"Yes," she replied, patting the fanny pack across her stomach.

"Don't drink too much, and don't let Hunter have more than a cup, okay?"

"How far are you going?"

"Not so far," he answered, digging into his pocket and extracting a small, skin-colored device. "After talking with Nick, I thought I would try this. It's called a hunter's ear. It amplifies sound so you can hear animals at a greater distance. The SAINT team told me that when Nick shot the second drone, it made a distinct buzzing noise. I want to see if we're being watched."

"If someone comes along, will you be able to hear me?"

Bishop nodded. "Yup. Yell like crazy, and I'll come running. Or, you can just fire off a shot... like the last time you had trouble in New Mexico."

Terri automatically checked again for a snake. While she'd thoroughly searched the area before sitting down, her husband's remark brought back memories of a very close call. "Oh, you don't have to worry about any of those little reptilian bastards getting close to me. I learned my lesson."

Nodding toward the device, she said, "I thought Nick was adamant about your not bringing any of your high-tech toys. Is it a good idea to have that... just in case we get surprised?"

"I can ditch this little thing pretty quickly. And it is not expensive or rare, so it wouldn't be completely out of character to have one."

"Yeah. I heard you try that same logic when Nick found out you planned on packing your night vision. I thought you were going to cry like a little boy when he said you couldn't bring along your favorite plaything," she teased.

Bishop, still fiddling with the tiny sensor, didn't react to her jab. "You know, this thing weighs about the same as a roll of toilet paper. I sure hope I made the right choice," he said with a perfectly innocent deadpan expression.

Growling a throaty, "Ohhhh... youuuuu... pigheaded...," Terri tried to stand, but her aching legs quickly discouraged a full frontal assault. She then looked around for anything to throw at her husband, but only pine needles were within reach.

Grinning like the cat who just swallowed the canary, Bishop said, "I'll be back in 10 minutes. Please don't shoot me on the way in."

As he turned to leave, she could only think of an old, childish insult. "Smell ya later."

Grinning at the witticism, he countered, "Sure enough, my little desert *flower*."

Terri watched him move away, inserting the electric doodad in his ear and then making adjustments to the device as he walked. Waiting until he was several steps away, she covered her mouth and started giggling.

Bishop quickly discovered his toy was worthless unless he stood very still and held his breath. Slightly larger than a common hearing aid, the operating principle was similar, but far more acute. His boots sounded like thunder rolling across the mountainside with each step. He extracted the device, deeming it more important to identify the easiest route down.

He had sensed Terri was struggling with the climb, shocked she had endured for so long. Even his own legs were aching, muscles tight and joints complaining of abuse. Her grit was amazing.

He continued down what was some sort of game trail or wash, the path zigzagging through the rocks and trees, leading into what appeared to be a lush valley below. *We'll camp there tonight*, he thought. *The hard part is over.*

As he tried to detect any observers, Bishop longed for his regular equipment. A thermal imager would spot someone hiding in the rocks, a good scope on his rifle would make him feel better about walking into an ambush.

Even a simple red dot optic would be an advantage. Nick's argument had been sage. "They're smart, organized, and somewhat skilled. Don't give them even a hint of what you really are. Make mistakes, make noise, pretend to be unaware and stroll into their territory like any old Joe Nobody on the run. It's the only way to get inside their walls... alive, anyway."

It had been so long since Bishop had used iron sights on a rifle. He'd had only a few hours on Bliss's range to zero his blaster, and he didn't like the setup one bit. Halo optics were faster, and if lead was going to fly, he wanted his airborne first. "You're not going in there to fight, dipshit," Nick had countered. "You're doing this to talk. The best possible outcome is if you never have to pull the trigger."

Even his selection of a weapon had been a point of contention. "You've got that fancy-smancy, piston-operated shooting iron. Not many guys carry those. You should leave that at home and carry a beat-up, old blaster like every other swinging dick who thinks he's a bad ass."

But Bishop drew the line at leaving his best gun at home. There wasn't any time to gain trust in a strange weapon. *Hell, if it were up to Nick, I'd walk in there buck naked. Enough is enough,* he determined. *It's not like I am going for an Academy Award here.*

Even his pack, armor, and load-vest had been left behind. "I can take one look at your rig and tell you're a pro," Nick had warned. "They'll be able to do the same. You're a vagabond, scavenging and clawing your way across a post-apocalyptic landscape, struggling to get your wife and kid to a better place. You'll use piecemeal, jerry-rigged crap to carry your stuff. Get a civilian backpack of low quality, tear it here and there and then patch it with duct tape. Tie some of your gear onto your belt using twine. Ditch the Camelbak and carry old plastic jugs for water. No MREs. No fancy fire starters. Get a crappy tent and use plastic bags like they're going out of style. Look the part," Nick had advised.

While all that sounded fine and good back at Fort Bliss, in reality, it sucked in the field.

Unbalanced loads caused more wear and tear on the body. That led to less energy and stamina, which resulted in a lower state of awareness. Being unaware in enemy territory wasn't a habit associated with long-term survival.

Human beings were worse at practically everything when worn down. They couldn't fight, hunt, reason, or react nearly as well or as quickly. Every step of the decision-making process was handicapped.

With his typical rig, Bishop could easily make 10 miles a day carrying 65 pounds of weapons, ammo, and kit. He'd be hurting at the end of it, but it was doable.

Now, with his hobo setup, he was barely toting 45 pounds, and only five miles had just about kicked his ass. And if they ran into trouble? Diplomatic mission or not, he was really fucked.

He had one magazine in the rifle, another in his pants pocket rubbing a blister already. Less than 60 rounds. Not enough to even break contact, let alone fight his way out of a bad situation. He had no blow-out bag, or IFAK (Improved First Aid Kit) as the Army liked to call it. If they were hurt, even an accidental fall on the trail, they were in trouble.

Continuing down the path, Bishop wondered how anyone managed to travel very far with equipment and limitations like Terri and he were using. Somehow they succeeded – the Alliance seeing a steady stream of "immigrants" every single day. Many arrived with far fewer possession than what he had brought along. Most looked worse for the wear.

Satisfied he had ascertained the easiest route down, Bishop paused for a moment to study the surroundings. He decided to try the hunter's ear again, just for shits and giggles.

Holding his breath and remaining motionless, he repeated the process of adjusting the unit's gain and volume controls and then listening intently.

On the second such iteration, he found he could indeed hear a rather vocal songbird from somewhere down in the valley.

On the third test, he was pretty sure there was running water beneath the canopy of trees below.

It was after the next adjustment that he heard a mechanical buzzing noise in the background.

Bishop then began adjusting his feet, turning his head, and

thus changing the position of his ear, a few degrees at a time. All the while studying the Columbia blue sky.

And then he saw it.

Even though he'd been searching for a drone since they'd unpacked the truck, his heart froze at finally seeing the thing. It wasn't large, maybe 20 to 30 inches across, he estimated.

It didn't seem to be armed or dangerous, nor did it act in any threatening way. But there it was, hovering maybe 200 meters above the ridge, some sort of camera or sensor hanging underneath. And it made his blood run cold.

There was something troubling about the robotic spy. It violated a core instinct and yielded to some primal fear of someone... or something being able to see you – when you can't see them.

"Gotcha," he whispered, trying not to stare or gawk. *Just act normal*, he thought, forcing himself to calm down. "Terri's going to love this."

Now, really feeling the role of an actor on the stage, Bishop turned and began hiking back up the trail. He tried to be carefree and confident, but it was extremely difficult. The hills had eyes.

He arrived back at the camp to find Terri feeding Hunter small bits of bread while holding his sippy cup. The moment she looked at Bishop's face, she could tell something was wrong.

"Shhhh," he hissed in as low a volume as possible, pretending to move close in order to help with Hunter. "They know we're here," he said into his wife's ear. "Don't look, but I saw the drone just to the south."

Despite his warning, Terri couldn't help herself and started to turn and look. "Don't!" Bishop snapped. "In a minute, we'll walk to the edge and look down. I'll point out some bird, and you can see it then."

"Okay... sorry... this all so weird. Really weird."

Pulling Hunter into his arms, Bishop did as promised, guiding his wife to a spot where they could oversee the valley below.

"Off my left shoulder," he whispered, pretending to point at the trail. "Just about 200 meters above the trees, straight above that outcropping of rock. It's red, a little bigger than a bird."

"I see it!" she announced.

"Don't stare."

"Okay... but... it's tiny. I was thinking of those great big things, like they used in the wars. I could swat that little pest with a broom."

"Or throw rocks at it," Bishop grinned, trying to lighten the stress. "Now, let's just act normal, and go back and get our stuff. I want to have tonight's camp set up early, well before it gets dark."

They proceeded down the mountain, the trip much longer than it had appeared from above. A few hours later, they came to a paved road, where Bishop spied a small gravel parking area.

They found a trail leading into a narrow gorge, a 10-foot wide stream running through the middle. It was stunningly beautiful.

The couple stood and stared for several minutes, taking it all in. Something caught Bishop's eye, and after parting a patch of overgrown weeds, he found a sign declaring the land was part of a national forest, and that they were at the beginning of a marked trail.

The pathway was covered in man-made gravel, about six feet wide, lined with stones, and meandering alongside the stream. The south side of the cut was a sheer rock wall, the Texan pointing out climbing anchors embedded here and there in the face. "This must have been a popular place before the apocalypse."

To the north was the brook, and then 100 meters of flat, heavily forested ground that ended in another vertical cliff face.

"I don't think I've ever seen anything so beautiful," Terri pined. "The word picturesque hardly does it justice."

The couple followed the path, the flat, engineered surface a welcome relief for their tired legs and sore shoulders. Even Hunter seemed enthralled by the surroundings.

A half mile in, Bishop stopped and pointed toward a muddy patch of earth between the trail and the stream. "Bear tracks," he stated without emotion. "Not a big one, but a bear nonetheless."

They approached a wooden bridge, the heavy, planked surface passing Bishop's test for weight bearing integrity. Crossing the bubbling waters, Bishop noted a school of fish swimming nearby. A few looked to be keepers.

On they journeyed, heads pivoting and fingers pointing out the natural beauty of the place. It seemed like every bend and curve in the trail rewarded the eye with an awe inspiring view.

And then another trailside sign appeared, the faded yellow letters accompanied by an arrow directing hikers to the "Loggerhead Primitive Camping Area."

Exchanging looks with his wife, Bishop said, "Why not? At least the ground will be flat for the tent."

Here, the path wasn't as smooth or wide, but on the other hand, it was well marked. After hiking another few minutes, they spotted the dead-end canyon, complete with BBQ grills and flattened spaces for tents.

"No showers?" Terri complained, checking out the facilities.

"Nope. Primitive camping evidently means just that."

After resting and drinking, the couple set about making camp. After the tent was pitched, Bishop found two sturdy trunks for his hammock lines but didn't string the net just yet.

Next came the always troublesome chore of water.

While they had a fire, plenty of wood, and a nearby stream, Bishop knew from experience that was only half the battle. There was never enough potable water.

Terri and he each carried large, steel cups in their kit. In addition, they owned an old Army mess kit, including a small frying pan. But that was the extent of their water-boiling capabilities, and it was never enough.

Terri would want to bathe Hunter with clean water. The two adults could both use a sponge bath. Then there were the requirements of refilling their travel jugs and the act of cooking at least one meal. Good hygiene demanded an abundance of the precious commodity for brushing teeth, rinsing any game or local plants harvested for dinner, and washing their hands. It all added up and would require several sessions of boiling, cooling, refilling, and starting all over again.

Bishop retrieved one of his big, black trash bags and headed toward the stream, taking time to study their new homestead in more detail.

From a tactical perspective, the campgrounds were a mixed lot. Unless a foe was willing to repel down 75 feet of sheer rock, there was only one way in, and that was a positive in the Texan's mind.

On the other hand, there was only one way out. Not a good feature for a lone couple in "Indian country."

What Bishop liked the most was the fact that it would be nearly impossible to spy on them from the air. Tall hardwoods and pines rose from the canyon's floor, their canopy dense enough to deny observation from above. "They'll have to come visit us face to face," Bishop mumbled, not sure if that was a good thing or not.

He returned, struggling with several pounds of water in the bag. After securing the soft-sided reservoir to a tri-pod of sticks, Bishop began filling every available container for boiling.

He was using the state-provided BBQ pit for purification, the flat, metal grill the best surface for balancing stainless steel cups and flat pan bottoms. Each batch required a glance at his watch to make sure the liquid spent enough time at bacteria-killing temperatures.

A short time later, Terri noticed Bishop whittling on a set of poles with his knife. "Punji stakes?" she asked, only half kidding.

"Nope, I'm going fishing."

"I didn't know you liked to fish," she said, tilting her head.

164

"Growing up in West Texas, the opportunity didn't present itself all that often. I always thought I'd try my hand at it after retiring."

"What are you going to use for bait?"

"Bait? You need bait?" Bishop asked with an expression of boyish innocence.

Terri bent and lifted Hunter into her arms, "Come on, son. Let's go watch your father not catch any fish. When you're older, remind me to be the one who teaches you how to drop a line."

The family trekked the short distance to the stream, Bishop carrying his survival net and stakes, his rifle slung tight against his chest.

Like any fisherman, he scrambled up and down the rocky bank twice, looking for just the right spot. Once selected, Bishop sat down and removed his socks and boots.

"Oh, shit, that's cold," Bishop protested, wading into the knee-deep water.

"Well at least your feet will smell better," Terri sniped.

The Texan began driving his stakes into the creek's bottom, spacing them like fence posts, about a foot apart. He then proceeded to weave the survival net through, front and back. When he'd finished, he had erected a vertical barrier across the deepest part of the water.

Next he produced a length of paracord, securing it to the tops of the outermost stakes.

He climbed back up the bank, slicing off two leafy branches. With his two fan-shaped bunches of foliage, he hiked upstream about 30 feet, studying the water closely, and playing out the paracord as he went.

Again, Bishop descended into the cold water, a branch in each hand. He clenched the paracord in his teeth and then submerged the leafy end of the trimmed bushes. Winking at Terri, he proceeded to step back toward the net.

Terri shook her head and whispered to Hunter, "Once a cowboy, always a cowboy. He's trying to herd the fish into the net. And you know what? I think it just might work."

Bishop continued walking, moving at a gradual pace, the bush-tips bouncing along the bottom. "I can see the fish," he reported through clenched teeth, now less than 20 feet from the net. "There are a couple of big ones."

When he was five feet away, Bishop started splashing his feet and waving the underwater blockers with more vigor. Next, he dropped the branches and began reeling in the paracord, hand over hand.

When he tightened the slack, the cord pulled both end-stakes over, and the net collapsed.

Terri was impressed... and excited... and suddenly hungry. "What's the catch of the day? I hope it's not an old boot someone discarded."

"I don't know," he replied, wading forward quickly to inspect the trap. "Yes!" he announced with glee. "I can see fins and scales in the net. Watch out!"

Bishop bent and scooped the entire apparatus in his arms, and then without additional warning, flung it toward the bank, barely missing his wife and child.

Scrambling to dry land, he began untangling the mesh and stakes, eager to examine the catch.

Mostly, he found small perch, barely larger than his middle finger. But there were two trout and one pan fish worth cleaning and frying. "Yes!" he celebrated, holding up the largest specimen with pride. "Make fun of this old cowboy, will ya?"

A short time later, Bishop was feeding small hunks of fillet onto a hand-carved skewer.

"I have to admit," Terri said, watching her husband prepare the meal. "That was pretty creative. I owe you an apology. I should've known you'd pull that off."

"Hell, I didn't know if it would work either. Let's just hope it tastes good."

"Anything would be better than salted beef," she said.

"I could try and gig some frog legs tonight," he grinned. "I hear they taste like chicken and ain't bad for breakfast."

Terri's face contorted with disgust. "Well, *almost* anything would be better than salted beef."

"Turtle soup?"

Chapter 13

Hack was displeased, to say the least.

His frustration was due to several factors, not the least of which involved his Native friends and co-workers.

"How is it that the man best qualified to run Valley Green managed to get himself killed chasing the Alliance intruders?" he inquired of the Apache.

"Men are men, Grandfather. He considered himself both an engineer and a warrior. When the call went out for more security here at the cabin, he responded with a warrior's heart. It is a sad loss for his family and tribe, but he died with honor."

They just don't get it, Hack thought. "And you were okay with this? You were fine letting the best civil engineer in all of the Caldera tribes risk his life?"

The Apache shrugged his shoulders, "He was a man. It was his right. Should I have denied him that?"

The toymaker wanted to explode but checked his temper. Over and over again the "Native outlook," on what was important and what was not had hampered the project. No matter what he said, no matter how strong his logic, they simply weren't going to change their ways. It didn't occur to him that maybe he should be the one to make adjustments.

A few months ago, he'd arrived at the construction site and found the area completely void of any workers, only to find out that a wedding was in progress. Time and again, the project had been delayed, most often for reasons that just didn't seem to be a high priority to Hack.

Just like the death of his best engineer, it all seemed so shortsighted. The project's completion would do more to secure the tribes' future than any rite of passage accomplished in the forest. Killing two or three of the enemy was nothing compared to the benefit of having a nearly unlimited food supply. Yet, for all of his persuasion, he couldn't make them understand.

Or maybe they did and just didn't care.

That thought had occurred to Hack on more than one occasion. If this were true, it was just something he'd have to learn to live with. No one person, society, form of government, or nation was perfect. The human model had flaws.

Heaven above knew the whites had their share of shortcomings. Images began to flash through Hack's mind, horrors of the events following the collapse that would haunt him the rest of his days.

Hack had watched the town tear itself to shreds, gang

rapes, arson, cannibalism, looting, and outright anarchy prevailing for weeks. But the Natives? Rather than prey on the weak, they had banded together to help the least among them. While the townsfolk looted, the pueblos donated. As Santa Fe burned, the tribes were calling for everyone to plant extra rows in their gardens.

Maybe placing a higher priority on weddings and ceremonies wasn't such a bad trade off. Perhaps the difference in how the two segments of society dealt with the apocalypse had nothing to do with differences in philosophy, but was merely due to the fact that the Natives had been living "without" for decades.

The Apache broke his train of thought. "We can no longer monitor the strangers from the desert with the drones. They have set up camp in Loggerhead Canyon, and the forest canopy is too thick."

"Are you sure they're still there?" Hack asked, having visions of sabotage delaying Valley Green even further.

"No, we can't be positive. I'm sending in three men first thing in the morning. They will have orders to question the strangers. If the answers don't make sense, then they are to kill the man and bring the woman and child here."

"Okay."

The fish had been five-star restaurant quality, Bishop allowing it to slowly smoke over the open fire. Even Hunter had seemed to enjoy the taste.

The rest of the evening had been spent recouping from their hike, neither of them having much energy. Bishop made one more trip to the stream, retrieving even more water, as well as a few hand-selected, extra shiny stones for Hunter's amusement.

"Boil those rocks," Terri ordered. "He puts everything in his mouth these days."

Bishop now had two leaf bags involved in their water assembly line, one for raw, the other potable after boiling and cooling.

Those two reservoirs were soon to be joined by a third, the Texan rigging up a plastic lined, rock walled pool for Hunter's bath. Mixing hot and cold water together, the parents enjoyed watching the naked boy splash with glee. Terri and Bishop each took a sponge bath with the remaining warm water.

Given their long, up and down trek, it was no surprise that

Terri nearly dozed off staring at the fire.

"Go to bed," Bishop suggested. "I'll tidy things up here and then hit the hay myself. I have a feeling tomorrow is going to be a long day."

"Do you think we'll make contact tomorrow?"

"I don't know. They may just choose to ignore us completely, which means we have a lot more walking ahead of us. But my gut says we'll meet the locals sometime in the next 24 hours. They could be watching us right now... with human eyes."

Terri shuddered, peering around at the dark, stone walls that surrounded the campgrounds.

After another yawn, she lifted a sleeping Hunter and made for the tent.

Bishop spent the next few minutes organizing their equipment. Given the bear tracks he'd spied on the way in, he used a length of cord to hoist their meager food supply, sure the scent of cooking fish would attract curious noses from far and wide.

Lessons learned from long ago drove Bishop to repack equipment he knew would be needed in the morning. The habit was born of the need to move quickly and the desire to avoid leaving any of their precious assets behind.

Given the local wildlife, he decided to keep the fire high throughout the night. That would also help him sleep.

Digging in his pack, Bishop had one last task that he'd been pondering all evening. Retrieving a spool of fishing line, the Texan took Hunter's rocks and put them inside his steel cup. He tied one end of the line to the container's handle, and then proceeded to run a trip wire across the box canyon's opening.

It was a bit out of character, he knew, but having just a few seconds of warning might make the difference between living and dying. He wondered for a moment if bears would smell and step over a tripwire, or just walk on through.

Balancing the heavy cup and keeping the line taut required more effort than he'd planned but was well worth the investment. Now he would be able to sleep, and that rest would help keep his mind clear for the rest of their mission.

Two more logs on the fire, and the Texan was rolling into the net-hammock. It seemed like he'd just closed his eyes when the cup of rocks rattled its warning.

His first thought was a bear.

Rolling out of the hammock, it took Bishop a moment to clear the sleep from his head. The sky was already brightening, the sun rising in the east. He'd slept like the surrounding rocks.

In they came, three men on horses, painted warriors riding high on garnished steeds.

They offered a more impressive display than any western he'd seen in a movie house or on television… and were far more intimidating.

Each of the new arrivals wore a layer of white paint on his exposed skin. Dark blue and black lines had been carefully drawn on the pale canvas of flesh, their angles and depth bringing forth an aggressive, hawk-like profile.

Instead of lances, the Indians carried battle rifles with feathers attached to the barrels. Bishop recognized Kevin's sniper rifle in one man's hand, and it pissed him off.

"Terri? Honey, it must be Halloween, because we've got trick or treaters at the door," Bishop announced in a calm voice, watching the three riders approach without hesitation or pause.

He sensed more than saw her head poke out of the tent flap, the Texan unwilling to take his eyes off the advancing threat.

"What are you doing here on our land?" came the harshly toned greeting. "You are trespassing."

"Well, good morning to you, too," Bishop replied with a cheery sarcasm. But then his tone went cold, "The sign said this was a national forest. It's nobody's land."

There wasn't an immediate response to his statement, two of the riders continuing past the lead man, trying to flank Bishop's position. The Texan wasn't about to let that happen.

Stepping back to keep all three of them to his front, Bishop ended up further away from the tent and his family than what he wanted. Still, given the rocks and trees, the riders didn't achieve their tactical goal. And they didn't like it.

"There is no more nation to own the forest. We now claim this land. Where are you from?"

"We came from back east," Bishop answered honestly. "We're just passing through. We don't want any trouble."

"And you walked all this way? Across the desert?"

"No, our truck broke down just on the other side of the mountains. We're trying to reach family in Arizona. Looking for work along the way."

With a nod from the leader, one of the riders dismounted, marching boldly toward the family's belongings and beginning to rummage through Bishop's pack. The searcher wasn't gentle about it, pulling out an item, holding it up for the others to examine, and then throwing it aside before reaching in again.

"Get the fuck out of my pack," Bishop growled. "You've got no right to...."

The objection was interrupted by the leader pointing his weapon at Bishop's chest, "We have to make sure you're not stealing from our people. We have no interest in your junk."

"Junk?" Bishop started to protest. "That's our life in that pack, friend. It's all we got."

Terri appeared just then, looking scared-shitless and clutching a wide-eyed Hunter to her chest. "Bishop? What's going on? Who are these men?"

"It's okay," he said, pretending to be brave. It didn't take much acting.

About then, the man searching the pack pulled out the Army's wanted poster. Unfolding the paper, the warrior read the words, did a double-take at Bishop, and then held it up to show the boss.

"This is you?" the honcho asked, holding up the paper.

"It was a misunderstanding," Bishop replied sheepishly. "A big misunderstanding."

"So you are a wanted man with a big reward, huh? Maybe we should take you back to Texas and collect that bounty?"

"That won't be easy, mister. A few have already tried, and they're now discussing their reward with Saint Peter," the Texan replied, tightening the grip on his rifle.

Bishop's threat didn't seem to have much outward effect on the Natives, the leader continuing with his round of questioning. "So you killed soldiers? A lot of soldiers?"

"Like I said, it was a misunderstanding, and none of your business. Now if you fine gentlemen don't mind, you're frightening my wife and son, and we haven't had breakfast yet."

Something in Bishop's bravado struck the leader as curious. "Are you a soldier?" the lead man inquired.

"No."

"Were you a soldier?"

"Yes, a long time ago. Before everything went to hell, however, I was an engineer. Since the lights went out, I've been anything and everything necessary to feed my family."

"What kind of engineer?"

This is it, Bishop thought. *This is where I use bait to catch the fish.* "I was a civil engineer back in the pre-collapse world. I specialized in fluid dynamics. I worked for a water company in Houston... but what the hell does this have to do with the price of tea in China? You're getting a little too nosey, Mister."

There was some truth to the Texan's response. His major in college had been in Fluid Dynamics, but that curriculum had little to do with water. Teenage aspirations of a career in the oil fields had evaporated long ago. The Texan hoped he wouldn't be pressed on too many details during the job interview.

But the rider didn't take the bait. The Indian tilted his head as if trying to judge the honesty of Bishop's answer. His gaze then directed to a wide-eyed, cowering Terri.

"And you?"

Bishop wasn't certain just how scared Terri really was. If she was acting, it was a damn fine job.

With a stutter, she managed, "And... and... me what?"

Terri's question didn't receive an answer. Instead, the rider guided his horse to an angle where he could see her backside. Eyeing her blue jean covered legs up and down, the Indian merely grunted, and then reigned his animal back to the original spot.

Seemingly no longer interested in the woman or child, Bishop saw the man's intense gaze refocus on him. It didn't stay there long.

The Texan saw the boss signal his dismounted subordinate, a slight, barely noticeable nod. Some instinct told Bishop that his death had just been ordered.

The man was quick, drawing a knife and lunging three steps in a blink.

But Bishop was ready, his rifle butt driving into the attacker's face with all the force he could muster. Down they went, the Indian badly dazed, but still putting up a struggle. The impact so jarring, the Texan lost his grip on the carbine.

They rolled once, twice, and then Bishop was on top, both of the Texan's powerful arms turning the warrior's blade against his own chest.

Desperation and adrenaline kicked in, the Native realizing the end of his life was only a few inches away from his heart. But Bishop was stronger, on top, and motivated by the thought of Kevin's rifle being carried by another man.

Sensing the other two Natives would be moving to help their friend, Bishop decided against having a seesaw battle with the blade. Like a diamondback striking at prey, the Texan's right hand left his foe's wrist and struck at the man's Adam's apple with tremendous force.

Bishop felt the sickening collapse of the man's throat, and knew the Native was done. Anticipating an attack from the other two, he rolled off, scrambling for his rifle.

Shots rang out, Bishop's body automatically cringing with the expected impact of bullets slicing through his flesh. His hand closed on the carbine at the same moment he spun to face the attackers.

One of the remaining Natives was just hitting the ground,

clutching his chest with a grimace as he fell off his horse. The leader, slumping over in the saddle, let out a low moan of pain, his hand at his stomach. Terri stood with her 9mm fully extended in one arm, a wide-eyed Hunter in the other. Bishop's son started screaming in terror just as the third and final foe hit the ground.

The couple exchanged a quick glance, Bishop mouthing, "Thank you," to his bride.

Two of the tree attackers were still alive, the man with the crushed throat trying desperately to breathe, the other survivor moaning in agony as he withered on the ground.

Bishop moved to make sure neither could reach a weapon, kicking away the two AR15s, and picking up Kevin's long gun. Terri tried to cover the bodies with her weapon while comforting a hysterical Hunter at the same time. As soon as her husband motioned the all clear, she returned the pistol to her fanny pack and began rocking and cooing her son.

"That poor kid is going to be deaf before he hits kindergarten," Bishop said.

"I stuffed his ears with cloth before we came out of the tent," Terri replied. "I think he's more upset over that than the gunfire."

"Well, take it out of his ears. These guys are out of the fight. It's over."

Nodding, Terri proceeded to do just that while Bishop walked between the two wounded men.

It was clear that neither of them were going to survive. For a moment, Bishop pondered putting both of them out of their misery.

As he tried to convince himself it was the humane thing to do, the guy with the crushed throat jerked with a series of violent seizures and then died.

Bishop turned to check on the second fellow just in time to see the man produce a small pistol hidden in his shirt. Before the Texan could shout a warning to Terri, the badly-suffering Native put the weapon against his temple, and pulled the trigger.

"Wow," was all Bishop could manage to mutter as he turned away. The explosive events of the last minute were staggering. It was all too much. "It's not even breakfast yet."

The couple was stunned, Terri walking and rocking Hunter around the campsite, avoiding the bodies that now littered the area. Bishop just went and sat on a rock, staring down at the ground in disbelief.

What had been a pristine island of calm and beauty was now scarred and polluted by violence and blood. It had all happened so quickly.

Hunter eventually settled down, comforted by his mother's embrace and soothing tone. Terri then sat beside Bishop, her voice sad and full of despair. "We are so screwed. You were right, Operation Sacagawea wasn't such a hot idea."

"That's not fair. It was a great plan," he replied, trying to comfort her. "Diana and you were right – we had to do something."

"No," she sniffed, the reality of their situation coming clearer every second. "I got us into this. Now, I've probably managed to get us all killed, and the Alliance will have to go to war. I should've listened to you. I'm sorry."

Bishop didn't respond, instead choosing to wrap his arm around Terri's shoulder and pull her tight against him. His other hand went to Hunter, rubbing the boy's chubby cheek. *This might be our last gentle moment together*, the Texan realized.

But there was no blaming his wife. He had agreed to all this. There wasn't any need for finger pointing or guilt. The locals would be coming… and almost certainly with more than three men. Was this the final chapter? Had their luck finally run out?

The emotion and stress boiled to the surface, sobs racking Terri's frame as Bishop pulled her close. They didn't move or speak, the water's distant babble the only sound in the canyon.

As he knew it would, Terri's inner-strength eventually won out. He'd seen it a dozen times since they'd been together. Where others would melt into a puddle of hysterical nerves, when it all seemed so hopeless, some fire would ignite in her belly and she would come up fighting. More than any other reason, it's why he loved her so.

The first sign of the transformation was the stiffening of her spine and straightening of the shoulders. He knew the words would come next, defiant and unwilling to concede. He waited, and for a brief moment, Bishop thought his wife would have made a great soldier.

"What do we do now? Make a run for Texas? You know they're going to come looking for their friends in a bit," she said, rubbing one last sniffle from her nose.

"They would hunt us down in a matter hours. They have the drones. They outnumber us, and they know the territory."

"We have their horses and guns. We might make it?" she said, trying to insert hope into the conversation.

Hunter reached up, wrapping his tiny hand around his father's finger and flashing a large, toothless grin. "Daaa, baaa," bubbled from the child's throat.

"Did you hear that?" Bishop brightened. "He said da da. He's talking to me!"

Terri had to smile at her husband's excitement. "Yes, I heard it. I think you're right," she agreed.

Bishop took him from her, the dead bodies and smell of

174

blood and cordite forgotten, their forthcoming demise pushed aside. For two minutes, the father tried to solicit another statement from his son.

Despite making every silly noise, funny face, and odd sound he could think of, Bishop couldn't get Hunter to repeat the word. But it didn't matter. Dad was sure he'd heard it, and impending doom aside, the jabbering lightened his mood.

Handing Hunter back, Bishop was inspired, "We're not going to go down easily, my love. Let's get to packing. I'm going to scavenge what I can from our deceased friends, and then we'll ride like the wind for Texas."

Glad her husband had recovered from the dark mood, Terri nodded. "I'm on it," and then hustled off, making ready to bug out.

Bishop approached the horses first, knowing the animals were their only hope. Skittish, and still nervous from the gunfire, he spoke to them in a tone similar to that which Terri had used to soothe Hunter.

After securing the animals, Bishop then began to search the bodies, quickly patting them down and separating the effects into two piles. One they would take with them, the other would remain with the departed.

It was a discomforting act, taking a dead man's possessions. Bishop couldn't help but wonder if the lifeless shells at his feet had families or children. Where did they live? What did they do before the collapse?

Standing over one of the gunshot victims, the Texan peered down at the deceased man's face and realized he didn't even know what the guy looked like. So heavy was the paint on the man's skin, Bishop doubted he would recognize the guy if he had met him just a few hours before. Even the fellow's build was distorted by the turtle shell pads, braided animals bones, and ornate chest plate.

Tilting his head, Bishop smiled. "Terri," he called out. "I've got an idea."

Terri stepped back to admire her handiwork.

Glancing between the dead model at her feet, and her fidgeting husband, she finally nodded. "I think that's it."

They had found pouches of some pigment on the bodies, Terri realizing that mixing the powder with proportional amounts of water resulted in a thick body paint.

175

While Bishop figured out how to don their garb, Terri had set about applying his "makeup."

"That's war paint," Bishop corrected. "Women wear makeup, men wear the colors of battle."

"Uh-huh. Whatever. Other than Mardi Gras, I wouldn't advise this get-up on a regular basis. I just don't think it's you."

She stepped closer, commanding him to "hold still," while she applied a few touchups. "There's my noble savage. You look ready to kick ass and take names. I especially like the long hair. It brings out the bad boy in you... and we all know the girls like the bad boys."

It had been so melancholy, using his knife to trim one of the local's hair from his corpse. Terri, with a patch of cloth, the Indian's headband, and a length of Bishop's fishing line, had fashioned a passable, makeshift "wig."

"War bonnet," Bishop had corrected with a grin.

She had to admit, it was difficult to tell her husband from the men who had just tried to kill them. A thick layer of black, then a second coating of the white and grey accents hid Bishop's naturally lighter complexion. His dark tan from working the ranch helped as well. Now, they had to hope no one else could tell the difference.

Nick said their security team was transient, living in tents, Terri reminded herself. Maybe the guards don't know each other all that well. Bishop might get away with this among strangers.

Bishop scanned the cloudy, grey sky. "Even the weather is with us. The lower the light, the more likely I'll get by with this disguise."

"Are you sure about this?" she asked for the third time. "Riding into the enemy's lair would seem to have its drawbacks."

"Our chances of escaping back to Texas are slim, even with the horses. And if we did manage to return home, that still leaves the Alliance with a huge problem. You wanted to talk to their leader, so let's go talk. The end result can't be worse than our fleeing the territory."

Terri rubbed her chin in thought and then nodded. "It's not any more insane than my little scheme. And like you said, we're probably both dead either way. Why not?"

Bishop grunted, cursed, and struggled to lift the dead bodies onto the horses' backs. When he came to the man with the crushed throat, he turned to Terri and said, "Let me borrow your pistol for a second."

"Huh?" she questioned, handing him the iron anyway.

"Cover Hunter's ears, please."

Using one of his trash bags as a splash guard, Bishop said, "Sorry," and popped two rounds into the dead man's face. The effect was devastating.

"What the hell are you doing?" Terri asked, thinking her husband had finally lost it.

"He's unrecognizable now. Being an imposter has two sides."

Terri got it, but still had to shake her head over the morbid act. "Ewwww," she groaned, turning away from the gore. "Let's hope they don't have a good CSI team. You'd never get away with that on those old television shows."

As Bishop hefted the last man, Terri watched as he managed to drape the corpse over a horse's back and then secured the poor fellow with rope. After double checking the animals were properly tethered together, the Texan mounted the last unoccupied saddle.

"Wait a second," Terri protested, realizing all of the horses were occupied. "Where are Hunter and I supposed to ride?"

"Squaws walk," Bishop said, sticking out his chest. "Especially when they're the spoils of war. Don't you know anything about Indians?"

"I got yer spoils of war... right here, buddy," she growled, pointing at her butt. "And you can just kiss it."

"We'll get around to that once we're back at the teepee," he said, trying to maintain a straight face. "For now, get your spoils of war walking out of this canyon before I decide to ravage my conquest right here and now."

With a defiant tilt of her chin, Terri began walking, grumbling something about paybacks being a bitch.

It was a safe bet that Loggerhead Canyon had never witnessed such a convoy passing through its rocky bastions. Terri and Hunter, the captured prisoners, were followed by Bishop in full Native regalia, the proud warrior returning home, eager to show all that he was still upright in the saddle. Behind the conquering hero plodded the fallen, draped over the remaining two pack animals, along with the prisoner's possessions. It was a procession that seemed to belong to another time and place.

Bishop let Terri pretend to steam, knowing full well that she was aware of how critical appearances were going to be if they had any hope of pulling off the deception.

The Texan-turned-warrior pulled a map from the saddle bag, already having a good idea of their route. Nick and he had studied the area thoroughly before leaving Fort Bliss, including the exact location of the mountain cabin that the big man said was most certainly the locals HQ.

"That's where the white-haired dude lives," Nick had briefed. "That's their primary command and control."

Bishop was also well aware of the ring of booby-traps. Like always, the smallest piece of information was proving critical. He recalled Nick's warning, the former Special Forces operative's voice still fresh in his mind. "The trees are notched about head high with a sideways cross. Stay between the notches, and you'll be fine."

They followed the meandering trail, Bishop's confidence in their route bolstered by a set of fresh hoof prints when the path crossed the stream.

They came to a fork, one branch leading off into the forest. "Go left," Bishop said.

As soon as they entered into the cover of the thick woods, Bishop stopped the caravan. "Okay, we're out of the open. Come on back."

After setting Hunter down, he lifted Terri onto the horse and then handed her the child. A moment later he was behind her, wrapping his arms around her waist and spurring the animal to continue. "Your ass looked so hot, baby, I just had to have you in my arms," he breathed in her ear.

"You smell so bad, I'm thinking it might be better to walk," she teased, knowing Bishop's snarky remarks helped him release stress in situations like this.

They continued, the trail gradually climbing into the mountains, passing through forests that in any other circumstances would have inspired awe with their natural beauty.

And then it began to rain.

It was just a spit of moisture at first, Bishop cocking his ear as the drops struck the canopy of green above them. What little light was penetrating to the forest floor dimmed, and then the clouds opened up.

"Shit, my makeup… err… war paint is going to run," Bishop complained, looking around for any type of shelter.

"To hell with your costume, Bishop. This rain is icy. Hunter and I will catch our death of cold in this crap."

Dismounting, Bishop rushed back to his pack, digging out two of the ever-handy leaf bags. With a flash of his knife and a section of paracord, he fashioned a quick poncho for his wife and child. A few moments later, he was covered in black plastic as well. The horses and the dead were on their own.

"I don't know if this hurts or helps," he said to Terri, climbing back up to sit behind her. "Do the Natives use trash bags for shelter?"

"Hell if I know," she said, obviously disgusted with the rain and cold. "You're the one who watched all those Old Western horse operas. How did the Indians keep dry in the movies?"

"I don't know. It never rained."

"Well, at least these hoods cover our faces. That should help... a little." she added, checking to make sure Hunter could breathe and was staying dry.

Onward they plodded, the horses splashing through the puddles while Terri continued to fuss with her raincoat, unable to keep all parts of her body dry at the same time.

Bishop was about to increase her misery. "You're going to have to walk again here in a minute. Sorry."

"Why?"

"We're getting close to the location where Nick said their security perimeter begins. If I was really a warrior with a captive, you'd be walking. You know that, right?"

"Yes."

"Sorry. You can keep the poncho though."

"Thanks."

The thunder and wind began to intensify as she dismounted, the blowing rain seeming to find every nook and cranny of her makeshift cover. "This sucks," she announced with little fanfare. "You're going to pay later when you have to massage my poor, little toes and wait on me hand and foot for a week."

"Keep your pistol handy," Bishop warned. "I'm not sure how thoroughly they will check us out."

"Gotcha."

"And try to look like a miserable wretch who just lost her husband and is sure she's about to be raped and plundered."

"That's not going to be difficult," Terri replied. "At least the miserable part."

"Which part?" Bishop shouted over the raging storm, unable to hear his wife's words. "The rape and plunder, or the losing your husband?"

Terri half turned and announced, "Undecided at this point."

On they plodded, fighting the elements, the uphill trail making it all the worse on Terri. Bishop's heart went out to her, the Texan occupying his mind with how he would make it up to his bride when all this was over. If they survived.

And then, in the middle of a pine thicket, there was a man standing in the trail, a battle rifle across his chest.

Bishop heard the others coming in from each side, four men surrounding them in less than a second.

The man in charge of the guard post walked up and looked at Terri, but only for a second. Without a word, he continued past her, making to inspect the bodies hanging over the pack animals.

"What happened," he said, looking up at Bishop's hooded face.

"The man put up a fight," came the Texan's reply.

179

The guard's attention went back to the dead, his hand grabbing a handful of hair to lift the head of the body adorned with Bishop's clothes.

Right as the hollowed, grotesque, half-face came into view, a bolt of lightning flashed, the effect causing the guard to jump back in horror.

Shaking his head in disgust and a little embarrassed at his reaction, the man then turned back to Bishop and questioned, "Are you hurt, brother?"

"Not too bad," Bishop replied. "I was lucky."

"Take them on up," came the reply. "Grandfather will want to interview the woman and see their possessions. There's hot tea at the camp."

And then they were past, relief flooding through Bishop's bones.

After they were well past the sentries, Terri chanced a quick glance back at her husband, a sly twinkle in her eye. "Love you," she mouthed, and they turned back to continue up the trail.

They came to a compound, three outbuildings appearing through the mist and rain. Just like Nick had described, Bishop made out the main cabin, garage, and what the big man assumed was a workshop or barn. The Texan's eye went immediately to the garage, looking for any sign of Kevin or the other prisoner.

"You there," he barked at Terri over the wind. "Go to the main house. Grandfather will speak to you there."

As they approached the home, another Native American appeared on the porch, his eye skeptical of the newly arriving rider and captive.

Rather than challenge Bishop, he asked, "How many did we lose?"

"Two," the Texan replied, keeping his head low so the rain would run off of his hood. "But her man is dead, and their goods are on my horse."

"And her?"

"She and the child didn't resist."

"Bring her and their possessions inside; leave his body out here on the horse. Grandfather will want to know what you learned from the stranger before he died."

Then he walked to the end of the porch, shouting orders to another group of men huddled under the workshop's awning where they were trying to stay dry.

Bishop tensed as three of the onlookers ducked into the rain and then scurried toward him. But they were only after the horses... and their dead comrades.

One of them handed Bishop his own pack, for Grandfather

180

to inspect, and then they were off, leading the animals and their ghoulish cargo away.

The porch-guard turned, meaning to walk inside. Bishop stepped up behind Terri and gave her a shove with his rifle barrel. "Go!" he commanded, hoping she wouldn't turn around and smack him.

They entered the log home, the room warm and inviting, a wood burning stove roaring away in the corner. Bishop reached up and roughly tore away Terri's poncho, and shoved her again, indicating she should stand by the stove.

He had to admit, she looked the part. With purple lips quivering from the cold, her hair was in complete disarray, a mess of wet, matted strands. Covering the captive with his rifle, Bishop set his pack down in the middle of the floor and stepped back to a carefully chosen position in the darkest corner.

The guard appeared again, this time followed by the now-infamous white wizard.

Hack ignored what he thought was one of the Apache warriors, moving instead to get a better look at Terri. The protective, shivering mother flinched when he reached for the blanket covering Hunter's face. "What is his name?" Hack inquired in a mellow tone.

"Hun... Hunter," Terri managed, her voice croaking in apparent fear.

"And how old is Mr. Hunter?" came the next question.

Before Terri could respond, Bishop moved, the flash suppressor on his carbine pressing against the guard's right ear. "That's enough," the Texan growled. "Now it's my turn to start asking questions."

Bishop took the stunned guard's weapon, and then pulled back his hood. "Allow me to make the introductions. My name is Bishop, and this is my wife Terri," he said. "We want to talk."

Hack was initially confused, his eyes darting back and forth between Bishop and the guard. Terri's voice came from the stove, "Actually," she said, pulling her pistol from under Hunter's blanket, "I'm going to do the talking, and you're going to listen."

"What is it you want?" came the old man's shaky voice, finally realizing what was going down.

"First things first," Bishop replied. "Where are the two men you are holding captive?"

Hack started to answer, but the bodyguard cut him off. "You'll never get out of here. Drop your weapons, and I'll give you my word you won't be harmed."

Pressing the sharp metal of the flash suppressor further into the guard's ear, Bishop said, "That's not what's going to happen, Chief. We are going to retrieve my colleagues, and then we can all sit around and have a nice, friendly, little chat. After walking through the rain and cold, I think my wife deserves to be heard. If you, or the men outside, decide to get clever, Grandfather gets it first. Understood?"

The Apache nodded, the motion causing Bishop's steel to dig deeper into his ear.

Bishop then turned to Hack and declared, "My friend and I are going to go retrieve the captives. If he tries any shit, my wife will kill you. She is a crack shot, and completely without inhibition. She's already sent two men to the happy hunting grounds this morning, and the day is still young. Do you understand?"

"Yes. But you people don't have to do...."

Terri moved forward, her pistol pointblank on the bridge of Hack's nose. "My husband, as usual, is being so politically correct. I actually *enjoy* shooting assholes."

With Apache Jack to his front, Bishop pulled up his hood and said, "Let's go. Get clever, and I'll give you a haircut with 5.56mm lead. And just so you know, I'm a horrible barber."

While Terri covered Hack in the main house, the duo went out the front door, Bishop's carbine ready to cut down the guard. They splashed through the rain, walking quickly to a side door of the garage where the Indian produced a key.

The on-duty sentry seemed surprised to see his boss entering at such an hour, his confusion increasing as Bishop followed Jack through the door. "What's going on?" he asked.

Bishop's rifle butt was his answer, the stroke knocking the sentry halfway across the tiny room.

In the corner, the Texan saw a man rise off a folding cot and knew instantly it was the Colonel's son.

"Unlock his chains," Bishop ordered, shoving the Apache toward the prisoner.

The PJ didn't make a sound as his shackles were removed, standing quickly and making eye contact with Bishop. The Texan said, "I'm an old friend of your father's from HBR. You okay?"

Sergeant Grissom nodded, "I can walk... and fight a little if need be."

"Good," the Texan noted before redirecting his gaze to Apache Jack. "Where's the boy?"

"In there," came the response as the Native nodded toward another door.

"Well, let him out," Bishop ordered, growing impatient with the fellow's negative attitude.

Again, the local produced a key ring and opened the door. "He can't walk," he explained, stepping aside so Bishop could see Kevin lying inside.

The lad looked up, unsure of who Bishop was given his

disguise. "Kevin, it's me, Bishop."

"Mr. Bishop?" the kid replied, obviously puzzled.

"Yup. Terri's with me at the house. We've come to get you out."

"How's my dad?" was the first question. "I saw him go down."

"He's fine. Grim got him back to the hospital at Bliss just in time. He'll be okay."

Kevin swung his leg off the cot, a heavy white cast covering the limb from mid-thigh to mid-calf. "I can hop, sir," the brave young man bragged.

Grissom stepped up, "I can carry him on my good shoulder... if we're aren't going too far."

A few minutes later, the foursome was again out in the storm, the Apache followed by Bishop and the former prisoners.

The gaggle of guards had returned to the dryness of the awning, obviously curious about all of the strange activity. One of the more observant sentries chanced the rain, wading through the muck to intercept his boss. "What's going on?" he challenged, staring hard at the previously confined captives.

Apache Jack, despite having Bishop's weapon at his back, shouted a string of words the Texan couldn't understand, and then took off running.

Absolute bedlam erupted.

"Go! Go for the house," Bishop shouted over his shoulder, bringing his carbine into play.

The group of loitering security men finally got it, two of them trying to bring their weapons around. But they were slow.

With a steady arch of brass ejecting from his weapon, Bishop poured lead into their ranks, splinters and chunks of the workshop flying in all directions. One of the sentries dropped instantly, the others scrambling, crawling, and running for cover. The Texan silently cursed his lack of practice with the iron sights.

The PJ did his best, groaning and sliding with the weight of Kevin's body and the rain-slick forest floor, but he was sluggish and clumsy.

To cover their escape, Bishop stayed at the PJ's back, throwing three rounds left, five right, and then spraying the center with an extended stream of suppressive pills.

The security men reacted quickly, an ever increasing amount of incoming fire chasing Bishop and his friends back toward the house.

Lead whizzed past the Texan's head, some of the rounds throwing up mud and grit, others zipping through the heavy air like angry insects hell-bent on revenge. Bishop felt naked without his armor. When his foot finally reached the porch's bottom step, the blizzard of bullets suddenly stopped.

They don't want to hit the Great White Wizard, Bishop thought. That's handy to know.

The Texan backed into the cabin, finding the PJ already struggling to load one of the weapons Bishop had captured at the campground. Kevin, having been dumped on the couch, was trying to reach his sniper rifle lying nearby on the floor. His wife had her pistol up against Grandfather's temple, Hunter still cradled in the nook of her free arm.

"I take it that didn't go as planned," she panted, charged-up from the eruption of gunfire and sudden rush of wet, hard-breathing men bursting into the room.

"You might say that," he responded, watching from the corner of the window to make sure the guards outside kept their distance.

With Grissom now covering Hack, Terri went to check on Kevin. "Miss Terri, you don't know how glad I am to see you guys," the kid greeted. "Can you hand me that rifle, please?"

"Get him some ammo, too," Bishop directed from his perch at the window. "We may need his help."

Once Kevin was again armed and dangerous, Bishop helped the kid hobble to the window, using the logs from the stove's wood basket to build the sharpshooter a nice little fighting nest. "Yell if they look like they're organizing for a rush," Bishop ordered.

"Yes, sir... and thank you, sir. I feel a lot better with my rifle back in my hands."

Bishop then recommended Grissom take the rear of the house, handing the PJ three spare magazines he'd taken off of the dead at the campground. "You got it," the sergeant replied. "How long do we have to hold out?"

"Well... I'm not sure," the Texan replied. "That kind of depends."

Grissom started to ask for clarification, but then just shrugged. "I've got the back side of this hacienda. You take care of business out here," and then made for the rear of the cabin.

"What is it you people want?" Hack asked, genuine fear finally sinking in. "Take what you want and leave me alone."

Terri exchanged looks with her husband, and then smiled at the toymaker.

"Let's go have a seat and talk like regular people," she said.

Bishop, now soaked and cold, decided he'd make coffee while his wife delivered her spiel. Digging through his pack for the makings, he gauged the amount of surplus water in his wife's clothes and asked, "Want a cup of joe while you're talking?"

"Coffee?" Hack perked at the word. "You have coffee?"

"Yes, we do," Terri responded. "Would you like a cup?"

Chapter 14

With his hands surrounding the cup of steaming brew, Hack sat at the kitchen table, studying the young lady and sleeping child across from him. "However this all turns out, I want to thank you for this," he said, nodding towards the coffee. "I thought I'd never enjoy the pleasure again."

"We actually came here to offer you similar goods and services, and much, much more," Terri began. "We are not your enemy."

"Who is 'we?' Are you from the Alliance or the U.S. government?"

"Both," Terri answered honestly. "But I can only make an agreement in the Alliance's name. The president in Washington must approve any negotiations for the U.S. side. I wouldn't worry about that too much, however. My husband and he are on excellent terms."

Hack shook his head, her words seeming so strange and out of place. "You'll pardon me, but I'm having a little trouble taking you seriously. The two of you look like common vagabonds to me, not a diplomatic envoy."

Kevin, listening from his perch at the front window, called back to the kitchen, "Believe her, sir. That's Miss Terri. She's the real deal."

With a slight blush, Terri grinned at the lad's statement, and then proceeded to answer in her own words, "We were in disguise for several reasons, not the least of which was we couldn't figure out any other way to approach you or your people. It seemed the previous two attempts had resulted in violence and death. We thought this was a better alternative."

Hack looked around at a house full of armed, diligent men holding him at gunpoint. "So taking me hostage was the preferred method?"

Terri snorted, peering over her cup with a sly grin. "This wasn't our intent. Actually, my husband is an engineer, and we hoped to be offered employment on your irrigation project. That, as the plan went, would allow us to meet whoever was running the show, and then we would approach peacefully."

"So you were going to resort to espionage and subterfuge, instead of an outright assault?"

"No, we were going to approach from a position of trust. We weren't spying on you. There's no need. We're well aware of exactly what you're doing."

Hack used a sip of coffee as an excuse to gather his

thoughts. After savoring the hot liquid, he responded, "Okay, I'll stop being contentious. Please continue."

"I'll be blunt and to the point, so we have a chance to make significant progress before your friends outside get stupid and try to storm the house. The Alliance will not allow its water supply to be cut off. We are willing to share, trade, barter, and enter into a formal treaty if necessary, but we won't allow our primary agricultural regions to be denied water."

As Terri expected, Hack's spine stiffened at the stark threat she had tabled. "I don't see they have much choice," he stated with an edge. "I'm sure, if you are who you claim to be, that you're aware of our recent acquisition of nuclear materials. We have a delivery mechanism and the will to use it if attacked."

"So you won't rethink your new irrigation system?"

"Why should we?" Hack said firmly. "Look, these people... the tribes, have been shit on and abused for over 400 years. Now, the tide is about to turn. With our agriculture output and rule of law, we can start all over again and eventually return the Indian Nations back to the prominence they deserve. Go find your own water – or attack if need be. But let me warn you, we will lay waste to vast stretches of Texas and the Mid-west. We have the materials and know-how to do so."

"Oh, no one is going to attack you. That option was taken off our table long ago, and Washington could care less what you do with the water. No, we pose no military threat whatsoever."

Again, Hack was confused by Terri's seemingly contradictory positions. "I don't get it. You make bold statements about 'won't allow,' yet you claim to be nonviolent."

"Simple," Terri grinned. "Even as we speak, Alliance engineers are in Colorado, just north of your territory." She then turned toward the living room and raised her voice, "Bishop? Do you still have that map?"

"Yup," he replied, joining them in the kitchen after changing into regular clothes.

The Texan unfolded a map and pointed with his finger. "This area is the San Luis Valley in southern Colorado. After approximately three months of earth moving with our heavy equipment, we can reroute the Rio Grande through northern Oklahoma and into the Texas Panhandle. According to the studies I've seen, this project would actually increase our agricultural output by over 40%."

Hack snatched the map, pulling it closer to study. After a bit, he glared at Terri with fire in his eyes. "You can't do that. You would starve out what little food we manage to grow now. This entire region depends on that river."

"Why not?" Terri shrugged innocently. "You didn't seem to

care if we starved. Good for the goose, good for the gander I always say."

The expression on Hack's face was cold and angry, but Terri sensed he was beginning to see the light. "What do you want?" he finally asked.

"We're willing to share the water, much like the pre-collapse arrangements that existed between the states. We also want to be your trading partner. Like that coffee in your cup, we have a lot to offer."

"Such as?"

Terri rolled her eyes, "Such as? It's Texas, for Pete's sake. We have fields of pipe and valves and all sorts of fluid handling equipment lying around. Our experts believe you can build a much more efficient irrigation system with plumbing as opposed to flooding. We refine gas and diesel. We have seafood, and are starting to produce medicines. The list could go on and on."

Glancing down at the map and then at Bishop's rifle, Hack said, "It doesn't seem like you're giving me much choice."

Terri shook her head, "No, we're giving you every choice. Believe me when I say that our ruling council had significant dissenting voices that opposed even opening a dialog with you. Many of them wanted to simply initiate the Colorado project, and let you wither in the sun.

"And why didn't you?"

"Because life is difficult enough these days. That's not what the Alliance is about. We all need each other more than ever before. So when the choice comes down to either establishing a strong trading partner or starving tens of thousands of people, our value system guides us to the high road. Hasn't there already been enough suffering and death?"

Hack looked sad, mumbled, "I see."

"What do you have to lose?" Bishop asked, not understanding the man's reaction. "Our estimates say that you were going to have enough irrigated land to grow ten times the amount of crops necessary to feed the local population. If we work together, you can still have an excess for export and trade, plus a strong ally to boot. I don't see the downside to this solution."

"Prominence," Hack replied. "Prestige, respect, security... a future for those people out there. They are good people. They deserve a land of plenty and the independence that excess capacity would provide them for generations. Now it appears that they are going to be denied yet again."

The discussion continued, Hack asking questions, Terri providing answers. The entire back and forth repartee annoyed Bishop, Hack seeming to want to know every possible detail of

188

the Alliance's offer.

Terri had just uttered "We can work out those details later," for the nth time when Bishop decided it was time to stretch his legs, and get out of the kitchen before he said something to undermine his wife's efforts.

"Mister Bishop," came Kevin's voice from the window. "Do you have a minute?"

Bishop left the kitchen, moving quickly to join Kevin. Peering around the window's edge, the Texan couldn't see why the kid had sounded the alarm.

"What's up, Kevin? Looks nice and quiet to me."

"Sir, I know it's not my place, but that's the problem. My dad once told me if things are going well, I'm probably walking into an ambush. I haven't seen anyone move out there for 45 minutes."

Scratching his stubble-coated chin, Bishop had to admit the kid had a point.

"Keep frosty," Bishop finally replied. "I'm going to go check around back."

Sergeant Grissom reported the same unnerving lack of movement. "I thought they were all out front," he said. "This can't be good."

It then dawned on the Texan that Hack was stalling.

Strolling back to the in-process meeting, Bishop remembered the stolen nuclear materials. "He's stalling. They're up to something," he growled.

He grabbed Hack's chair, spinning the shocked man around and coming nose to nose. "Where are your Indian friends, sir? I know you're stalling... what are they up to?"

Whether from fear or pride, Hack didn't respond, and it pissed Bishop off. He could see the loathing in the man's eyes, almost a celebration of having deceived them for so long.

Without hesitation, the Texan turned to his flabbergasted wife and barked, "Hand me your pistol."

"What?" Terri started, "What are you doing, Bishop?"

"Hand me the fucking gun," he snapped, reaching for her belt and the holstered weapon.

Terri knew from the look in her husband's eyes that something was terribly wrong. Before she could even reach for her sidearm, he had yanked it from the leather.

Bishop flicked off the safety and pointed the barrel at Hack's foot. "You better start talking, right now, or I'll use 9mm lead to chew off parts of your body until you're singing like a bird. Now, out with it... what are your friends up to?"

Hack's mouth twisted into an evil grin, "You're too late, asshole. It's already done."

"What's already done?"

189

Hack hesitated, his mouth firmly sealed, the twinkle of skullduggery glinting behind his eyes.

Bishop fired.

In the enclosed space, the roar of the handgun made everyone jump. The deafening report was immediately followed by a howl of pain coming from deep inside the toymaker's chest.

"What's already done?" Bishop screamed, moving the pistol to the other foot.

Hack was trying to cry, breathe, moan, and protest all at once. "Fuck you!" he yelled between gasps of breath. "It's over! I warned them! I told them to stay away!"

Bishop fired again, watching as Hack's body seized, bouncing up and down in the chair, the man's eyes rolling into the back of his head. No one noticed that the Texan had intentionally missed the inventor's other foot by more than an inch.

"This gun holds 17 rounds," Bishop screamed, fury and rage thick in his throat. "I've got 15 left. Now start talking before I move on to more painful parts of your worthless carcass."

When the pistol moved between Hack's legs, the man found words. "They're launching the balloons, you fool. There's no stopping them. They're automatic."

Bishop paused, trying to figure out what Hack was saying. His mind went back to a cautionary phrase he'd heard his father use long ago, "… when they send up the balloons."

It was slang from a period when the old Soviet Union and the United States threatened each other with thousands of intercontinental ballistic missiles. "Sending up the balloon," meant launching those weapons - and the end of the world.

Turning to Terri, he said, "He's been stalling you while his friends are doing something with that stolen radioactive shit."

Back to Hack, "What are they doing? Where are they?"

Nearly hysterical with pain, Hack was sobbing so badly he could hardly speak.

Bishop didn't know the capability of the stolen materials. He had no clue as to their capability, range, or potential. What he did know was the fear he'd seen in Nick's eyes and the grim expression on General Owens' face when the topic had been broached.

His mind filled with visions of more bodies, more graves, and droves of sick and dying people. He pictured vast swaths of unusable land, dying crops, and suffering livestock.

Those grave thoughts were soon replaced with the Colonel's face, twisted in anger over the Alliance's meddling in the affair. Tanks, gunships, and artillery would soon follow, the United States provoked to the point of war. More dying. More suffering. More bodies.

And all because of one man. All because of the individual sitting right there, defiant and proud of the horrors he'd just unleashed on mankind.

Bishop grabbed a handful of white hair and with strength born of pure adrenalin and wrath lifted Hack from his perch.

He didn't hear Terri's protests, couldn't register Hack's screams of pain and torment.

Hack still managed to kick both of his feet despite one suffering a bullet wound. He howled in misery as the Texan dragged him into the front room and toward the wood burning stove.

With his free hand, Bishop opened the iron door and gazed for a moment into the licking flames and glowing embers.

He released Hack's hair, allowing the injured man to fall with a thump to the floor. And then Bishop had the man's arm in an iron grip, pulling it toward the stove's inferno.

Somehow the Texan's intent registered in Hack's mind. Whether it was the heat on his skin, or the look of pure hatred in Bishop's eyes, the toymaker realized what was about to happen.

"Wait! Wait! No!" Hack pleaded in a shrill voice. "Oh, God! No!"

Bishop didn't heed the request, his eyes reflecting the red and yellow blaze inside the iron belly. "This is a preview of hell," he grumbled as Hack's now-closed fist was poised at the threshold. "I'm going to burn both of your arms down to stubs."

"I'll tell you! I'll tell you!" came the screamed surrender as the heat from the coals flooded Hack's brain.

Bishop paused, holding tight, Hack's struggles to withdraw his limb worthless against the vice-like grip that held it.

"They're at the mine. They're launching weather balloons with the Cobalt attached to detonators," tumbled the rushed confession.

"Where is the mine?"

"Just northwest of here. On the ridge. Less than a mile. There are seven balloons, seven cases of Cobalt."

"How do I disable them?" Bishop asked.

"You can't. They're on automatic altimeters. When they reach 80,000 feet, the radiation will be released."

Bishop released his grip on Hack's arm, motioning for Grissom to tend the toymaker's wound. Turning to his shocked wife, the Texan shook his head. "I think we're fucked."

"Can we get in touch with Bliss? Have them send airplanes to shoot them down?"

Bishop looked out the window, noting the dusk. "I don't know.... Even if we could call them, can the plane's radar see the balloons? It's going to be dark in just a few minutes. No way they'll be able to see them at night."

"They can't be shot down?" Terri asked, getting desperate.

"Hell, I don't know. Who has ever shot at weather balloons?"

"What about this, Mr. Bishop?" Kevin said, holding up his sniper rifle.

The Texan paused, trying to run the numbers in his head. "Maybe I can stop some of them."

"Every one you bring down means fewer people that will suffer," Terri added.

Nodding, Bishop rushed to fill his pack with magazines. Grissom looked up from Hack's bleeding foot and said, "My night vision and equipment is in the back room. I saw it there. That will help us."

"You have to stay here, Sergeant. You're hurt and besides, somebody has to protect my wife and son and keep an eye on this madman," Bishop said, glancing at Hack.

"I can help, sir," Kevin announced, reaching across for one of the guard's discarded carbines. "I can't walk, but I can still shoot."

Terri was holding her pistol, "Don't go alone, Bishop. Take Grissom with you. Kevin and I can hold down the fort until you get back."

Nodding, Bishop motioned for Grissom to get his shit together. "If you slow me down, I'll leave you behind. Let's roll."

As the PJ was scrambling around, Hack continued to moan and whimper. A thought occurred to Grissom. Reopening his medical kit, he produced an item resembling a cigar tube. "This will make him easier to manage, and reduce his whining," he announced.

"What is it?" Terri asked.

"Morphine," came the response. "He'll be in happy land in less than five minutes."

Everyone watched as Grissom flipped off the end cap with his thumb and then plunged the device into Hack's thigh. The reaction was nearly instantaneous.

The Texan saw the PJ stuffing something in a pouch on his vest. "What's that?" he asked, a hint of hope in his voice.

"It's my Sat-phone," came the reply. "Will that help?"

"Can you call Fort Bliss?" Bishop asked.

"I can't call anyone unless they have a telephone system up and running. I only used it to file our status reports. I don't even know who I was talking to or where they're located."

"Could they radio Bliss?" Terri continued to push.

"I'm not sure. We can try."

The PJ switched the unit on, punching a series of buttons while studying the screen. He held the unit like a phone and waited.

"CONUS CIC, state your business," came the warbled answer.

"This is Rat-pack 3. Repeat, this is Rat-pack 3, I need to speak with the OD (Officer on Duty)."

"Wait one."

The sergeant's eyes darted between Bishop and Terri, knowing they were very short on time. Finally, after what seemed like forever, a voice came on the line. "Go Rat-pack 3."

"I need a communication sent to Fort Bliss. Is that possible?"

"Umm... I'm not sure. Describe the situation, please."

Rolling his eyes at the desk-jockey's fear of messing up, the PJ stated the main reason. "There are 90 pounds of highly radioactive material that may have just been launched toward Texas. I need help in stopping the attack. I need to get a message through to Bliss – right now."

There was a pause at the other end, Grissom sure he could hear voices talking it over. "What's the message, Rat-pack 3? We'll do our best."

It dawned on the PJ that he didn't know what to say. Frustrated and knowing time was running out, he said, "Details to follow," and handed Bishop the phone.

The Texan didn't hesitate, "This message is for General Owens and Diana Brown. Sacagawea requires extract at HQ. Repeat, Sacagawea requires extract at HQ. Come heavy."

The officer on the other end read Bishop the message back, and then the call was disconnected.

Three minutes later, Bishop and Grissom were rushing out the door.

Diana was at the base hospital, nervously speculating over Bishop and Terri's progress. A knock on the doorframe caused both patient and visitor to glance up, a bright faced young man in uniform standing in the threshold.

"I have an urgent message for Miss Diana Brown," he said, producing a sealed envelope.

After thanking the messenger, Diana tore open the package and pulled out a single sheet of paper. She read it aloud to Nick, unsure of the meaning.

193

The big man tried to sit up, a grimace of pain stopping that maneuver cold. "They're asking for someone to come and get them," he said. "General Owens needs to know about this right away."

Diana scanned the paper again, "It says here the general was copied on the message."

On cue, the base's commander appeared in the doorway, getting right down to business. "I've been on the radio with the Pentagon. It was one of their original team members who called this in. He said that their PJ made the call, but then a strange voice sounded the message. What do you make of that?"

"Can we listen to a recording of their call?"

"Yes, it's on the way over here. Sorry to interrupt your rest, Nick, but there's something on this transmission that wasn't included in the original message."

"Oh?"

"You'll see... or rather hear it for yourself in just a moment."

A few moments later, another soldier knocked on the door, carrying a laptop computer under his arm. With the general's permission, he opened the lid, and the room was filled with a voice identifying himself as Rat-pack 3.

And then Grissom's statement about the 90 pounds of Cobalt-60 played, the two Alliance leaders both growing pale at the same moment.

Diana and Nick continued to listen intently, some relief filling the room when Bishop's voice streamed through the speakers. "They're still alive!" Diana reacted happily.

Owens quickly put a damper on any celebration. "My friend at the Pentagon warned me not to send in troops. They are hopping mad about the radiation release, and even more pissed that we have people inside New Mexico. What are your orders?"

Nick and Diana exchanged a glance, Nick knowing exactly what the Alliance leader had in mind. "If we can get a couple of Blackhawks ready, I think we have a reasonable solution to the political side of the problem," Diana said.

"My birds are your birds," Owens replied. "What's the plan?"

Grim was just retiring for the evening, bored with his book, and having already cleaned his weapon twice. His wife had made a grand dinner, sensing her husband needed a pick-me-up. As usual, the contractor didn't volunteer any information about what was troubling him so.

The small bungalow in Alpha had been a gift from the Alliance, allowing Grim to relocate his wife and daughter away from Memphis and The Circus. Everyone seemed to be happier in the small Texas town.

Normally, when at home between missions with the SAINT teams, Grim was all about spending time with his family. He'd learned long ago that time was precious, and he might not be coming home from the next deployment.

Every minute he could spend with his girls was priceless and to be relished.

But not this time. Grim had returned from New Mexico sullen and withdrawn. His wife had seen the same pattern of behavior a few times before, some female instinct apprising her that her husband had suffered the loss of someone near and dear. She'd found quiet, unconditional love was the best therapy.

Peeking in on his sleeping daughter, Grim heard the car engine. Even in Alpha, with the supply of fuel increasing every day, a motor at this time of night was unusual.

The knock on the front door was really weird.

With a pistol in his belt, Grim answered, surprised to see a soldier in uniform standing on his porch. The first thing that went through the contractor's mind was the ruckus he'd caused at Bliss. Had some asshat officer decided to press additional charges?

"Yes," Grim answered, trying to decide if he was going to cooperate with the young man.

"Sir, there's been a message received from New Mexico. Councilwoman Brown has requested your presence at Fort Bliss. She further added that you should come ready to deploy, sir."

A smile stretched across Grim's face when his wife appeared from the bedroom in her robe. "What's wrong, hun?" she asked with a sleepy voice.

"They need me at Bliss," he answered, kissing her cheek as he went by. "Sorry... but I have to run."

Grim's kit was all packed and ready in the corner. Hefting his weapon and ruck, the contractor turned and dashed back to his wife. "Tell my little girl her daddy loves her. And the same goes for you. I shouldn't be gone long. Just going out for some milk."

That last statement caused his wife to smile. "Going out for some milk," was their secret code phrase meaning, "I'm all right. I'll be back soon. I love you. I have to do this."

After a quick hug and kiss, Grim was eagerly bounding down the front steps, hefting his pack toward the waiting Humvee.

"I'm coming, Kevin," he whispered. "I'm on my way, kid.

We're walking out together this time."

It didn't take Bishop long to find the balloon launchers.

The first hint was one of the silver colored units reflecting a glowing silver as its height caught the last of the sun's rays. It was nearly impossible to miss against the backdrop of the dark sky.

"Aren't you going to shoot it?" Grissom asked, pointing toward the still low balloon.

"If I do, they'll know we're coming. I want to get as many as I can in the first salvo. That thing's not moving very fast. I don't think it will escape."

The next clue regarding the location of the launchpad was the sighting of several beams from at least a dozen flashlights moving in every imaginable direction.

"Shit... looks like there are a lot of guys down there," Bishop noted.

They continued stalking through the woods, coming close enough that they could make out the distant sound of human voices.

Grissom motioned with his hand, indicating a nearby hill. "The high ground," whispered the PJ.

Nodding, Bishop headed toward what he hoped would be a good position to snipe the balloons. They climbed briefly, Grissom moving as well as any man Bishop had ever worked with. *This guy knows his shit*, Bishop thought. *I'm glad Terri made me bring him along.*

They advanced to an overlook, gazing down on a meadow bustling with activity. There were at least 20 people below, scrambling back and forth between the old mine and an open grassland.

Bishop counted four balloons in various stages of being inflated, one in the final preparations of being launched.

"How many holes do I have to punch in one of those things before they plummet back to the ground?"

"No idea. Like you said back at the house, who shoots down balloons?" Grissom responded.

"So there are three in the air," Bishop said, turning to examine the one that had just floated overhead.

"I can see two of them," the Texan whispered, clearly excited. "One is just a speck, but the other two... I think I've got a shot. They sure don't move very fast."

"I bet all that nuclear junk is heavy. Hell, that guy back there might have it all wrong. Maybe they won't climb so high."

Scanning the sky with the big rifle's optic, Bishop found the third. "I've got all three of them. One is way, way out of my range. But the other two... maybe."

"Do it," Grissom replied, readying his carbine to protect their position.

Bishop chambered a round in the .338's massive breech and began prioritizing his targets. "When I open up on the balloons that are already aloft, you start poking holes in the ones down there."

"Got it," the sergeant replied, taking aim.

The Texan first examined the closer targets, bringing the nearly inflated unit into the rifle's powerful optic. He judged the size between two of the hash marks in the scope's glass, and then looked back to see if he could estimate an accurate range to the furthest airborne target.

Judging the significant bullet drop, Bishop centered above the floating target and squeezed the trigger.

Kevin's blaster kicked a lot more than Bishop's .308 or carbines, the impact against his shoulder surprising the Texan. It was a lot louder, too.

He watched eagerly, waiting to see if his bullet did any damage. After three full seconds, it dawned on Bishop that he had no idea if he was hitting the target – or not. It was frustrating, ramping up the already high levels of stress.

Sergeant Grissom soon offered a solution.

After waiting to see if Bishop's attempt provided any results, the PJ opened up on the valley below, picking the balloon nearest departure. With one shot, the entire thing exploded in a brilliant flash of light and flame that sent shadows across the entire mountain.

Bishop pivoted, wondering what the hell had just happened.

"They're using hydrogen to fill them. You'll know if you hit one," Grissom reported. "Remember the Hindenburg!" he shouted, firing another round into the next target. It too erupted in a brilliant flash of flame and thunder.

That was all Bishop needed to know.

Now he wasn't so concerned about bullet drop, spin, and wind.

Shouldering Kevin's mega-blaster, the Texan cut loose, rapidly working the bolt and walking his rounds into the drifting prey.

Three shots later, a micro-sized yellow and red sun appeared in the New Mexico sky, the sphere of light indicating the Texan had found the mark.

The closer balloon exploded with only two attempts.

Just when Bishop was beginning to feel better about the whole thing, bullets started whacking and thumping into their hide.

"I think they found us," Grissom reported as he nailed the last balloon.

"I think they're pissed that we shot their toys," Bishop responded, bringing his rifle around.

He scanned the valley, able to pick out only vague shadows and glimpses of rushing bodies. "They'll be coming this way soon," warned the PJ. "I'd prefer not to be here when they get their shit together."

And then something different came into the Texan's optic. For less than a second, he thought there were hot water heaters down below. "I've got the hydrogen tanks," he announced to Grissom. "This ought to slow them down a bit."

Centering the cross-hairs, Bishop fired. The result was spectacular.

With an ear-splitting clap, the entire area was bathed in a white-hot flash of heat and light. Both of the snipers were temporarily blinded as the thunderous report rolled and echoed over the mountains.

The return fire from below ceased.

"Let's get the hell out of here," Bishop directed, taking a last, long look at the balloon that got away.

Chapter 15

The two men hustled back to the cabin, finding Terri anxiously waiting by the door. "What happened? I saw and heard explosions and gunfire."

"I got six out of seven," Bishop answered. "The last one was out of range."

Hack, lying on the floor, was obviously high on the morphine. With glazed eyes, he slurred, "S-s-s-o you couldn't get them all, huh? There's no stopping the balloons," his words blending slightly. "Even my best drone would have trouble bringing one down."

Hack's statement caused Bishop to tilt his head in thought. Ambling over and taking a knee beside the prone inventor, he goaded the tipsy fellow. "Oh, now don't be telling stories. There's no way your drone could catch one of those balloons. That thing must be 10 miles away and four or five miles high by now."

"My latest one could," Hack bragged. "It has a 30,000 foot ceiling and a 30-mile range."

"Bullshit," Bishop challenged. "Those little pipsqueak toys? No way."

The Texan watched Hack's dilated eyes, trying to judge if the medicated man was going to take the bait. *And Terri didn't think I could fish*, he thought.

Finally, Hack dismissed Bishop's unbelieving attitude with a wave of his hand. "You know nothing of aeronautical design, young man. You're nothing more than a hired gunman for a group of thugs. My Big Red can climb that high... maybe more, if the air is right."

"Oh, yeah. And which one of your toys is this supposed Big Red?" Bishop asked.

"Well, that's obvious.... It's the biggest one in the garage. Thus the name, dunderhead."

After exchanging looks with Terri, Bishop exited the door and scurried to the garage. Heaving up the bay door, he found a drone that was impressibly larger than all the others. It was painted fire engine red.

He retrieved the device, as well as a tablet computer lying next to the flyer on the workbench.

Hack became distraught when he spied Bishop carrying his pride and joy. "What are you doing, you... you... you Neanderthal? Put that down this instant. That is a sophisticated scientific instrument, not some toy for you to break."

"This thing?" Bishop mocked. "I don't even think this unit will fly, let along track down a balloon. You're pulling my leg."

"I'll prove it to you," Hack said, trying to upright himself.

Between his injured foot and the narcotic surging through his system, Hack had no chance of standing. With Grissom under one arm and Bishop under the other, they assisted the wounded man to the front porch.

"You there!" the old inventor ordered Terri, "go s-s-sit Big Red in the driveway," Hack slurred. "Let me show you a thing or two about aerodynamic design."

Terri, following with the drone, did as the toymaker instructed.

Taking the tablet, Hack fumbled with the unit, his unsure fingers having trouble with the controls. "My apologies," he offered to his audience. "I seem to be having trouble controlling my hands."

"Let me help you," Terri offered with the sweetest of smiles.

With Hack's instruction, Terri soon had the rotors spinning with a powerful hum. Like a grandfather boasting in front of his granddaughter, the toymaker wanted to show Terri everything. "Touch this," he said with pride, "and watch Big Red blast off."

Terri did exactly that, pretending to be so excited when the drone shot skyward with impressive thrust. "How do I make it go really high?" she beamed.

Again, Hack provided the necessary instructions, pointing to the tablet's controls.

After Bishop whispered the direction in her ear, Terri continued her charade, "I want it to fly northeast. Can it do that?"

And then she wanted to turn on the camera, control the gimbal, and go higher.

Hack seemed to be enjoying it all, happy to have a pretty girl so excited with his creation.

"What's that?" she asked, looking at the camera's point of view on the tablet's screen. "It looks like a really big star."

"I don't know," Hack said, obviously having forgotten about the balloon. "Let's go see what it is."

With Bishop and Grissom looking over their shoulders, Hack instructed Terri on how to manipulate the drone's controls and in a short time, the image of the balloon became clear.

"Ram it," Bishop told Terri. "Kamikaze that damn thing and knock it down."

"What? Wait… what are you talking about?" Hack began to protest. He started to reach for the tablet, but Bishop stopped him cold, gripping the toymaker's wrist before he could interfere with Terri's piloting.

"No… Please don't hurt Big Red," Hack pleaded, enough of his neural pathways functioning to grasp what the strangers around him intended.

Grissom was there to help, Bishop nodding with his head that they needed to get the ever more belligerent man back inside.

As the two men lifted Hack by the arms and legs, Terri turned and sneered, "Watch this. Nearly the entire display on the computer was filled with the silver outline of the balloon, the drone obviously closing the distance rapidly.

Then the screen flashed white, and the transmission stopped sending video.

"I think you got it," Bishop said, relief dominating his voice.

"Is this finally over?" Terri wondered.

"Maybe," Bishop answered. "Now we wait and see if Diana got the message and can get us out of here. We're still trapped miles behind enemy lines."

The tarmac at Fort Bliss was a riot of activity, men rushing in every direction, shouted orders trying to override the growing howl of two Blackhawk helicopters spinning up their turbine power plants.

Grim arrived via speeding Humvee, the contractor badgering his driver the entire trip from Alpha to hurry, worried the copters would leave without him.

Exiting the transport and retrieving his gear, Grim scanned the hustle and bustle, quickly identifying a group of armed men gathering to the side.

Trotting up to what appeared to be a rifle squad, Grim easily identified the man in charge. "Which bird do you want me in?" he asked, having to shout over the din.

"Who the fuck are you?" came a hard reply. "We've already got enough volunteers."

The rebuttal took the contractor by surprise, but only for a moment. "I'm the guy ordered by the Alliance to go along and keep your ass from being shot off," Grim snapped back. "Stand down that attitude, trooper, before you go someplace you don't want to be."

Grim's counter took the leader by surprise, the man looking the contractor up and down, unsure what to make of the stranger.

No one was wearing any badges, insignias, or rank, a fact that tended to confuse military units. The men surrounding Grim were accustomed to a hierarchy and chain of command. Without a clear indication of rank, the young soldier didn't know if the new arrival was a colonel or a private.

Finally deciding it didn't matter at the moment, the soldier pointed a finger at Grim and countered, "I don't give a shit if you're General Owens, my squad was assigned to this clusterfuck, and I don't need some outside amateur mucking things up. Is that clear?"

"He's not General Owens. I am," boomed a clear voice across the tarmac, the officer and Diana walking briskly toward the departure point.

"Tennnn hut!" someone shouted, realizing the big brass dog was present.

"At ease," the senior officer commanded. "You men, carry on. Sergeant, can I have a quick word, please?"

"Of course, sir," Grim's antagonist answered, hustling over to speak with the general.

"That man you're speaking to in a most disrespectful way is a former Marine Corps Recon operator... and the veteran of more deployments than anyone else on this base. In addition, he is one of only a handful of people who have actually had eyes on your objective. I suggest you welcome his experience and expertise."

"Yes, sir! I had no idea, sir."

"No problem, son. All of this is being thrown together at the last minute. That man's name is Grim. I'd advise you take his counsel seriously. Carry on, and bring everybody back in one piece."

"Yes, sir!"

The NCO stepped up to Grim and offered his hand, "Are we square? I didn't know."

"We're good," Grim answered, accepting what was in reality an apology. "Which bird do you want me in?"

"Number one," the sergeant replied. "Up front with me. You've been where we're going?"

"Yes. I know a great spot for the insertion. It's within the ring of their trip wires and security."

"Roger that," came the reply, and then the sergeant was off, making sure his shooters were ready.

Diana approached Grim, something clearly on her mind. "I have a message for you," she shouted over the ruckus. "Nick wanted to be here, but can't. He said to tell you, 'Bring him back.'"

"I'll die before leaving that kid again, Miss Brown," Grim replied. "Never again."

Diana was about to wish Grim good luck when another Humvee came speeding up, the driver dodging through the crowd. "Now what?" she mumbled.

Butter appeared from the passenger side, the other SAINT member hefting his pack and weapon from the back seat.

"And just what the hell do you think you're doing?" Grim snarled, marching toward his teammate. "You're supposed to be in the hospital."

"I'm fine, sir," Butter responded with his usual boyish smile. "I'm going with you."

"No, you're not!" Grim replied. "The last thing I need is a sub-par man along on this little venture. Now get your muscle-bound ass back to the infirmary, before I have those troopers over there carry you back."

For the first time since he'd met the big ranch hand, Grim saw Butter's face paint mean. Ice-fucking-cold mean.

"I'm going," Butter growled, glaring at the rifle squad with a dismissive sneer. "And there ain't enough of them to stop me. Kevin and you are my teammates, and you'll have to shoot me to keep me off of that whirlybird."

Grim tilted his head, smiling inside. A replay of the conversation he'd just had with the Army NCO ran through the contractor's mind, and then he nodded. "I understand. Just don't get in my way. Got it?"

"Yes, sir," Butter grinned, back to his normal, happy demeanor.

Grim pointed to the NCO and said, "Go tell that guy I said to find a place for your oversized carcass."

"You got it!" Butter replied, rushing toward the NCO.

Turning back to Diana, he noticed a frown on her face. "That boy should be in the hospital," she said. "Are you sure that's a good idea?"

Shaking his head, Grim said, "It would take Godzilla to keep that kid off this mission. I understand what's going through his head. He'll be fine. He just joined a very exclusive club. I like him."

Throughout the night, they took turns standing watch so everyone could get some sleep. No one but Hunter managed any real rest.

Bishop fully expected the locals to assault the cabin after his sniping their airborne armada, but the forest and mountains around Hack's cabin remained quiet throughout the night.

It was Kevin who spotted the first movement, his warning

203

rousting Bishop from his nap on the couch. "Sir... Mr. Bishop... I see people out there."

A surge of energy shot through Bishop's exhausted body, the Texan rolling off the couch and heading to the window with his rifle primed and ready.

The dawn was just old enough to allow a view of the perimeter of Hack's compound, and Bishop didn't like what he saw.

There were at least 50 people there, all of them standing in plain sight, staring at the cabin. "What the hell are they doing?" the Texan asked, not really expecting an answer.

Moving to the back of the home, he spied a nearly identical picture. Dozens of people, all just standing still and staring back at him as if they were waiting for some sort of announcement.

The ruckus woke Terri and Grissom, both thinking something was wrong. After studying the gathered throng for a few moments, the PJ reiterated, "At least they're not armed. I was half expecting pitchforks and torches."

"Or a full frontal assault," Bishop added. "Why just stand there and stare at us?"

An hour passed, more and more people gathering on the perimeter. "There must be 300 people out there," Terri observed. "Maybe more."

To the holdouts inside the cabin, it was unsettling.

Bishop paced front to back, his weapon never leaving his hands. "Why don't they do whatever they're going to do? Just get it over with."

Terri had decided to ignore the multitude, feeding a ravished Hunter his breakfast instead of worrying about it. "Maybe this is how they handle hostage negotiations?" she answered. "It seems to be working – at least on you."

Kevin's voice sounded from the living room, "Mr. Bishop, something's happening."

"Finally," Bishop growled, flicking the safety off his weapon and moving toward the front of the home.

Peeking around the window frame, the Texan spotted three elderly men walking toward the front porch. They were unarmed, at least as far as Bishop could tell.

They stopped 30 feet short of the stoop, staring up at the cabin, otherwise unmoving.

"An envoy?" Bishop asked Kevin.

"No white flag," the kid responded.

"You've been watching too many cowboy movies," Bishop grinned.

Terri flashed her husband a nasty look, and then stepped beside her mate, a content Hunter bouncing gently on her hip.

"I'll go see what they want," she announced with a casual tone.

"You're acting like it's the paperboy wanting his money," Bishop chided, shaking his head. "May I remind you that we've killed a bunch of their people in the last few days? I don't think it's a good idea for you to invite them in for coffee."

"Well, then you go see what's going on. It's rude to just let them stand out there."

Bishop's head pivoted between his wife and the three men on the lawn. Shrugging his shoulders, he nodded and moved to the front door.

Having visions of some yahoo with a deer rifle zeroed in on the cabin's threshold, Bishop opened the door and jumped back, waiting for a bullet to come flying. None did.

Exposing only a slice of his head and staying back in the shadow of the doorway, Bishop called out, "Good morning."

Terri flashed her husband a look that said, *"That's it? That's the best you got?"*

"We would like to talk," came the response from the yard. "And only talk."

Bishop was suspicious, shaking his head at Terri. "I don't like it."

Rolling her eyes, she pushed past her husband, mother and child strolling out onto the porch. "That would be wonderful," she told the three men. "We would like to resolve a few things as well."

Bishop appeared next to his wife, his eyes scanning the horizon, perusing the crowd for the flash of a weapon or any other indication of a threat.

"There is nothing to resolve," one of the men declared. "We only wish for you to return Grandfather's body to us. He was important to our people, what you would call a hero for our cause. We would like to bury him with honor."

Terri was a bit taken aback by the request. Again, with a pleasant smile, she said, "I'd be happy to give you his body, but I don't think he'd like the burial part. He's still alive."

The three men exchanged frowns, finally offering, "You haven't killed him?"

"No," Terri replied, now clearly intrigued. "Why would we do that?"

"He guided our actions and attacked you with the poison material. His metal hawks led to the death of several of your men. Valley Green was his idea. Why wouldn't you kill him?"

Terri was sincere in her reply, "Because that's not our way. We think this has all been a big misunderstanding. We're not your enemy. We don't want any more killing."

"We are going to have funerals all around the Caldera

today," spoke another. "So many of our people have died. If you're not our enemy, then how did this happen?"

Much to Bishop's dismay, Terri stepped off the porch and approached the trio. When she was closer, she responded, "Because mistakes were made on both sides. That's why I'm here – to talk, not fight. Let's sit down and have an honest discourse so no one else has to die."

"You've already won," declared another of the three. "We assume your armies are on the way. We know we can't stop them without Grandfather. We will not resist."

It took Terri a minute to grasp their perspective. She shook her head, "No armies are on the way. We have people coming to take us back to our homes, but just a few. We only want to share the water and have fair, open trade with your people. That's it, nothing else."

Again, the three elders exchanged unreadable glances among themselves. The apparent leader spoke again, "So many things in this world have changed so quickly. If what you are saying is true, then how did this all happen? Why did so many die?"

Terri hesitated in her answer, so Bishop filled in, "Because people... all people... get things set in their heads and lose faith in other men. They stop believing the world can be a better place. The man you call Grandfather told us last night that he wanted the Nations to have respect and dignity... and to be a proud people once again. He just naturally assumed we wouldn't let that happen, and that led to all the trouble. In reality, we all want the same thing."

Terri continued, "I have a favorite saying that applies to all that has happened in the last few days. One of our great leaders once said, 'Comparison is the thief of joy.' Too many people looked at life as either win... or lose. They judged their dealings with others like some sort of sports contest that ended in either victory or defeat. We believe that outlook is part of the reason why society collapsed. We have learned our lesson. Now, we want strong neighbors and partners. Both sides can walk away from this better than we were before."

"She quotes Teddy Roosevelt," one of the elders commented, surprising Terri with his knowledge. "Maybe we should listen to her."

But not all of the trio were convinced. "You'll understand if we're skeptical of your words. There's a history of deceit, broken promises, and unfulfilled dreams with our people," said another.

Bishop nodded, "We aren't promising you anything. As far as your dreams, well, those are your own. Consider our people a mirror. How you decide to interact with us is how we will respond in kind. It's really that simple. If you reroute the rivers, we will do the same. If you share the water, we will as well. If you are hostile towards us, then you can expect us to be violent in return. As I'm so fond of saying, it's your call."

The three local leaders were exchanging glances when a slight vibration broke the stillness of the morning air. Without warning, a Blackhawk zoomed over the gathering, flying low and fast with a deafening roar. Bishop looked up in time to see a row of eager faces peering down from its open bay. The rifles and helmets made it clear Fort Bliss had gotten his message.

Shocked by the helicopter's sudden appearance, the three elders were spooked, glancing up and around nervously and then throwing a look at Bishop and Terri as if to say, "You lied again!"

Bishop let his rifle fall against the sling, holding out both hands, palms down in a calming motion. "They're here just to take out our injured men. They're not here to invade or fight," he soothed.

Right when it seemed like the elders might believe Bishop's explanation, another, more constant whine came from behind the mountain.

All eyes searched for the source, another Blackhawk rising slowly from the tree line, a six-barrel mini-gun sweeping the hundreds of milling Indians surrounding the cabin.

"Oh shit," Bishop said, seeing the machine gunner covering the crowd with his ultra-deadly weapon. "They think the cabin's surrounded and under attack."

Bishop knew that mini-gun could fire over 100 rounds a second, images of a hailstorm of hot lead slicing through the throng of peaceful folks surging through his brain. They would die by the hundreds if that gunner cut loose.

Bishop glanced right and left, looking for anything to signal the distant bird. Hunter's blanket came into his view, the bright white cloth exactly what the Texan needed.

Terri initially jumped when Bishop grabbed his son's warmer, roughly unwrapping the bundle containing the wide-eyed boy. Then she got it, instantly helping the Texan with his task.

Bishop stepped forward, placing himself between the menacing copter and the three elders, wildly waving the white blanket in the air.

The Texan exhaled in relief when he saw Grim's face behind the gunner, tapping the trigger man's shoulder and pointing toward the Texan and his white flag.

A moment later, the Blackhawk tilted its nose and flew away, hurrying to join its sibling now landing to the north.

"That was close... damn close," Bishop turned and said to

Terri. "From the air, it had to look like we were under attack."

He then faced the three elders, an apology forming on his lips. But something in their gaze stopped Bishop before he could utter a word.

"You put yourself between us and what was surely instant death," one of the men said. "You didn't run or think of your wife and child. Thank you."

Bishop nodded, slightly embarrassed.

"We can talk," offered one of the local leaders. "You obviously understand the value of our people and were willing to sacrifice yourself for our brothers and sisters."

Turning back toward Hunter, Bishop returned his son's blanket. "Welcome to the team, little hero. Let's hope that's the last time you have to bail your old man's ass out."

Chapter 16

Bishop stood in line, one of a dozen Alpha residents waiting his turn at the Alliance Business Office.

The building, formerly the First National Bank, had been skillfully repaired and showed few signs of the looting or vandalism that had left the former landmark a hollowed-out shell less than a year before.

As Bishop meandered his way through the queue, the roped posts guided him past the windows facing Main Street, his view of the busy thoroughfare partially blocked by one of the remaining signs of the apocalypse.

Glass was one of a long list of items still in short supply throughout the Alliance. During the violence that followed the collapse, millions of windows had been broken, and many buildings still suffered the scars.

In this particular case, some crafty individual had painted a colorful mural on the otherwise uninspiring sheet of plywood. One section was dedicated as a community bulletin board.

Bishop grunted when he noted a picture of Pete's smiling face atop one of the posters. "Get Your Identification Card Today!" the cheery piece instructed the passing citizen. "ID cards and Driver's Licenses are available at this location!"

As the line shuffled forward, Bishop came eye to eye with the *Alpha Bulletin*, what amounted to the fledgling first attempt at a newspaper.

Like glass, paper was also in short supply, so the publishers had taken to posting limited copies on several boards all around the town.

Bishop smiled, shaking his head at today's headlines. Under the caption of "SAINT Team Rescues New Mexico Envoys," was a picture of Grim and Butter carrying Kevin on a stretcher toward a distant Blackhawk.

As Bishop examined the snapshot accompanying the article, he grinned. Grim must have known someone was snapping a picture, the gruff old warhorse bent low like he was taking fire, his expression indicating the patient was critical, and he was braving numerous machine gun nests to save his friend. It was probably fortunate Butter's mug was out of the picture, no doubt the big man's toothy grin would have ruined the dramatic moment.

Bishop started to read the story, wondering if Grim had granted an interview with the local newshounds. Secretly, the Texan hoped the contractor had made some gaffe or foot-in-mouth remark so he could relentlessly tease his friend.

A rumbling through the marble floor paused Bishop's review of the piece, the two ladies in front of the Texan glancing nervously toward the street through a still-intact pane of glass.

"It's just one of those pipe trucks heading to New Mexico," the calmer of the two informed her friend. "I read where the Alliance is shipping almost a million feet of pipe to help the Native Americans irrigate a valley."

"I heard the same," replied the second, fussing with her Easter-like hat. "I sure hope the vegetables they grow over there are better than the ones we're getting from down south."

"For a minute, I thought it might be another one of those scary wagons hauling all that radioactive material back east. I don't know why they routed those dangerous things through Alpha," continued the first, having to fan her face at the mere thought.

"I know. But I saw Sheriff Watts personally escorting them through town, so that made me feel like they must have been safe. That man wouldn't let any harm come to any of us."

Bishop barely contained the chuckle, not wanting to let his two line-mates know he was eavesdropping on their conversation. Sheriff Watts had just about had a kitten when the council had ordered him to provide security for the Colbalt-60 being transported back to the U.S. It was the only time anyone had ever seen Watts frightened of anything.

The line inched forward, the conversation about nuclear waste diverting the Texan's thoughts to New Mexico and his wife.

Terri and Hunter were still there, negotiating the final stages of a trade agreement that would greatly help both sides in the recovery. It would all have been over and done a week ago, but Washington had demanded to become a third party to the negotiations.

In Terri's shrewd assessment, "Those guys from D.C. could fuck up a two-car parade."

According to his wife, Hunter was now consistently asking about "Da-da," and had on one occasion muttered, "Mama." Bishop had his doubts about the accuracy of her report, knowing Terri was stone cold green over the fact that their son had chosen to address his father first.

And then it was the Texan's turn in line, a smiling lady behind what had been a teller's counter back in the old days. "Good morning, sir, how can I help you today?" she greeted.

"I have a voucher," Bishop responded, handing over a piece of paper Diana had given him just a few minutes before. "I was told I could exchange it for cash at this location."

Nodding, the lady responded, "That's correct. Now, let me

take a look and see.... Oh, my, this is for a lot of money."

She turned, motioning over a supervisor, showing the older gent Bishop's chit.

"Could I see your identification, sir?"

Oh, no, here we go again, Bishop thought, his blood pressure rising. "I haven't managed to acquire one the new cards," he explained. "I do have my old, pre-collapse driver's license, but it's seen better days."

After digging in his wallet, Bishop produced the faded card, the laminated surface showing the wear and tear of it's owners hard life.

Both workers studied the ID, glancing back and forth between Bishop's face and the not so clear picture. "I'm sorry, but this license is so damaged, we can't...."

The rejection was interrupted by Diana's voice carrying across the lobby, "I thought I might catch you here," she gushed in a happy tone.

"Miss Brown," both workers greeted as Diana smiled and cut past the waiting queue and came to Bishop's side.

"I forgot to give you a card to take to Nick when you visit Bliss. Give him my love," she said, handing over the envelope.

Bishop nodded, accepting the correspondence. And then, with a touch of embarrassment, said, "Could you help me out here? These nice folks are questioning my ID, and I kind of need some money."

Diana glanced at the government workers and then at the license they were holding. "Is there an issue?" she asked.

"Is this man the individual who should receive payment from this rather sizable voucher?" the teller asked, handing Bishop's document to the Alliance's leader.

Diana, with an absolutely straight face, glanced at the document, and then at Bishop, and said, "No. This man is an imposter. Please call the authorities, immediately."

Bishop's mouth dropped open, a protest forming in his throat as Diana handed the tellers back his paper and then pivoted to leave.

"Wa-wa-, wait just a damn minute... Diana!" the Texan pleaded, his voice sounding far whinier than he intended.

Bursting out in laughter, she turned back, having to cover her mouth again when she saw Bishop's helpless expression. "Oh mercy," she breathed deeply, trying to stop. "If I only had a picture of your face to show Terri."

Nodding quickly at the two tellers, Diana added, "I was joking. Yes, he's one and the same as the name on the voucher. I just signed it personally less than an hour ago. Give the man his money; he earned it."

The councilwoman gave Bishop a hug and said, "Gotta run. I owed you that one. And tell that big lug of mine I love him, and that he'd better hurry up and heal, because there are other gentlemen showing interest."

And then, just like always, she was gone, a virtual whirlwind of energy and purpose.

Bishop turned back to the tellers, the nice lady now counting out a significant stack of bills. "I would like to remind you, sir that the bank will be reopening soon. They will be offering secure saving accounts, and may even begin paying interest in a few months."

Bishop nodded, smiling politely. "Thank you."

Then, hunching forward and lowering her voice like she was about to divulge a secret, she said, "And I just want you to know, it's not safe walking around with this much cash. While it's rare these days, thugs and muggers do still exist in Alliance territory. I'd hate to see some mean hoodlum steal your money, young man."

It was all the Texan could do to keep from laughing, the irony of someone robbing him - after all he'd just been through. "Thank you for that advice, ma'am. I appreciate your looking out for me. By the way, what all is involved in obtaining a new driver's license?"

Thirty minutes later, he stepped onto Main Street, the bright sunshine, a just acquired driver's license, and a pocket full of money brightening Bishop's face.

Looking up and down the street, he began mentally prioritizing what was sure to be a busy day.

Probably the most difficult item on his list was a surprise for Hunter.

According to the last shortwave conversation with Bishop's better half, Hack had built his son a solar powered, electric train. Terri reported the boy was fascinated by the small engine going round and round.

Hack, it seemed, had taken a liking to Hunter, probably in no small part due to Terri pressing the U.S. government to grant the inventor full amnesty. "It turns out he's a brilliant man who simply got caught up in a world gone crazy, not a criminal mastermind or insane megalomaniac," she had informed Bishop. "Right now, humanity needs every speck of genius we can get our hands on, especially these folks out here."

Bishop wondered if the man still held a grudge over having his foot shot. *Just another smart guy you've pissed off,* he chided himself. *You've gotta stop doing that.*

And then there was his wife's opinion of the tribes. "Do you remember talking about that prepper guy from the gun store?"

she had asked. "The locals have a similar point of view, and in a way, it's refreshing. I think you would actually appreciate how they live their lives. Hell, I might even consider moving here. It's beautiful, and I love the people."

But today, on payday, with cool weather and crisp air, the Texan wasn't going to worry about any of it. The truck needed fuel. He wanted to get something nice for Terri to celebrate when his family returned home in a few days. He needed seeds and perhaps a new windmill pump. He was hungry.

Using his thumbs like he was hiking up a gun belt, Bishop then tipped his hat low, and began sauntering down the sidewalk. "I wonder where a man can get a bacon cheeseburger in this one horse town."

THE END

A note from Joe:

To all of the loyal readers of the Holding Their Own series, I'm pleased to announce that there will be an 11th title, currently scheduled for release mid-summer of 2015. Thank you one and all, and God bless.

42593378R00123

Made in the USA
Lexington, KY
28 June 2015